W9-BOK-317

the

first

time

she

drowned

the

first

KERRY KLETTER

PHILOMEL BOOKS

time

she

drowned

PHILOMEL BOOKS
an imprint of Penguin Random House LLC
375 Hudson Street, New York, NY 10014

Copyright © 2016 by Kerry Kletter.

Philomel Books is a registered trademark of Penguin Random House LLC.

Library of Congress Cataloging-in-Publication Data
Kletter, Kerry.
The first time she drowned / Kerry Kletter.
pages cm
Summary: Committed to a mental hospital against her will for something she
claims she did not do, Cassie O'Malley signs herself out against medical advice
when she turns eighteen and tries to start over at college, until her estranged
mother appears, throwing everything Cassie believes about herself into question.
[1. Self-actualization (Psychology)—Fiction. 2. Emotional problems—Fiction.
3. Family problems—Fiction. 4. Mothers and daughters—Fiction.
5. Memory—Fiction. 6. Sexual abuse—Fiction.] I. Title.
PZ7.1.K65Fir 2016
[Fic]—dc23
2014045881

Printed in the United States of America.
ISBN 978-0-399-17103-1
10 9 8 7 6 5 4 3 2 1
Edited by Liza Kaplan.
Design by Siobhán Gallagher.
Text set in 10.25 Monticello LT Pro.

To Beth Macdonald and Susan Nagin Thau for everything.

In Memory of John.

prologue

MY MOTHER WORE the sun like a hat. It followed her as we did, stopping when she stopped, moving when she moved. She carried her beauty with the naiveté of someone who was born to it and thus never understood its value or the poverty of ugliness.

As children, my older brother, Matthew, and I were drawn to her like tides, always reaching our arms up to her, pulled to her light. If she had shadows, I did not recognize them as such. I saw her only in her most perfect form, and any suggestion of coldness or unkindness was merely a reflection of me. This was the unspoken agreement I had with her, suspiciously drawn up before I was old enough to understand its cost.

Until I was a teenager, my family lived on the poor side of a wealthy town in Pennsylvania. It was a washed-out-looking neighborhood where the colors of the houses were tired and peeling from neglect. Still, we had a huge backyard that stretched wide and ripe with all things wonderful to children. On its left seam it was lined with blackberry bushes whose purple juices stained our fingers as we stuffed them into jars for jam. On the right and perched tenuously on a hill as if cresting a wave of green sat an enormous yellow boat, so old and weathered, it had undoubtedly crawled its way to the shores of our yard to die. The boat was as big as our house and about as seaworthy. When I once asked my mother why we bothered to keep it, she looked not at the boat but at my father, who was tooling uselessly about its deck.

"It's a fixer-upper for sure," she'd said. "But maybe there's something we can salvage." She didn't sound very convincing.

If nothing else, the boat was the perfect venue for playing pirates. Every weekend, Matthew, who loved to wield his authority in being three years older, played the role of the good captain while I, in a flash of prescience, was relegated to the part of the doomed and hated buccaneer. He would order me to move here and there, serving as both actor and director of our little scenes, and I would follow his instructions dutifully because Matthew was always better at pretending than I was.

Meanwhile, my father cleaned and fussed with the old boat, muttering and sighing as if his repetitive efforts might someday induce its spirit back to life. My brother and I would race wildly around him, as heedless of his frustrated cursing—the background noise of our childhood—as he was to our presence. For it was not for him that we played and scrambled about, maybe not even always for ourselves, but for her, the one who wore the sun like a hat, who was the sun to us. Because she mattered more. And because I sensed on some subterranean level that she needed us to, sensed that if we did not play the role of happy children, she might break like the Atlantic upon us.

Yet, for all my efforts, there were moments when I would catch my mother looking at that broken boat with the strange and startled horror of the drowning. This frightened me, and always I looked to Matthew to see if he too noticed the seas rising behind my mother's eyes. He did not. Or if he did, he did not acknowledge it. But I saw too much. And I was never as good at pretending as Matthew was.

one

DR. MEEKS'S OFFICE is on the other side of the hospital and sometimes, if the weather is decent and the nurse escorting me is kind, we take the outside route to get there. I see him on Tuesdays and Thursdays and it's a five-minute walk, so if I'm lucky, I get ten extra minutes of sunlight on top of the four hours we are permitted each week. By comparison, even murderers on death row get out more than that. I know this because James and I looked it up. I once complained to Meeks that my vitamin D level is probably dangerously low, and he replied that if I'm so concerned about my health, I shouldn't smoke so many cigarettes. I told him I smoke only because there is nothing else to do—which there isn't. He suggested I could be "spending my time working on myself." I told him I refused to take advice from a man who wears jazz shoes and a fake orange tan. Ever since Meeks agreed to have me committed here for something I didn't do—something that never even happened—we haven't gotten along so well.

The hospital grounds are lush and vast with grass the color of Ireland. The beauty is not for the patients but for the visitors, to protect them from the bleak, stretched-time despair behind the façade. It's like the white picket fence that masks the ugly truth of a suburban family. Or in my case, the sprawling lawn, the sunlit mother, the large boat that doesn't actually sail.

Those of us inside the hospital walls spend most of our time staring out of locked windows with steel mesh screens at all that beauty we cannot have. But today on the way to Meeks's office, the outside world feels different, like something that belongs to me too, not just a piece of sky I get to borrow for four hours a week from a nurse with keys. I have just turned eighteen, old enough to sign myself out of here AMA—Against Medical Advice. Yesterday I turned in my seventy-two-hour notice, which means I will be leaving this hellhole in two days. Two days. Hallelujah.

Nurse Mary and I enter the waiting room with its beige and brown tones and the single, uninspired painting on the wall of a small child with her back to the observer, playing in the sand. All of the decor is designed to soothe, or at least not provoke. It's just one of the many insidious ways they suck the spirit out of you in here, make everything so bland and dull that your limbic system just shrivels up like a raisin and dies.

Dr. Meeks cracks open the door to his office and sticks his big llama head out. "Cassie," he says in the same morose way he always says it, like he's about to show me a dead body. He has tight curly hair and milk-white teeth and looks like a second-rate game show host on cable. He opens the door wide and I walk past him to the couch, sit down and wait for this to be over. One last session and I'll never have to see him again.

"So. You're really going through with this," he says.

For the past two and a half years I have hardly looked at him, fearing that to allow even a moment of connection is to risk breaking, just like most of the other kids here. But today I look directly into Dr. Meeks's eyes, and when I do, my whole center of gravity shifts, moves lower like a stake in the ground, making me sturdy and immovable. He has no power left. "Try not to miss me too much."

"I still wish you'd reconsider," he says. "I'm worried about you." But he doesn't look worried. He looks irritated that I have refused to accept his diagnosis that I am sick and in need of the medicine he's been trying to shove down my throat for the last two and a half years. "You haven't really addressed your problems here."

"What problems?" I say. I've already explained to him that the biggest problem I have is people like him believing that I'm the problem. But he won't see the truth. None of them will. Adults always believe the parents over the kid, it's a fact of life.

"For instance . . . you still haven't talked to me about your nightmares."

Just the mention of my nightmares makes something seize up inside of me. But there's no way in hell I'd ever talk to Meeks about them. Or about anything else for that matter. I pull a loose thread of fabric from my shirt and examine it with my fingers. All I have to do is sit here quietly and bide my time for one hour and I'll never have to do this again.

"I wish we had more time," he continues, "to develop a trusting relationship."

"Trust?" I say with a laugh. I know it's not even worth engaging at this point, but it's just so irritating. "Maybe if you'd tried listening to me instead of falling for my mother's—"

"Cassie, your mother loves you. She brought you to us because she wanted you to get well. We all do."

I shoot forward, unable to stop myself. "Really? My mother

loves me? 'Cause you've said that before and I'm curious: what has she ever done to make you think that?"

"Cassie . . ."

"I mean, putting aside the vicious lies—is it the once every, what, six months that she managed to visit? The letters she never wrote, the phone calls she never made?"

"Cassie."

"Or is it just that you've fallen for the myth that all mothers love their children?" As if all people feel the same way about anything. As if there's only one feeling you can have. "I'm being serious here, because maybe there's something I'm missing. I need to know why—"

"You don't know what you need, Cassie!" he fires back.

I put my hands up and fall back into the couch again. "Okay," I say. "That's helpful." I turn away from him, the internal shield hardening as if my organs have been injected with concrete. I look to the open window beside his desk and think of how often over the last few years I fantasized about making a run for it, leaping out. I turn back to him. "I wonder if you'll ever look back someday and consider that maybe, just maybe, I was telling the truth all along. I hope you do. I hope you wonder about that."

His face is without emotion, cold and reptilian.

"Then again maybe you always knew my mother was lying, but what did you care, she was paying the bills, right?"

"I think you need to take a deep breath, Cassie," he says, folding his arms across his chest. "You're getting out of control."

I can feel it in my stomach, the grenade he has just deposited in me. He watches now, waiting for it to explode so he can sit back, satisfied, and say, "See!"

I clamp my teeth down on the anger—just two more days here—and turn back to the window, letting my mind drift beyond the glass, floating high into the treetops. All that's left in this room is my body—my breath and my blood circulating at the energy-conserving level of a child's night-light. The rest of me is gone. Dr. Meeks calls this dissociation.

I call it escape.

The truth is I have mixed feelings about leaving this place. I desperately want to go, but I have spent half of my teenage years here, insulated as an oyster and so far from the real world that I no longer know what it is or how to live in it. I feel like a newborn about to be dropped off on life's doorstep, totally unequipped to navigate the world outside these doors. It's no secret that Dr. Meeks thinks I'll fail, that I'll be back. Or worse, that I'll be just another statistic. Another kid found too late, bleeding out in a bathtub or beside an empty bottle of pills.

Sometimes I worry that he's right.

I wonder if it would feel different if I were going home. Not that I've been invited or that I think it would be a good idea, but the known universe always feels easier even when it's miserable. Most of the kids here talk constantly about the glorious day when they will finally be reunited with their families, never mind the fact that it was their screwed-up parents who messed them up and then dumped them here. That's another fact of life—it's really hard not to love your parents, even when they suck. But I'm not like that. I try to have as little contact with my mother as possible. Every once in a while this primal longing erupts in me, a sort of lost-alone-in-the-dark desperation that strikes deep in my chest. But as soon as that happens, I hold my breath and suffocate the feeling until it passes. I don't want anything to do with her. Not after what she's done.

But the thing is, when you don't have a mother, you don't have a home, and when you don't have a home, there's nowhere to go when you're sad or scared or alone, even in your own mind, there's just nowhere to go.

As if from a great distance, I hear Meeks ask me if I have anything I want to say to him before our final session is over.

"Actually," I say, leaning forward, "there is one last, very important thing I want to tell you."

He blinks and his head jerks back slightly in surprise. "Okay," he says, summoning his best impression of a serious doctor—cupped hands, level brow, listening eyes. But his mouth betrays him, twisting as if to suppress the hope that he is finally about to get his breakthrough.

I take a deep breath. "I don't know how to tell you this, but . . . I guess I'll just go ahead and say it. Right now, at this very moment . . ." He leans in. "There are . . . little blue men climbing up the window behind you. They're, oh my God, Dr. Meeks, I think they might be Smurfs!"

He leans back and sighs and rubs his temples. "Cassie," he says.

"You're not even going to look? You just want to believe that I'm crazy."

I pretend to cry for a second, terrifically bad acting until he says, "Okay, Cassie, our session is over."

"Free at last!" I jump happily to my feet.

He walks me to the door and then waves in his next patient.

It's James, my best friend here and the only reason I have made it through this place with my sanity intact.

Just as Nurse Mary and I are leaving, I hear James scream, "Holy crap, Dr. Meeks! There are Smurfs climbing up your window!" and I laugh all the way back to the ward. It's been almost two and a half years that James and I have been screwing with Meeks, and it never gets old for me. *Two and a half years, and now only two days left.*

Instinctively, I look down at my wrists where the rope burns once were. Even though the years have passed so slowly, it's still hard to believe it's been that long since the day my parents dumped me here, since that terrible, terrible day.

two

IT WAS FEBRUARY, and I was fifteen when I woke to my mother, my father, and Matthew standing over my bed. They were backlit by the early morning sunlight, their shapes ringed by the glare. I blinked up at them, squinting through unadjusted eyes. It was so disconcerting to find them there and to realize that they had been staring at me as I slept that it took a moment to register their serious faces.

"What?" I said.

They watched me with cold detachment, the way one might examine a bug getting sucked down a drain.

Then I noticed the ropes in their hands.

I looked up at their faces.

Down at the ropes.

Faces, ropes, faces, ropes.

I sat up. "What the hell?"

"Get up and get dressed," my mother said. "We're taking you to a hospital."

"A hospital? Why?" I said, and then, in my disoriented state, worried that something was actually wrong with me. I flashed back to the night before and then looked down at my body as if finding it covered in blood would explain things.

My mother glanced first at my father and then at Matthew, who flanked her on either side like foot soldiers. They moved in closer. She took a breath. "It's a psychiatric hospital," she said. "You can come willingly or we'll tie you up."

I looked at my brother and laughed. "You have got to be kidding me." There was no way this was happening. No way this was real. And yet.

I turned to my father.

He wouldn't meet my eyes.

I looked back to my mother, at the curl of satisfaction on her lips. This was her doing.

I glanced at the door. No way to make a run for it.

Slowly, I removed my blanket and swung my legs over the side of the bed.

There was so much light in my bedroom. It seemed too early for such blinding sunlight, and when I looked down at myself, moving in this strange space between dreaming and not, my skin and clothes seemed bleached out by it, my whole body a fading stain.

I picked a sweatshirt off the chair and threw it on over the big T-shirt I had slept in. "Are you going to watch me put my pants on, too?" I said. All three of them continued to stare at me. I guessed that was a yes. I turned my back and slipped on my jeans as fast as I could. My body was shaking, yet my mind was completely still, completely stunned. I knew I had to figure out a way to save myself, but I could not form a thought beyond that.

They marched me out of my bedroom and down the stairs. Matthew was in front of me, his now six-foot frame blocking all chance of escape. I watched his back as he descended the steps— the one person I'd always believed could keep me from falling through the Earth now leading the way down. I thought of the Matthew I had shared a childhood with, the one who had taught me how to skateboard, who sang "Jimmy Crack Corn" to me when I was scared or sad, the perfect older brother whom I followed and imitated as if I could fill my half-formed self up with him like plaster into a mold. I knew he had been under the spell of my mother for years now, had become in essence my mother's surrogate husband once she'd decided that my father was useless. But I never imagined he could become this brainwashed. I wondered how, in his mind, he could justify this, what she must have told him.

We reached the kitchen. The reality of what was happening seized me all at once, shook me in its teeth like a small, helpless animal.

"You ASSHOLES!" I screamed. I swiped my arm across the countertop, bringing everything on it crashing to the floor. Then, in the chaos of that instant, I took off.

I was out the door and down the driveway, the houses and trees blurring in my panic. The sound of my own terror roared in my ears as I ran for my life. I was almost to the sidewalk when Matthew sacked me from behind. The asphalt rushed at me. A vivid memory dislodged with the impact, the image of Matthew and I running around on the boat, him playing the good captain and me the interloper, the doomed and hated buccaneer.

We are given our roles so young.

In an instant, all three of them were on top of me, tying my wrists and ankles while I screamed for help that I knew—in this neighborhood where everyone minded their own business—would never come. Matthew and my father carried me to the car, stuffed me on the floor of the backseat like an old sack and slammed the door shut. I struggled uselessly to untie myself, screaming screams so bloodcurdling, I didn't even recognize my own voice.

The door opened again and my mother helped my baby brother, Gavin, ten years my junior, into the car. She buckled him into the car seat right above me. His little face looked stricken when he saw me tied up and sobbing on the floor.

"Help me, Gav! Please! Untie me. Don't let them do this to me!"

His forehead furrowed with conflict. He looked pleadingly to my mother. She gave a cold, authoritative shake of her head, closed the door and climbed into the front seat. "Let's go," she said.

My father started the engine.

"Please, kiddo," I said to Gavin. "You know what's right. You know I'm not crazy."

"I know," he whispered, his voice choked with apology. "I want to, but Mom said no."

The sorrow in his face broke me. A single fragment of love in such a loveless place.

My father backed out of the driveway and down the street in silence. From my vantage point on the floor I could see nothing but Gavin's anguished face reflecting my horror. We drove for hours and I pleaded with him the whole way there to help me. I shouldn't have—he was too young. But then, so was I.

three

AS NURSE MARY and I reach the ward, I pause and look back at the garden path we have just walked, this small patch of land and sky, the only landscape I have known for so long. I commit the scene to memory, imagining that just two days from now I'll be able to look back and say, "I lived there once," and I'll marvel at the strangeness of that fact. Then Mary sticks her key in the heavy metal door and I am still a patient, back on the ward, the door banging shut behind us. I have become immune to the sound of keys and of doors slamming, but even after all this time, I still have the queer sensation when I walk through these halls that I am watching my body from above as if it belongs to someone else.

The ward is an L-shaped corridor, bookended by a television room and a "game room," which consists only of a pool table that's missing three balls. None of us know how to play pool anyway.

I remember my first day here, being half dragged onto the ward by two aides as I tried to resist, pleading with them to see that I did not belong here, that I was the one being victimized. The aides handed me off to a nurse with short, practical hair and a bland, cheerless face.

"I'm Kay," she said. "Come with me." We walked toward the

TV room as she rattled off the facts of this place. "Breakfast is at seven. Lunch is at twelve. Dinner's at five. Lights-out is ten o'clock. School is five hours a day on-site. Group therapy is on Monday and Wednesday, and attendance is mandatory. One fifteen-minute phone call allowed each day. No cell phones. Pay phone is on your left. No razors, knives, scissors, glass or cords. No lighters or matches. No physical contact with other patients." She paused in front of an empty, boxlike room. It had nothing but a bed with a bare rubber mattress and a small wooden desk. There was a narrow window with a thick steel mesh screen over it. "Yours," she said.

I stepped inside. It smelled like cleaning fluid and salt: sanitized tears. *Not mine,* I thought.

"You can't stay in here right now," she said, ushering me out again. "You're on supervised watch in the common area until tonight."

I tried to imagine night in this place and felt ill. Back in the hall, a group of kids who looked around my age were gathered by the door, docile and obedient as they were herded two by two like kindergartners on a field trip. They eyed me suspiciously. I was afraid to even look at them. I wondered what they were in for, what brand of crazy. They waited patiently for the door to be unlocked and then filed out, chaperoned by nurses on either side.

Nurse Kay caught me watching them. "They're going for ice cream," she said. "We do an outing once a month here. You won't be able to go this time, but as long as you're on good behavior, next month for sure."

"My parents will have me out long before then," I said.

"Okay," Kay said, as if she were too bored to refute it.

I went and sat down by the window where I could watch for my parents, and put my hand on the steel mesh screen.

"You can't get out that way," a voice said from behind me. "I've already tried."

I turned to see a boy peer out from behind a high-backed chair. He had shaggy shoulder-length hair and pool-blue eyes that seemed to flicker between humor and sadness. The heavy metal T-shirt he was wearing had the sleeves cut off, revealing bruised and scrawny arms. He seemed like the kind of kid found cutting class and smoking Marlboros on the steps of any high school in America. In contrast, I had never touched a cigarette, and listened to cheesy pop ballads and old rock. He pulled out a cigarette and waited for Kay to light it.

"This place is locked up tighter than death row," he said, blowing smoke out of the side of his mouth. "Only they don't treat you half as nice." He gave Kay a pointed look. "Isn't that right, Kay?"

"Please don't be like that in front of our new patient, James," Kay said, retreating to the nurses' station.

James jumped up from his chair, thrust his arms wide in the air and sang after her, "I gotta be meeeeeee!" Then he winked at me and shrugged as I stared at him wide-eyed. He sat back down and flipped on the TV.

Kay turned around and sighed. "Everybody's a clown."

Just then, a frail, sickly-looking boy with huge dark circles beneath his eyes shuffled slowly and silently past us.

"Not him," James said dryly.

"Do you know when my parents are coming up?" I said to Kay as I watched the zombified kid shuffle down the hall. He couldn't have been more than twelve.

"Did they say they would be?"

I nodded, and my voice got caught on the answer. "To say good-bye."

James jerked back around to look at me. The humor was gone from his eyes, replaced by wide, open compassion. He stood and came over. He was short, maybe five foot five, and walked with a bounce as if to acquire more height. "First day's the hardest," he said, sitting down beside me. "I'm on my second month." Then he added, "Actually, the second month sucks too," and handed me a stick of gum from a pack in his pocket.

I turned back to the window, swallowing the fresh onslaught of tears his kindness threatened to unleash, and waited for my parents to come up as they had promised. I was sure that as soon as they stepped foot on the actual ward, they would realize what they were doing, change their minds, take me home.

I waited there for hours. They never showed.

Later that afternoon of my first day in the hospital, the door swung open, and the ward, which had been quiet and inactive, was filled with the voices of the returning patients, loud with their achievement of temporary freedom and intimidating in their sheer numbers and togetherness. I was surprised that most of them looked like regular kids up close. I don't know what I was expecting.

They said polite but not particularly friendly hellos to me and then split up into smaller clusters and whispered to each other and glanced over at me while I pretended not to notice. It was only when night descended and I'd been in the common area long enough to become a familiar object in the room that they began to approach me and to ask me what I was in for. I told them it was all a misunderstanding, that I'd be out by the weekend. They all laughed. Every single one of them laughed when I said that.

It didn't take much longer for them to tell me their own reasons for being there—stories that, in the mere hearing of them, made me older than I was ready to be. There was fifteen-year-old Eric, dark skinned with braces, whose father had walked into his bedroom one night, put a gun to his head and pulled the trigger. Eric was diagnosed with "behavior disorder," as if there was a right way to behave after something like that. Fourteen-year-old Shelly was pale and fragile as a cloud with a neat row of razor-blade scars up both of her wrists. She was raped by her father's best friend at a picnic, but no one in her family believed her, so she kept trying to die. Sweet, stuttering twelve-year-old Brian was born of heroin addicts and had never, to anyone's knowledge, received a single phone call or letter or visit from anyone.

I sat and listened to these stories, all the while struggling against my own terror as if I were sitting on the steep ledge of myself and trying not to look down into the void. It wasn't just the sadness of their lives that horrified me. It was the fact that most of these kids had been here for a long time, locked up in this place where no touch was allowed, where you couldn't blow-dry your own hair without supervision, where every right was stolen, and yet, none of them seemed to mind all that much. This locked-down, lifeless hallway had become more comfortable to them than the outside world.

It was 10:00 P.M. before I was allowed to go to my room, away from the watchful eyes of the staff. Nurse Kay escorted me there, and I followed, dazed and disbelieving. Just that morning I had woken up in my own bed, and now I was going to sleep in an insane asylum. I reached my room and put on the hospital scrubs they had provided as pajamas. I climbed into bed, thinking it would be a relief to finally be by myself, but the darkness stared back at me, filled with strange shadows and the reality of abandonment.

From a window above mine, an old lady's voice croaked, "Help me!" over and over into the pitiless night.

A few minutes later a flashlight shined in my face. "Fifteen-minute room check," a nurse said. "Just making sure you're still alive."

Define alive, I thought.

four

IN THOSE FIRST few months of my hospital stay, I rarely left my self-appointed position at the window in the common room. I watched the sky change, the days newly bright and scented with spring, the nights softening after a brittle, cold winter. I'd close my eyes and imagine what my friends back in Pennsylvania were doing, what the second half of the school year was like, all the fun things I was missing. I pressed my face up to the steel screen, and I waited for my mother to come take me home.

I didn't eat much, couldn't bear to swallow over the perpetual lump in my throat. The nurses kept threatening me with an IV if I didn't stop losing weight, but I did not know this body that was trapped here in a loony bin and I did not want to feed it. I wanted to shed it, to slip away from it, felt as imprisoned by my body as I was by the locked doors. I wanted out of the hospital and out of my gray, bottomless despair. I cried myself to sleep each night, torn between the relief of dreams and the fear of waking to discover that the nightmare was real. Each new day was like coming to in the middle of the ocean to find that the ship has left.

I wanted my mother. That powerful and primal longing for her bubbled up constantly against my will, leaving me with the paradox of wanting to be rescued by the very person who had imprisoned me. I did not want to wish for her. And yet, to not wish for her—the one person who could reverse my situation—was to surrender all hope. She was my torturer and also my potential savior, and since it was impossible for her to be both at once, my thoughts became hopelessly ensnared, spinning and slamming into walls at every turn like a bug in a jar. To hope was to believe that my mother was good and that she loved me and that soon she would come take me home. But that would require me to accept that I was bad, that I deserved to be there, that it was all my fault. On the other hand, if I maintained my experience of her as tormenter, I could hold on to my sense of self and truth, but I had to give up all comfort, reconcile myself to the despair of nothingness and nobody there and nobody coming and no way out.

I celebrated my sixteenth birthday with a piece of cafeteria cake and a bunch of mental patients. I received a postcard saying that my uncle Billy had died of cancer. I started forgetting the names of streets in my neighborhood, and how it felt to ride in a car, or sit in a movie theater and wait for the lights to dim.

Eventually my parents did come to visit, if only for appearances. My father would sink deep and low in a chair, almost swallowed by it, his face tight and strained, while my mother blew in behind him as if the sun had followed her inside, blinding her to the darkness around her, acting as if this place, my being here, this horror, had nothing to do with her.

On one of their first visits, she told me they were moving. My father had just received a huge promotion at work, elevated to a level beyond his competency, she said, but they finally had enough money for a house on the right side of town, where my mother had always felt she belonged. She seemed happy, untouched by my absence, talked at me about all the great things Matthew was experiencing in college as if the words wouldn't cut. Sometimes Gavin came with them, bearing colorful drawings and eyes full of love and innocence that seemed to fill the depressing hallways with life. Matthew never came. He was embarrassed, my mother said, to have a sister in a mental hospital.

Each time, I cried and begged them to take me home, promised I would be the daughter they wanted. But when visiting hour was over, they walked out the door and watched it shut on me and went back to their lives. I wanted so badly to be driving off with them that my state of longing began to feel like perspective. Maybe it really had been me, maybe my mother really was just trying to help, maybe if I could fix myself, they would love me and take me back.

I posed this possibility to James one day when he sat beside me at the window as I watched my parents' car pull out of the parking lot.

"Cass," he said gently. There were tears in his eyes too. "I don't know much, but I know you don't belong here. Don't believe the lie, okay?"

I looked one last time at the station wagon retreating out of the long driveway. "Okay," I said, and in that moment my tears stopped instantly and finally because someone saw and understood and said out loud what I knew in the tiny, quiet temple of my soul to be true.

After that I stayed away from windows. I accepted the sentence I had been given and waited for the day that it would end.

James tried hard to resuscitate me with laughter. In the dining hall he sat beside me and stuck packets of ketchup into his breast pocket and then pretended to stab himself with his plastic knife, throwing the nurses into a panic. During visiting hours, he introduced himself to everyone's guests and then casually mentioned that he was in for murder. "It only happened twice," he said, and then winked at me as the visitors' eyes bugged out.

When Dr. Meeks encouraged him to speak about his upbringing in group therapy, James was near tears as he relayed the time he was kidnapped by carrot-colored midgets from a chocolate factory after he turned into a blueberry. Another time, he raged with bitter indignation over the merciless teasing he got at flight school for having a nose that was too red and too bright. When Dr. Meeks suggested that James was afraid of letting us know who he really was, he jumped to his feet, thrust his arms into the air and sang, "I gotta be meeee!" Then he looked my way to see if I was laughing.

Eventually, I did begin to laugh again. It was all there was left to do.

five

BACK ON THE ward, Nurse Mary and I part ways, and I go seek out my friend Trish as I always do after my sessions with Meeks because it's the hour when our favorite soap opera, *Malibu Dreams*, is on. Today is the last time we will ever watch it together. I find her in the room next to mine, poised in front of her warped plastic mirror, applying foundation to her cheeks with one hand and smoking a cigarette with the other. Impressively large smoke rings float above her head before they break up and disappear. I pause in the doorway, taking in this scene so familiar, soon to be a memory.

"What's up?" Trish says without looking at me. She has been avoiding eye contact for the last couple of days, and I know it's because she wants to make me matter less now that I'm leaving.

I shrug, a sudden lump in my throat. I always imagined that leaving here would be the best feeling in the world, but these friends are like war buddies, all of us deeply bonded because we have survived the worst of our lives together. Once I walk out that door, I won't be allowed back to visit.

I notice the small hole above her bed and laugh. "Remember that?"

Years back, when I first discovered that pea-sized opening in our shared wall, I would occupy myself at night by sticking raisins through it and waiting for Trish to notice. For weeks, I amused the hell out of myself by imagining the small pile of fruit accumulating on her bed. Then one night, I had my face up to the wall, preparing to squeeze another raisin through it, when a sudden blast of lotion squirted through from the other side and nailed me in the eye. "Gotcha!" Trish had said, and the two of us laughed until we were sobbing and the nurses came running to see what was wrong.

"I taught you early on not to mess with me," she says now, allowing a small smile as she takes a drag off of her cigarette. I pull one out of my own pack and light it off of hers so I don't have to track down a nurse to do it for me. On occasion, I have seen a nurse let Trish light her own cigarettes even though it's against the rules. They won't let me anywhere near fire.

I sit down on her bed and ash into a small plastic cup on the windowsill. Technically we aren't allowed to smoke in our rooms either, but I think the staff is secretly afraid of Trish. Actually, we are all a little afraid of Trish, who is tall and blond and strikingly beautiful but carries herself with a streetwalker's edge. She has been here longer than any of us, but I have no idea what she's in for, what label of crazy they have tagged her with. I suspect there was some pretty major shit in her past, because despite her toughness she jumps about six feet if you surprise her from behind, and she doesn't like anyone to touch her. Even if you just accidentally brush her arm as you're passing by, she freaks out.

Trish is the one who taught me how to properly smoke a cigarette, as well as how to score an extra ice cream cup at dinner and which nurses will let you stay up past curfew to watch the late-night talk shows. She has a boyfriend named Van who hops the fence to visit beneath her window. So many nights I have spent listening to their whispers, my ear pressed up to the screen, trying to make a study of the way they flirt with each other in case I ever get the opportunity to flirt with a guy myself. They tell each other about their day, and Van pretends to climb the hospital wall and jokes that he's going so crazy without her that soon he'll be locked up too.

I have tried to make sense of the fact that he's still around after all this time, that he stays with Trish even when she is at the bottom of her life and the whole world thinks she's crazy. Trish says it's love and maybe it is, I've just never seen love that looks like that—so entirely unselfish and without judgment.

I've daydreamed about having a boyfriend of my own someday, and now that I'm getting out of here, it's weird to think the opportunity might actually present itself. The thing is, I wouldn't even begin to know how to act, and the fact that I have no experience at all makes the whole idea seem daunting. I've never even kissed anyone, which is humiliating considering that I'm eighteen, but it's not like there are a lot of prospects on a psych ward.

I watch Trish apply a heavy line of electric-blue eyeliner, her brows creased in concentration as if she is preparing for battle. I remember the first time she showed me how to wear makeup, how amazed I was afterward to find that I didn't look anything like myself. Since then I have never left my room without it, even though there's exactly no one here to impress. There's a sense of security in the mask, in the daily burial of myself beneath layer and color, concealing the girl who walked in here two and a half years ago, so exposed and rejected and easy to wound. The act of putting on makeup is like covering up a secret I don't want anyone to know. Now when I catch a glimpse of myself in the mirror, I don't see ugly and unlovable anymore, I see mascara, cherry lip gloss, bright pink blush. I see an illusion I'm hoping to pass off as truth, as the real me.

We are about to head over to the TV room when Shelly of the sliced-up wrists passes by, sobbing. I rush over to find out what's wrong, but Trish stays put. She can't tolerate tears, doesn't let herself have them either. I find Shelly in her room stuffing an overnight bag with clothes. She tells me that her nana, the only real mother figure she's ever had, the only one who comes to visit, who bakes her cookies and strokes her hair, has been hospitalized nearby and is not expected to live through the night. I start to cry too because it's just so freaking sad and because this is what happens when twenty-two heartbroken kids get locked up together on a small hallway—everybody's emotions get all mixed up with each other.

Then Nurse Kay, who has mastered the art of being disaffected, struts in and informs Shelly that Dr. Meeks has denied her a pass to see her grandmother, having deemed her too much of a suicide risk. Considering the razor-blade scars up her wrists, he's probably right, but all Shelly knows is that she won't have the chance to say good-bye to the only person who ever loved her. She sits down on her bed and cries quietly, her pale face turning red and puffy. Soon, the crying moves, becomes something more guttural and desperate.

"Please," she sobs. "I just want to say good-bye!"

"I'm sorry," Kay says matter-of-factly.

Shelly stares up at her, dazed, blinking through tears. Then she jumps up suddenly and runs past us down the hall toward the door. "You have to let me out of here!" she cries, pounding her fists and yanking the knob. "You have to let me out!"

I run after her and put my hand on her shoulder, but Kay steps in front of me.

"No physical contact," she says. Then, instead of providing Shelly comfort, Kay turns and marches into the nurses' station and flips the emergency alarm. The piercing sound shatters the air, a high-pitched scream that runs laps around my head. Everyone stops, hands to their ears, fixed by the blaring sound we know too well. Only Shelly seems mobilized, thrashing harder to get out.

Within seconds, six huge male aides from other wards are running down our hallway. Shelly turns and sees them and screams louder than the alarm at the sight of all those men coming at her.

"I just want to see my nana!" she pleads.

They are upon her in a flash, manhandling her to the ground. She cries out for us, for someone to help her. I think of her rape as the men trap her arms and legs.

"Get off of her!" I scream. I know they'll try to take away my privileges like they always do when I stand up to them, but I've never given a shit before and I'm not about to start now.

"Please don't do this!" Shelly pleads with the aides, and her screams are so penetrating and desperate, they sound like they're coming from my own head.

Nurse Kay gives her a shot that silences her, and the aides drag her by the arms to the Quiet Room to "get herself together." Even after she is drugged and muted, I can hear her screams reverberating: the sounds of helplessness and grief, the horror of indifference.

The alarm stops. All is immediately and terribly quiet.

"You didn't have to do that," I say. "You could have just talked to her."

Kay ignores me, turns to the gathered crowd. "Okay, everybody, show's over."

"Some show," I say with disgust. And just like so many times before, I glance around at the other kids, hoping to see shared outrage in their faces. But the system that punishes feelings and rewards obedience has robbed them of their fight. Me, I don't know any other way to survive.

Finally, I spot James, just back from Meeks's office. He walks over and stands beside me, allying himself with my fury—me and James against the world.

six

LATE THAT NIGHT, my second to last here, James and I are sitting just inside the doorway of our respective rooms, James slouched against the doorjamb. The hallway is near black and quiet as sleep.

"So," he whispers into the watchful silence. "How's it feel?"

"What? Being a super-genius?"

Even in the dark I can see him roll his eyes. "Flying the coop."

I look down at my hands, which seem larger in the darkness. For the first time in my life, my entire future feels wholly dependent on me, and I can't think of anyone I trust less not to screw things up. I can't even think about it. It's too scary.

"You realize how hard it's gonna be, running this place all by myself?" he says.

I look up and smile. "All those damsels in distress and no one but you to rescue them."

He smiles back, but the air between us grows heavy with unspoken sadness. I look away.

"Anyway . . ." I say.

He watches me.

"What?"

He pauses. His face grows serious. "Who's gonna have your back when I'm not around?"

"Come on. I'll be fine."

He looks away, chews his lip. "I hope so."

"What's that supposed to mean?"

"Nothing. I just think your mother's gonna try to make you think you owe her now and suck you back into her control."

"Owe her for what?"

"Gee, I don't know . . . Twenty grand tuition for starters. Strings pulled to get you in."

I shrug. My mother's surprise offer to pay for college was made after I mentioned to one of the nurses that I wanted to go. At first, my mother was completely against me leaving this place, but then out of nowhere she came up with the idea that I should apply to her alma mater, and all of a sudden my going to college was a brilliant decision. She even got me an application and arranged for me to take the SAT. As soon as my dream became a possible reality, I was sure they wouldn't accept me, a mental patient. But then I learned that the hospital's on-site school would discreetly show up as a satellite to the local high school. I didn't meet all of the math and foreign language requirements, but my mother somehow worked her strange magic and *voilà*, I was headed to Dunton College, the place I had heard a million stories about, where my mother had gone to study art.

Since my acceptance, I have felt my anger at my mother not exactly dissipating but receding, slipping back below the swampy surface like an alligator head. I have seen this happen before, how one act of parental kindness across a history of cruelty can make a kid in here forgive everything that came before simply because they have been deprived of kindness for so long. But I tell myself I'm tougher than that.

"Just because she's paying for college doesn't mean I have to . . . like . . . talk to her or have a relationship with her."

"But why would she go to all that trouble? To get you into *her* school? There's gotta be an agenda there, right?"

"I don't know," I say with a sigh.

He's right, of course. I know how dangerous it is to let go of memory, to forget for even a minute who my mother is, but I don't want to think about that right now. The constant vigilance is exhausting and with less than forty-eight hours left, I just want to focus on hope.

"I need you to give me your word," James says.

"Okay. What for?"

"That you won't fall for the lie."

"This again?" I laugh. "You're so dramatic."

"Your word."

"Stop worrying. She doesn't have any power over me anymore."

He gives me a look.

"Good night," I say, and turn away.

"Wait! Cass," he whispers. "I've been thinking."

I return to the door. "Well, that's new."

He glances down the hallway and back to me. His face is serious. "I'm breaking out of here tomorrow. First thing. I'm gonna meet up with you in Rhode Island."

I laugh, lean my head against the door. "I'd love that," I say, touched by his fantasy. "But you know it'll never happen. Tighter than death row, remember?"

Kay's flashlight hits the far wall of the hallway, and James and I exchange looks. We have only seconds to hit our beds before Kay catches us.

"See ya in the morning," I whisper.

"Love you, Cass," he says.

I pause, trying to soak in the words, to hold them and keep them with me for when I go.

"Love you too, James," I say finally, but he's already in bed with his headphones on.

seven

IN THE MORNING, James is nowhere to be found. The nurses look everywhere. They tear our rooms apart. They check behind sofas, behind desks, in the Quiet Room. He is flat-out gone.

For the first few hours I don't even let myself get my hopes up, certain that he'll be caught and dragged back here. Instead I just sit back and enjoy his antics along with the other patients as we watch the nurses scramble around in a panic, everyone trying to figure out how the hell he managed to get out. But as the hours pass and a quiet unease descends upon the nurses on the ward, the air heavy with anxiety like the waiting room of an ER, I start to believe that maybe, just maybe, James has pulled it off. He has gone to Rhode Island. He is waiting for me there. Soon I am making plans for the two of us on the outside, how I'll hide him in my dorm room and sneak home food from the cafeteria. Then James can get a job at a beachside café or nearby coffee shop where I can go after classes and find him, where I can sit with someone who knows me and knows where I've been and cares about me anyway.

For the first time, the future doesn't seem quite so scary. For the first time, everything seems like it might just be okay after all.

+ + +

The hours tick into nighttime. The cafeteria is quiet at dinner, the reality of James's absence settling over the other patients, who, caught up in the excitement this morning, now realize they have lost something. I alone am happy, a quiet but deep relief expanding in my chest, making it easier to breathe.

At 9:00 P.M. the doorbell rings. The fantasy shatters. James has been captured by the police, I am sure of it. But when Nurse Kay unlocks the door and opens it, it is James, alone, standing in the doorway, no officers or hospital aides accompanying him. He saunters in smelling like late summer air and cigarettes lit by his own hand, acting with his usual cocky bravado, as if he had just been out for a stroll.

But something is different. Something is wrong. He won't look at me.

We all rush around him to hear the details of his escape, and he boasts to the others about how he slipped out with the laundry, stealing through bushes and jumping on a bus—to where he does not say. Everyone else laughs too loudly and listens too eagerly and speaks over each other with their endless questions. I stand at the back of the group and wait for him to give me some sign, some sense of explanation, something, anything. But he will not meet my eye.

I get frantic, chasing reasons in my head for why he came back, for what might have happened, for what he found out there that made him turn around and choose death row instead. Because if James couldn't make it, if James with all his fearlessness and charm went out into the world only to rush right back, then what hope is there for the rest of us? What hope is there for me?

I want to ask him, but he's not looking at me and there are too many people around, and then a nurse is leading him to the office, where they will check him for contraband: razors, knives, pills— anything you can off yourself with.

I head toward my room; my body, which was just this morning light with hope, is heavy now, waterlogged with dread and fear. In the hallway, James and the nurse pass by me on his way to being frisked. Once again I try to make eye contact, but instead James slips a small brown bag from under his shirt into my hand.

"Sorry, Cass," he mumbles to the floor, and disappears down the hall.

I go to my room and tear open the bag. Inside is a candle shaped like a Smurf and a small blue lighter to match. I think I'm supposed to laugh, but all I can do is cry.

In the morning, I go through the motions of packing, moving slowly as if through a thick fog. I wish James was with me, teasing me and making me laugh, but he is still unable to face me after coming back. I dump all of my accumulated belongings into one small suitcase: makeup purchased from the gift shop, a bunch of letters from when I first got here sent from old friends who slowly trickled away, the bedsheets and towel and clothes my mother packed for me the day she put me in here. Most of the clothes were already baggy when I bought them to hide all the weight I had gained in my early teens. Now, after years of inedible hospital food, they pretty much hang off of me.

I try to figure out what to wear for my first day of both freedom and college, but it's not like I have a lot of good options. Finally

I choose a T-shirt, an oversized sweater and a pair of jeans. Just the act of putting them on feels like a restoration of sonhood after not bothering to wear anything but hospital scrubs and pajamas for so long. And yet to see myself in these old clothes invites the intrusion of my mother's voice back into my head: "All my life, I dreamed about having a daughter . . . how I would dress up her up like a pretty little doll. I just don't know why you won't be the daughter I wanted."

I sit on the suitcase and zip it shut.

In front of the distorted plastic mirror I do one last check of my makeup and wonder what the kids at college will think of me, if they will be able to look in my eyes and know where I've been. Just to be on the safe side, I add more eyeliner and mascara.

I'm about to head out into the hallway when Nurse Kay pops her head into my room.

"The time has come, eh?" she says, smiling for once.

"Yep."

"Who's picking you up?"

"No one," I say. "I'm taking the bus."

"Oh," she says. Her eyes go sad. Just for a moment. Just long enough to let me know I was wrong in thinking she doesn't care about us kids or that she doesn't see the reality of our situations. "Don't miss your stop," she says then, and disappears down the hall.

I take a deep breath, grab my suitcase, and allow myself one last look at this room that has seen so many of my tears. It appears now exactly as it did the day I first saw it: the bare mattress, the small desk, the window with the steel mesh screen. There is no trace

n my memories feel somehow packed up and
's just a strange room I passed through in the
ny life. I think of the kid who will move in here
if they will be afraid like I was, if they will cry
like I did, if they will make friends here who
through. I go over to the desk and write a note,
let them know that they'll be okay, let them see that there was a
girl here before them who survived this place just as they someday
will. I leave it in the drawer and walk out.

At the end of the hallway, the other patients have gathered in a
semicircle by the door to see me off. When I see them there, whatever composure I have managed to assemble collapses. One by one
I hug each of them, defying the "no physical contact" rule. James
stands back from the rest, watching. He wears a blazer over his hospital scrubs and dark sunglasses as if it's a funeral. The sight of him
dressed like that makes me laugh and cry harder at the same time.

With each good-bye, the idea of this last, most painful good-
bye to James gets more difficult. My throat tightens around the
thought of it. I go to hug Trish, a quick hug, but it means something that she lets me. I slip a good-bye letter into her hand because I know she'll never let me say to her face all the corny things
I want to tell her.

"Don't let me catch you here again," she says, and I can swear
there are tears in her eyes too.

I go to Shelly next. I grab her wrists and glance down at all
those pink scars on white skin. "I'll see you again soon. On the
outside, okay?"

She looks at her hands as if surprised to see them there. When she raises her head to meet my eyes, her nod is small and unconvincing. I feel a pang of foreboding.

By the time I get to James, I am ready to call the whole thing off. I stand in front of him. His eyes are hidden by the sunglasses. I need so badly to see his eyes. All of my fear accumulates in the space between us, in the space of his absence from me before I have even left.

"I don't think I can do this without you," I say quietly.

He is silent for a moment, and then he takes his sunglasses off, revealing the James I know, the friend I love, my safe place. His eyes are tired and sad and far away. "I'm a call away," he says, handing me a folded-up piece of paper with the ward's pay-phone number on it. "You'll always know where to find me."

"I don't want to find you here. I want to find you out there!" I say, tears threatening.

"Listen to me, soldier," he says, grabbing my shoulders and looking into my eyes with mock seriousness to make me laugh. "Run! Save yourself!"

I manage to smile back and put my hands up in surrender. Then Dr. Meeks unlocks the door, looks at me with his well-cultivated expression of concern and hands me his card. "Just in case," he says.

I walk out the door and turn to watch it shut on James.

He moves to the window—all the kids do—for one last wave. I stand just below them and pull out the lighter James smuggled in for me. Then I hold up Meeks's card and set it on fire. I watch as everyone, James especially, cheers.

"You're going to do great!" he calls after me through the steel mesh screen.

He sounds so sure.

eight

I START DOWN the hospital drive, glance back one last time at James in the window. Then off I go, rolling my suitcase behind me through the high gates and onto a main thoroughfare where the loud whoosh of cars is startling after so much time spent inside. All at once and shockingly, I am back in the world.

The bus stop is on the corner. A large woman is spread out across the bench, two shopping bags at her feet. She stares straight ahead and clutches her purse when I sit down on the edge beside her. I wonder if she knows where I've come from, if she can smell the hospital on me the way certain dogs can sniff out a tumor.

"Do you know if the twelve thirty to Newport has come yet?" I ask. She looks at me and then away. I am suddenly certain that I will get on the wrong bus, find myself in some strange place— Siberia, maybe, or worse, New Jersey—where I will be forced to cap bottles in a hair spray factory, never to be seen again. I think of James hopping a bus from this very spot yesterday, hopeful and free and full of dreams before something made him change his mind, go back in.

The bus arrives with a squeal and a hiss. I step up to it. "Is this the one that goes to Newport?" I say. The driver grunts something that I can only hope is a yes and then sighs as if the effort to deal with such an idiot has taxed him tremendously. I climb aboard and hand him a ten from the large wad of guilt-money that my dad gave me on his last visit. It's a struggle to get down the aisle with my suitcase, and I feel the need to apologize for my presence as the other people on the bus stare miserably at me. Finally I make my way to an open window seat, the bus lurches forward and we are in motion.

For the next two hours, I watch the moving landscape provide proof of my freedom as the hospital, the town, the city, the state all fall away behind me. I stare at myself in the window glass, trying to recognize the girl reflected back at me, to make a friend of her, to make the hope stick. But worries bully their way into my brain, insisting that I am not equipped for this adventure, that I will be completely lost amid a world of strangers with no one to offer direction or guidance, that I will ultimately collapse and break apart beneath the unsupported weight of myself out here on my own. The absence of love, that barren, hopeless place revisited, will destroy me once and for all. I'll end up back in the hospital. Or worse, on the wrong end of a looped rope.

"Next stop, Dunton College," the bus driver says, jolting me from my thoughts.

I grip the seat in front of me as if bracing for a crash. The moment I have been both waiting for and dreading is finally here, only now the roar of terror that has reared up completely trumps the excitement. All at once, it's way too real and I just want to stay on this bus with these harmless strangers, close my eyes and go to sleep, wake up when life no longer feels exhausting.

Suddenly, the Atlantic Ocean comes into view. "Can I jump off here instead?" I ask, standing abruptly. The bus driver sighs again, pulls to the curb and deposits me on a street corner across from a beach. Then the bus is gone and it's only me.

It's windy and cold for August. The air is different here, dense and heavy with the sea. I walk up to the small, rocky beach, eager to answer the call that pulled me here. It all comes back to me like a once-elusive dream: the welcome of the ocean, its wide arms reaching. I breathe the whole of it, the smell and the size and the melancholy beauty of it into my lungs. The Atlantic has had a hold on me since the first time I saw it many years ago. I am drawn to its detachment, its mercurial nature, its violence. In these things I find a comforting familiarity.

The coastline is empty except for two homeless guys sitting shoulder to shoulder on a nearby bench, sharing a drink from a paper bag. Their friendship makes me think of James, of how connection can lift people out of their circumstances. They ask me for a cigarette and I give them two. Their gratitude is so genuine, their two rotten-toothed grins so drunkenly cheerful and thrilled that I immediately hand over the entire pack.

Then I start toward the water. The sky is stone gray and sunless, all the light wrung out of it like wet from a cloth. In front of the empty lifeguard stand, a few surfers zigzag up and down the waves, black as birds against the gloom. I watch them for a moment with yearning, imagining that graceful unity with the world. In the distance, I recognize Dunton's famous clock tower from the college brochure, its stately brick buildings sitting high on a cliff. I keep walking down the shoreline until I'm far enough away that no one should be able to see me. At any moment kids from school could show up, and I don't want anyone to see me with my makeup washed off. After all, if I have one hope for my first year of college, it's that I can rid myself of my ugly past, maybe even find love. Not that I'd ever openly admit that I want it. Or that I have the remotest clue how to get it.

The sea is the color of metal, the white waves disheveled and sloshing in a tantrum. The ocean calls to me with its baptismal promise. I shed my jeans and sweater. Today I leave my history behind. Make the past the past, as James always said. Today, right now, I start over. A new me. Or something like that.

The water is a shock of cold. It knocks the breath out of me before it reaches my knees. I look out at the wild, breaking ocean and take a deep breath, summoning all the hope I have in me for what is possible. Then I charge the surf and launch myself toward a wave about to crash. The instant before it does, I dive. For one moment my body is anesthetized. My thoughts frozen. Everything still and cold and silent. I emerge on the other side like something new, whooping with the rush. A second wave follows, mountainous and fast, and I rush into that one too, laughing as I go, the child in me released by the sea.

I move a little farther out where I can still find the bottom. My tiptoes are attuned for the brush of a crab as I lean my head back, let the water rinse my hair, rinse everything. I imagine my old self pouring out of me like octopus ink, black ribbons slipping into the current, disappearing into the depths.

There is no one around in any direction as far as I can see, and there is so much peace in that, in the absence of human voices.

Sometimes it seems like everybody wants to put their noise into the world until you can't have enough quiet to even know you exist.

A spot of light peeks out from the gray sky, and I close my eyes and push onto my back to bathe in it. The chop splashes in my face and stings the back of my throat, but I don't mind. It's this total merge with the ocean that I love so much: its tingling touch, salt taste, smell of fish, yellow underbelly, the sound of its roar and of its nuzzle. It is a return to the state of indistinguishable bodies, the gurgle of breath and heartbeat, the sense of being home. I tell myself I'm washed clean now, made new, that the flailing and wailing is over. I float for a long time.

Then suddenly, a flash in my head as if sparked by this new quiet and stillness. The voice from my nightmares. Reciting a nursery rhyme. "Georgie Porgie puddin' and pie." Startled, I gasp and flail, taking in water as I come back to the present.

I look up to realize that the shoreline has moved, the brick buildings of Dunton seeming much farther away and small. I go to stand, but the bottom is long gone. I recognize instantly that I'm in really big trouble. After all, I have been in this state of drowning before. So many times before.

nine

THE FIRST TIME I drowned, I was six years old. It was July and we were in the middle of a monthlong heat wave. I was dragging ass behind my family, already wearing my life preserver and tripping over the too-long beach towel in my hand as we approached my grandparents' house.

All morning my mother had been quiet. The last few weeks she'd been strained, probably because of the heat, and had been wearing an increasingly wilting smile. My father, who never noticed anything, had also not noticed this. But I was exquisitely attuned to my mother, needing the security of her steadiness, aware of its fluctuations, anxious when I felt it slipping. I raced to catch up to her, reached out my hand and grabbed hers.

"I'm so sick of having to come here like this," she said, dropping my hand to yank at the hem of her sundress and then pausing to smooth down her polar blond hair. She glanced back at our old beat-up car on the street and then up at the mansion before us. "I feel like Cinderella returning in her pumpkin."

My father seemed to register this as the accusation that it was, tucking his head into his shoulders like a turtle. We never visited his parents. My mother claimed they lived in an armpit (Cleveland). But her parents lived just on the other side of town and, unlike us, had air-conditioning and an in-ground pool, so we saw them often in the summer.

"Don't let them get me," my mother said. She took a step back so that my father could enter first, and Matthew and I gathered on either side of her like chess pieces to the queen. As always, my mother had the ability to pull people around her, compelling them to protect her no matter the cost to themselves.

My father sighed and pushed open the back gate as if it were heavy, which it was not, and we followed him through it.

My grandmother was in her usual habitat by the pool area, drink in one hand, cigarette in the other. She looked like an aging movie star, with hair the color of sharkskin that swooped away from her forehead and stayed put in a poof with at least one can of hairspray. Even in her bathing suit, my grandmother wore all of her jewels: twenty-four-karat bracelets that jangled when she smoked and gold earrings that sat like fat snails on her lobes.

When she saw us, she gave a small patrician wave to my mother and called out, "Bevy, darling," in her thick British accent. My grandmother was not actually British, and the details of how she acquired this accent, having never left the state of Pennsylvania, remain a mystery.

Posed like an antonym beside her, in jeans as old and wrinkled as my grandmother's knees, was my uncle Billy, my mother's younger brother. Billy weighed in at over three hundred pounds but was also tall, so my grandmother liked to say that he was not fat, "just big." He was big and also fat. And he lived in my grandparents' basement. As soon as Matthew and I were old enough to walk, he took us down there to see his porno magazines and his bong. He was our favorite uncle.

"Hello, Mom. Hello, Bill," my mother said with a hopeful smile. She bent over the lounge chair to give her mother a hug, but my grandmother held her at arm's length like a dirty diaper and blew air kisses at her cheeks. My mother drew up abruptly. Her beautiful smile twitched. She stepped back toward us, and I was shocked at how someone so large to me could be made to look so small, how one person could shrink another so easily.

"This bloody heat is awful, isn't it?" my grandmother said. "But I guess you would know that better than me, considering that little sweat box you live in! Your father is hiding out in the den with the air-conditioning turned up so high, I'm afraid we'll find him frozen solid in there. Thank God you have us to come to."

"We are lucky indeed to have you!" my father chimed in with petlike eagerness. My mother gave him a withering gaze and he slunk into a plastic chair, removed his glasses and rubbed some sudden speck of dirt off of them with his shirt.

My mother nudged Matthew and me, and we both mumbled hello to my grandmother, who insisted we call her by her first name—Leigh—lest anyone within screaming distance hear that she was old enough to be a grandparent.

"Hello, children," she said with a sigh.

Sometimes we called her "Pee" behind her back.

Uncle Billy complimented me on the pretty sundress I wore over my bathing suit and then took a hand out of his pocket long enough to ruffle my hair and call me "sailor" for the life preserver around my neck. Then he pulled a quarter from behind my ear and handed it to me before jamming his hand back into his jeans.

Suddenly, the back gate swung open again.

"Ohh, my darling!" my grandmother exclaimed. She leaped to her feet and pushed past my mother to envelop her other son, Paul, in a warm embrace.

Paul was a soon-to-be divorcé who declared everything was "magnificent." "It's a magnificent day, isn't it?" he'd say. "I'm going to take a dip in this magnificent pool. Won't that just be magnificent?" Even as a child, I knew he was full of shit and sensed that whatever was underneath all that magnificence was entirely unmagnificent and very, very angry. I avoided him.

"Come! Come!" my grandmother said. "Would you like something to drink? Bevy, why don't you get the men something to drink?"

"The men have legs too," my mother said as she headed toward the pool.

My grandmother ignored her and linked her arm in Paul's. "I'm so glad you came! Billy and I have been *dying* for some good company."

My mother perched herself at the water's edge and dangled her bare legs into it. "Cold," she said to no one in particular.

I plopped down beside her on the concrete. Behind us, my father was chatting up Paul with the loud please-don't-hit-me voice he used in all social interactions.

My mother glanced over at him, shook her head and sighed. She stared deeply into the pool as if she were seeking her reflection in it, her face blank and still as the water itself. I wanted to say something to break the spell of her unhappiness, which I could feel heavy inside me. I looked down to see what she saw, but there was only the bottom.

"Cannonball!" Matthew cried suddenly. For a moment he was tucked and suspended like a home run, catching the light before shattering the surface.

"How many times have I told him not to do that!" my grandmother yelled as she stood to wipe the splash off her lounge chair.

But my mother just smiled wide as a day as the emptiness into which she had been staring was replaced with the happy, wet face of my brother, appearing like a newborn from the depths.

"Oh!" she giggled, flicking water at him with her toes. "That was a good one!"

"Did I get you?"

"You know you did!" she said, pulling her own wet shirt away from herself. "You always get me."

Her whole demeanor changed as she beamed into Matthew's face, and she was still laughing, high and bright, when I slid off the ledge to join him. I gasped. The water was February-cold and sharp with too much chlorine. The life preserver pushed against my jaw and half strangled me as I bobbed by the neck like a buoy. But I was happy, so happy with my mother laughing and the sun in my face and the water so cold but so clean.

"Look, Mom!" Matthew said, treading water by the diving board. The rest of my mother's family retired to the upper patio for drinks, and my father shuffled uncertainly behind them. My mother stayed with us, watching Matthew.

"My God!" she said as the minutes passed. "Aren't you getting tired yet?"

"Nope!" Matthew gurgled. "I could go for hours."

"All right, I'm timing you. I bet you can't go five more minutes."

Even I knew he could go five more minutes.

"Piece of cake," Matthew said.

"It's not that hard!" I called out, eager to show that I could do it too.

"It doesn't count when you have a life preserver on," my mother said, with a roll of her eyes.

Forty-five minutes later we were out of the pool and my mother was presenting Matthew to her family as if he were made of gold. "Can you believe that he just now finished treading?" she bragged happily. "I'm telling you, Mom, my son is going to be an Olympian."

I was jealous. I wanted to be an Olympic water-treader too.

My grandmother finished off her Scotch in one gulp and sized up my brother. "Big deal," she snorted, lighting a cigarette and exhaling smoke through her nostrils.

My mother winced. She wrapped her arms around Matthew like a second towel and looked toward my father, who stared with sudden interest into the bottom of his glass.

"Jesus, Mother," she said. "Why do you have to be like that?" She glanced once again at my father as if he might stick up for her, then spun around and marched toward the house. Matthew and I followed her.

She slammed the kitchen door behind us so hard that I could feel the slap of its wind, her fury—the house and I both shuddering with it.

"Don't you listen to her," she said to Matthew. "Your grandmother just doesn't want me to have anything good in my life."

She bent over the sink and splashed cold water on her face.

"Why?" I asked.

"Because I'm a woman." She shut off the faucet and stared out the window. "And she doesn't like women."

"Why?"

"Because they remind her of her mean, miserable self, that's why." She turned to us then. "You kids love me, right?" she said, and she said it like she hadn't asked us a million times, like we hadn't shouted a million times, "Yes!"

"More than anything!" I cried, throwing myself at her legs as if I could fill her whole being up with myself so that my love would be inside of her. I wanted nothing more than to be the good in my mother's life.

We headed back out, and the first thing I noticed was that the air had taken on the peculiar smell of Billy's basement. We came upon my relatives collapsed over the patio table, pounding their fists and laughing so hard, they were crying. Even my grandmother, whose expressionless face was locked in by one too many face-lifts, was doubled over, killing herself with giggles, which she somehow managed to do with a British air. But the weirdest thing, the positive indication that the world had flipped on its axis, was that they were all laughing at a story my father was telling. No one ever laughed at my father's stories.

"What's going on here?" my mother demanded.

"Oh, Bev," Uncle Paul replied, wiping tears from his eyes, "you never told us that Ed was such a magnificent comedian."

"See, Bev!" my father said. He turned to Paul. "I've been trying to tell her!"

"Shut up," my mother said. She faced the rest of the group with her hands in tight fists at her side. "I can't believe you assholes are smoking pot with my children here!"

Suddenly the laughter stopped. Uncle Paul coughed out a mouthful of smoke. They all looked at each other with eyes wide and spooked, as if they were staring into the spotlight of a police car.

"And I," my grandmother declared finally with haughty indignation, "can't believe that your children are here while we're trying to smoke pot!"

Of course, that did it. They howled with such glee that Uncle Billy choked briefly on a martini olive and Uncle Paul fell backward in his chair and cackled all the way down to the concrete. Even my father, who couldn't have had more than a contact high, laughed eagerly as he always did when other people laughed—happy, I think, to have been given a recognizable social cue. And the sight of everyone laughing and falling all over themselves made me laugh too, even though I had no idea what was going on.

"Relax, Bev," my grandmother said through her giggles. She pulled out what looked like a lit cigarette that she'd been concealing under the table. "Here. Have a pull. God knows you could stand to chill."

"It really is magnificent stuff," Uncle Paul added.

"Go ahead," my grandmother said. "Spark it up."

There was even more laughter, so much laughter and such contagious laughter that I became swept up in it, overcome by anxious hysterical giggling. I did not notice at first that Matthew was not laughing. As soon as I saw the seriousness of his face, I looked to my mother and realized that there were tears in her eyes. I wanted to tell her that I didn't mean it, that I didn't even know why I was laughing, but I couldn't stop. She looked at all of us with a sad knowing smile, lingering on each face, as if recording us. When her eyes landed on my father snickering into his hand, she watched him for a long moment without blinking, and as she did, her sad smile dropped slowly and something else came over her. It was an expression that I'd never seen before, a frightened look, a panic even. She took several steps back, wrapped her arms tightly around her shoulders and squeezed. I had seen her mad at my father a million times but this was something else, something worse, something animal and desperate. It was as if she saw all the chess pieces had come to life, they were all on the other side of the board and they were gunning for her.

I moved toward her with a sickening feeling in my stomach.

She stepped back as if afraid of me and pulled Matthew close like a shield. Her frightened eyes darted between me and her family and my father as if we were all one, all the enemy.

I think, looking back, that that was the moment. I didn't know it then, but I felt it happen. I felt the Atlantic break.

And I had to do something. I had to fix the thing in my mother's face that looked broken. The thing I felt that *I* had broken. The solution was obvious to me. I turned and headed for the pool.

"Mom, look!" I shouted over the laughter as I threw off my life preserver and climbed onto the diving board.

The sun had taken its own dive behind the trees, and the water looked darker without it. I took a big breath before pushing off from the tips of my toes. My knees went up to my chest. I was going to be the something good in my mother's life.

I sank like a quarter. I don't remember being scared. Only that it was quiet. So quiet. And I was swimming, treading water at the bottom of the deep end in a wet and quiet room that felt like God. I looked to the surface, through all that trembling blue and the diluted sun overhead, and I waited for my mother's smiling face to appear.

Back on dry land, according to Matthew, no one heard the small splash of my body hitting the water, which was more than enough proof as far as he was concerned that I couldn't cannonball for shit. My mother, so disturbed by the scene of her family, grabbed him and headed out the back gate as my father followed, calling, "Wait!"

They were in the car, Matthew said, my mother hunched over herself and my father gunning the engine when Billy knocked on the glass, holding up my life preserver.

"Cassie forgot this."

My mother rolled down the window to grab it. But it was Billy who noticed, Billy who glanced into the backseat and said, "Wait. Where *is* Cassie?"

I thought I was dreaming and in the dream my mother was screaming, "This is all your fault!" Then I heard my father say, "How is this *my* fault?" and I opened my eyes and wondered why everyone was staring at me.

"Welcome back, Sailor," Uncle Billy said. His wet curls were dripping on my face. "Did you have a nice trip?"

I went to smile and coughed up a lung full of pool.

"She's okay," someone said, and the next thing I knew I was being hauled over my father's shoulder, watching the gate to my grandmother's house swing shut.

My mother was behind us, and her angry face appeared to bob up and down with the motion of my father's footsteps as he carried me.

Suddenly she drew back and chucked her damp towel through the air. It hit me square in the face. "Sorry, Cassie," she said. "That was meant for your father."

My father swung around and now I was looking in the direction of the car. I wanted very much to be in it and heading home. I didn't feel so good.

"That's not nice," my father said.

"Don't talk to me about nice! I can't believe you just sat there like that."

"Well, I would've jumped in, but Billy got to her first."

"I'm not talking about her, you imbecile," she said, and her voice sounded like it had been put through a cheese grater. "I'm talking about how you sat there and laughed with those assholes and let them get stoned in front of my kids!"

"They weren't getting stoned," my father said with a straight face. At times, you really had to respect him for his awe-inspiring capacity for denial.

"You're out of your damn mind," my mother muttered.

"What was that?" My father spun around again.

I was getting dizzy.

We reached the car and my father unloaded me into the

backseat. My mother climbed into the front and slammed the door.

"And you," she said, swiveling in her seat to face me. "What were you thinking, going into the deep end without your life vest? You just made me look like the worst mother in the world! Well . . . second worst."

"I didn't mean to," I said.

She looked at me hard for a moment as if she was trying to decide if she believed me. Then her face crumbled and she began to cry. "Oh, kids," she said. "Don't ever let me be a mother like her! It's my worst fear . . . It's . . . Oh God, promise me I won't. Promise me you won't let me turn out like her."

"You won't!" Matthew and I both assured her at once, believing with all our little hearts.

"Really?" She wiped her face and looked hopefully into Matthew's eyes.

"Yes," he told her, "it's impossible!"

"But how can you be sure?"

He thought about this very seriously for a second. Then he said, "Because, Mom, you do the worst British accent I've ever heard."

My mother giggled, then did a double take. "But wait a second! So does she!"

"Oh well," Matthew said, shrugging. "I guess we're screwed then."

They both laughed at this and she grabbed his hand and squeezed it. "Oh, Matty. You always make me feel better."

Then she turned to my father and her voice turned colder than

I had ever heard it before. "I'm telling you right now, if you don't get me out of this hellhole for a proper vacation—"

"Yeah, Dad!" I said, shoving my head through the space between the front seats. Already I was learning to want only what my mother wanted, to want it with life-preserving desperation. "Let's go somewhere fun!"

My mother turned and stared silently out the window while I continued to plead with him all the way home, believing somehow that a vacation could fix things, that my father, of all people, could save us.

ten

TWELVE YEARS LATER, there is no Uncle Billy to rescue
me as I move farther and farther from the shore, wondering if this
is really how I'm going to die. It's like I'm watching the whole
thing happen from outside of myself, completely detached and not
terribly surprised.

I've always had this vision of how my life would end. I wonder
if everybody has an idea of their worst imaginable death, an image
so explicit you could almost wonder if it is prophetic.

Back when things were really hairy, I used to have this story
play out in my mind so often that it feels like I have already lived
it: Someone is drowning, someone I love, and I race out to help
them. I'm a good swimmer, unafraid of the ocean, confident in my
ability to rescue. I reach them quickly but the victim is panicked.
Their arms lock around my neck and in their desperation for air,
they try to climb me, pushing me under. I shout at them to stop,
but the word itself gets drowned. I go under and they follow. We
are almost face-to-face. I grab at their arms to calm them, to make
them look into my eyes and see what is happening. But they can't
see past their own distress, can't see me as anything more than
a buoy to put their weight on, do not care that in their efforts to

survive they are killing me. I try to kick them, punch them, but it's no use. I can't get free and there's no more air and we sink into the darkness, fighting each other the whole way down. It's not like I made that up either. It's something that really happens to people. I just never imagined the person I'm trying to save would be me. Somehow, I always thought it would be her.

I start to swim hard, remembering what I've been taught about riptides: to move parallel to the beach, away from the channel. Only when I try, I can't do it. The current is too strong, too fast. I paddle desperately, but the Atlantic has an umbilical hold on me. I tell myself not to panic. The panic is what kills you. As soon as I start thinking about the panic killing you, I start to panic.

The wind is up. A fog sits. The brick buildings of Dunton College disappear behind it. My mouth fills with salt when all I want is air. My hair is in my face, eyes and mouth. I tilt my head back, frantic for breath, for someone on the shore who can help me.

No one sees. No one is there.

My thoughts spin in a whirlpool, sad and angry and frightened and pointless. Mostly, I just want to go home. Mostly, I'm just wondering why I always screw everything up.

The ocean has me by the legs. I can barely keep my head above water. That's how quickly the fatigue of drowning hits; it hits all at once, like I've been swimming my whole life and I'm just too tired to take another stroke. I want to cry, but know it will only make me drown faster. I think of how easy it would be to surrender, how drowning would take me like sleep. They say it's quite peaceful once you stop fighting.

Then suddenly, I hear a voice in my head again. Only this time it's my own—a little, quiet voice that somehow breaks through the chaos and struggle and self-flagellation and tells me quite simply that I will be okay. I have no reason to believe it, but my thoughts quiet anyway. And in the momentary quiet of my mind, I remember something else I once learned about riptides: that sometimes, the only way out is to quit fighting, to let it take you back and back and back until the current emancipates you.

I bring my legs up and let myself float, watching the reach of shore expand with terrible regret, an aching good-bye in my chest. Back and back and back I go, being asked to trust that this will save me when every part of me wants to do the opposite, to break free by moving forward. I think of my suitcase sitting on the sand, waiting for me to return to it. *At least someone will know I was here.*

Then it happens so slowly that I'm not sure if I'm imagining it, but I start to feel the sea releasing me, like a roller coaster easing gradually into the gate. My arms are both heavy and without bones, and I've swallowed so much salt water, I could puke up a whale. But as I start to move inch by inch diagonally across the ocean, I see the arch of waves in front of me, the brick buildings of Dunton College reemerging beyond that, and this new hope lifts me out of myself, shifts my perspective. I can hear birds and the lap of sea, the distant roll of breaking water. I find new energy to swim, which drains and pulses again and again. The distance is so much farther than it looks, and it is not until I feel the catch and the rise beneath me that I'm sure I am among the waves. One carries me, delivers me into a dump of white water where I am buried again, fighting to keep my chin above the whirlpool of froth. Another comes and I am drilled into the sand.

The sand!

I crawl and am knocked down, clawing my way to shore. Even in two feet, the current, so insistent, tries to suck me back.

Finally, I am on the beach. Gasping and happy. I collapse and cough and throw up water. I consider what a colossal failure my little baptism was, though it is a thought uncharged with feeling, likely to be revisited when I have more strength to hate myself. Instead I am taken by such a blissful state of peace, unlike anything I've ever felt, that it seems rooted in something bigger than just my relief. It is a bone calm, a soul calm, as if the unnamable but constant rattle inside me has been silenced for a moment, given a source to express and extinguish itself. I think back to that saving voice in my head and I wonder how I can find her again—the me who is wise and unafraid, who believes I will be okay.

Upwind, the sound of another human voice shatters my serenity. The rattle inside me stirs. I glance up. It's one of the homeless guys now standing on the bench, a hand cupped to his mouth while the other waves the pack of cigarettes in the air like a rescue flag.

"You okay, girlie?"

I start to laugh, but it feels like crying so I stop. I raise my head, triggering more coughing. Eventually I manage a limp wave.

"I'm fine," I call back, though my voice has no sound.

I'm fine. I'm fine. I'm fine.

Because just like all the other times I've drowned in my life, I'm determined to keep paddling forward, to believe that none of it has affected me at all.

eleven

I SPEND THE next hour in a dirty gas station bathroom changing out of my clothes, blow-drying my wet hair with the hand dryer, reapplying my makeup—trying to make myself perfect so no one will be able to guess what's underneath, see the girl who can't stay afloat. I light a cigarette from the new pack I've just purchased and immediately start coughing again. I've been hacking almost nonstop since I left the beach, trying to eject something lodged deep in my chest. The moment my lungs settle down I check my reflection once more. No matter how many hours I spend in front of the mirror, I can never hold on to what I look like the second I turn away. I'm like a vampire's opposite, existing only in the glass.

I leave the gas station and walk toward the brick buildings of Dunton, dragging my suitcase behind me. The campus appears to be straight down the road. I can't tell how far exactly, but I don't mind the walk. I'm still adjusting to how strange it feels just to be able to move through the world without supervision, to light my own cigarettes, to know the wind on my skin won't be taken away from me. Besides, I'm in no rush to get there. I'm scared shitless.

Forty-five minutes later I am at the main entrance to the Dunton campus where a big sign hangs, welcoming incoming freshmen. I stop and look around, taking everything in. The sun has come out over buildings so large and old and Gothic that everyone looks misplaced in time beside them. The ocean is present in the hang of salt in the air and in the coastal breeze that tosses the hair of both girls and trees. All around me, kids leap out of minivans and station wagons like they've just arrived at a party while their parents organize missions to unload their crap into the dorms. I stand alone with my suitcase and try to figure out where I'm supposed to go. A small voice in my head keeps saying, "I want to go home." I have no idea what I even mean by "home," which somehow makes the refrain harder to ignore.

Finally I take a deep breath and drag my suitcase across the lawn toward an orientation booth, threading through preppy parents and their loud, happy teenagers. Everyone around me is wearing T-shirts and shorts in the latest styles, while I am in my oversized jeans and sweater. Already I feel like I'm advertising that I don't belong here. I push my shoulders back and lift my chin higher, trying to appear cool and confident, like I don't care.

After standing in a long line of eager, boisterous freshmen, I eventually get my student info packet, which includes my dorm assignment, key code and meal card. Then I wander around until I find my dorm—an industrial-looking building with interior cinder-block walls and a concrete staircase. A disturbingly cheerful resident adviser greets me at the door, checks my name off a list and then points me toward my room. I reach my hallway and see a blond girl and her mother at the other end, struggling to hoist a huge picture frame through their doorway.

I summon the courage to say "hi" when I reach them, but in the same moment, their frame slips and crashes to the floor and they both erupt in hysterical, exclusive laughter. I turn and punch the pin number I've been given into the keypad on the door, push it open and step into silence. The room is painted stark white and contains a broken window shade, a single bare bed, a small desk and a chair.

Instinctively I assess my surroundings, calculating the distance between the bed and the door, the number of windows, the type of locks, the quickest escape. Ever since I was a kid, I've had a deep-seated fear of being trapped, and it's only gotten worse since I got locked up.

On the wall above the desk, I notice a fire alarm. I climb up and pull out the battery and then flick on my lighter, watching for a moment the vitality of the flame, feeling the heat of its nearness against my thumb. Then I spark up a cigarette and plop down on the bed. There is a phone on the floor beside me, but when I pick it up, there's no dial tone. I have no idea why or what to do about it. I imagine my mother helping Matthew with things like this in his first year of college. I stuff the phone under my bed so I don't have to see it.

The coughing starts again, so deep and persistent this time that little diamonds of light flash across my vision. The taste of seawater scorches the back of my raw throat and I feel kind of light-headed, like I can't get enough air.

I lie down on the mattress without bothering to put the sheets on and stare out the undressed window until the only light comes from the embers of the cigarettes that I light back to back and ash onto the floor between coughs. Music and laughter and the sounds of new friendships developing float under the door. I fall asleep questioning my decision to get a single, wondering whether it's worse to be with other people and have nowhere to hide or to be so alone that no one can find you.

At dawn I wake up coughing violently and dimly recall having done so throughout the night. When I stand, the room spins wildly. I sit back down and cough specks of blood into my hands. It kind of freaks me out, but I tell myself I'm fine, that if I ignore it, it will eventually go away. I eat half a Snickers bar from the vending machine down the hall, drink some water from the tap, lie back down and pass out.

Early evening again. My clothes and the mattress are drenched. My teeth chatter nonstop. It hurts to breathe. I don't know what to do, where to go. I barely have the strength to get out of bed, but all I can think about is the pay phone down the hall, how much I want . . . well, not *my* mother, but *a* mother, and if not a mother then someone. But I can't think of anyone to call. Then I remember the piece of paper with the hospital pay phone number that James gave me. I find it in my still-unpacked suitcase, then stagger over to the door and sit against it. I don't want anyone to see me like this, so I press my ear to the wood and wait for the hallway to quiet, wishing I had a cell phone like everyone else in the free world. When I'm certain most everyone is at dinner, I slip out and stumble down the hall.

As soon as I reach the phone and start to dial, I feel better. I can picture James slouched in a chair in the main room with his feet on the table, his arms behind his head, flirting with the nurses as they walk by. All I can hope is that he'll be the one to answer.

The phone picks up. "Hel-hel-hel-lo." It's Brian. The stutterer.

"Bri," I whisper as if somehow the nurses might hear me, "it's Cass. Can you get James for me?"

"Oh, sh-sure," he says. Then he shouts at the top of his lungs, "Ja-Ja-Ja-Jaaaames!"

I wince, in part because my eardrum has just been blasted and in part because I am sure his yelling has alerted the staff, thus ruining my chances of getting to talk to James, the one person who could make me feel less alone. But then I hear, "Looney Tunes Institute. This is James speaking." The sound of his voice is so comforting and familiar, I want to cry.

"Hey," I say and lean my head against the cool cinder-block wall.

"Cass!" He sounds so genuinely happy to hear from me that I grip the phone cord, wanting to hold on to his excitement, prop myself up with it.

"What's wrong?" he says when I don't respond right away. His voice is so full of worry that I can't bring myself to tell him the truth.

"Nothing!" I start coughing again. "Everything is great!"

"You sound like hell."

"It's just a little cough."

"It sounds like you need a doctor."

"I'm *fine*," I say. "Quit acting like I'm dying of cancer."

On the other end of the line, I hear Nurse Kay bitching at James for being on the phone outside of calling hours.

"I bet you don't miss that," he says to me. To her he says, "It's Cassie. She has cancer."

I laugh, and he whispers, "Quick, tell me everything. What's the first thing you did when you got out of here?"

When I tell him about my little swim, he is not amused. "Were you *trying* to kill yourself?"

"I was baptizing myself!"

"Uh-huh."

"Oh, stop," I say, though my voice comes out sharper than I mean it to.

"Cass," he says, his tone serious. "Please don't be a statistic."

It was something we talked about often: the high rate of suicide after release. With twenty-two troubled kids on the ward, we knew there were bound to be ones who wouldn't make it. I wonder how he could think I might be one of them.

"Anyway . . ." I say. But before I can continue, I start hacking really badly and look down the hallway, worried that someone might poke their head out and see me like this. "I should probably go."

"Promise you'll see a doctor," he says. "You need to learn how to take care of yourself."

"I promise," I lie.

Then I hang up the phone, go back to my room, climb into bed and go to sleep.

twelve

I DON'T GET better, I get worse. I sleep. I wake. They seem like the same thing. Days exist in a blurry, subaquatic state, separate from the college life outside my dorm window, the moving light and the sounds of voices, louder as they near, fading as they pass. Even my usual nightmares are underwater and without the serrated edges that typically wake me up gasping.

I have a vague recollection of having heard knocking one night, of my RA asking me from behind my closed door if I was okay, of me telling her I was fine. But I don't even know if it was real or a dream.

Friday becomes Tuesday becomes Friday again, announced by the late afternoon keg party breaking out on the campus lawn. Time has become a meaningless abstraction; there is only this moment and then the next. Sweating and then freezing, a stabbing so violent in my chest and ribs that I sometimes lose consciousness.

I get my food from the vending machine, slipping past other students who look at me strangely as they give me a wide berth, making me feel even more like an outsider. The rest of the time, I flit in and out of lucidity, one minute imagining I'm getting better, another so disoriented that at one point I wake thinking my mother is here. I hear her voice clear as glass. "I'm sick," she says. "Take Cassie to the hospital." I am confused by this, then angry, then my whole body disintegrates like light snow on pavement. Finally I realize that I'm still inside a nightmare, that I never woke up at all.

When I actually do awaken, I long for the comfort of a mother, an ache as physical as the illness itself. I do not long for a father, mine or even an imaginary one, although I suppose in some way they are the same thing. My father is a shadow person, a chalk outline of a body, nothing inside the lines—or at least nothing accessible. I know in my heart that he doesn't agree with all the things my mother did. But we both know that if he dared voice his opposition, she wouldn't listen or care, and then his irrelevance would be confirmed. So he went along.

I lie drenched in my bed, my wet lungs sucking for air that comes like little breaths through a straw, and like a sense memory, it pulls me into a particular moment in time, the moment that we all—the whole family—started going under. I close my eyes and slip down down down into blackness. Cars and landscape whiz by me. I feel the jerky rumble of the old station wagon. My father's voice comes into my head, loud and jarring. And all at once, I am back there on that fateful vacation, the one my mother demanded my father take us on, the one I begged for, the trip that marked the beginning of the end.

It was just days after my near drowning in my grandmother's pool. My father, eager to get on my mother's good side, had arranged everything at the last minute. Our luggage had been packed and piled into the back of our car in such a hurry that we reached the end of our block before I realized I had forgotten my favorite doll, Betty—a plastic Jamaican girl with a basket of fake fruit on her head—and screamed bloody murder until my father agreed to turn the car around and go get her. Once Betty was safely in tow, we were off again in our station wagon, aptly named the Blue Bomb for the explosive grunts of its tired engine. My mother had promised Matthew and me a nickel for every time we spotted a license plate that was not from Pennsylvania, and I'd never seen anyone so thrilled to lose money as we moved farther out of state and away from her family.

Meanwhile, my overly eager father, who might have been a taxi driver for all the attention we paid him, was shouting out every single sign that we passed along the highway.

"Boston! Ten miles ahead!" his voice boomed through the car like a train conductor.

"Stay alive. Drive fifty-five!"

"Slow for construction!"

"Who's he talking to?" Matthew finally asked.

"God only knows," my mother said with a sigh.

The two were discussing the various ways they might dispose of his body without drawing suspicion when at last my father called out the one sign that everyone was waiting for.

"Welcome to Maine!"

My mother clapped like a little girl, and Matthew threw his head out the window and howled into the warm summer air.

"Just wait till you see the house!" my father said. It was clear he'd been merely biding his time, waiting until he could pull out the trump card that would win my mother over. "It's practically on the water. I've heard it's almost impossible to get a house like this so late in the season. Okay, everybody, keep your eyes peeled. Ours is going to be the red one, number 377."

"Look at these gorgeous homes!" my mother said, and in a moment of clemency, she gave my father's arm a quick squeeze. He was so pleased with himself that if he'd had a tail it would have been wagging.

"Number 377," he shouted. "Here we are!"

My mother squealed. The house was small but lovely, hugged by a sprawling porch and surrounded by wispy green grass that lay down in a breeze.

"It's not red, though," I pointed out.

"That's because you're looking at the wrong house. It's just behind this one."

We all leaned forward.

The dread in the air was palpable.

"Where?" I said.

"Right there!" He pulled down the driveway and pointed to a second house that sat directly in back of the first.

I could barely bring myself to look. My father was famous for his "Reverse Midas Touch": Everything he touched turned to shit. I wrapped my arms around Betty and dared a glance out the window.

"Oh my God," Matthew said for all of us.

We all gasped. The house was amazing. It was a huge, sprawling place, the red color of a barn with white clapboard shutters and windows that opened almost onto the beach.

"The original renters bailed at the last minute, so I got it at a great price. Talk about good old-fashioned O'Malley luck, huh, kids?" He turned to my mother, his eyes hungry for her joy. "What do you think?"

She got out of the car and stood silently before it, her hair blowing against her face as she stared, stunned and agape, at my father's miracle. We all held our breath as we waited for her reaction.

"It's beautiful," my mother said finally. She turned to smile at all of us. Then she looked back at the house and her smile faded. "There's no porch, though."

We had barely unloaded our bags into the house before Matthew grabbed my hand and pulled me out the back door.

"Come on," he said, dragging me behind him into a wind that lifted the back of my dress like a kite. "I've got something to show you."

"Matthew, wait!" my mother shouted.

But we were already gone, running, running away from the house and over the sand dunes. I had no idea where we were going, only that I was with my brother and released into wide-open space, taking flight. The air was thick with the sea I'd never seen, so salty I could taste it when I breathed. Then all at once, it rose up before us, or we rose up to meet it, and I was standing for the first time before the deep blue waters of the Atlantic.

I gasped. Its enormity stunned me, ripped me out of the small ecosystem of my family and propelled me into a world far larger than I'd ever imagined.

"What do you think?" Matthew said, smiling proudly as if he had built the ocean himself.

I turned to my brother, seized and silenced by the beauty of this other realm, and it was then that he pointed out the sailboats, brilliantly colored triangles that square-danced against the sky. I watched them, captivated, watched the seagulls rise and fall with the waves, squawking into the wind.

Matthew led me gently down to the ocean's edge, where, in a small cove with shallow pools, we kicked off our shoes and let small fish scoot around our ankles. I felt that I had come home. I never wanted to leave.

We must have been out there for an hour, wading in the water, watching tiny crabs scatter and trying to scoop up fish with our hands when my mother appeared on the sand dunes, my father trailing behind her.

"Come on, Matty," she called, waving. "Let's walk down to the harbor."

Matthew raced up to her while my father and I followed, carrying between us the awkward silence of those who are left behind. We came upon the docks, where rows of sleek powerboats and boats with majestic fruit-colored sails *thwapped* in the breeze, and the voices of happy men shouted to one another over water that smelled like fish and gasoline.

"What do you think, Matthew?" my mother said. "Should I tell your father to rent us a boat?"

"As long as this one floats!" Matthew said.

"And no pirates," I added.

My father disappeared inside a ramshackle shop that sat as wobbly legged and filmy white as a seagull on the edge of the pier. When he appeared again, he was below us and teetering in a rowboat so tiny and old and tired that it seemed to be drowning beneath his weight.

"Ahoy, maties!" he called as he maneuvered the boat to the dock's edge.

My mother groaned.

"Sorry—it was all we could afford," my father said sheepishly.

Matthew and my mother climbed in, and the boat rocked and drifted under new weight. My mother shrieked, laughing nervously like a young girl on a Ferris wheel. Her face was flushed and happy when she turned to me. I stood on the dock and watched as a thin highway of murky sea quickly opened up between us.

"Looks like you'll have to jump," she said as the boat continued to move away.

I glanced down at the water, hungry and lapping against the docks. I couldn't see the bottom, only the vision of myself tumbling into the depths.

My father struggled to steer the boat closer to me, but, as in all situations involving my father, the opposing current was stronger.

"I'll catch you." My mother held her arms wide. "Now hurry up before your father manages to steer us to Cuba."

"But I don't want to go to Cuba!" I said.

"Believe me, we'd be dead before we ever reached Cuba," my father said, chuckling.

"You're not helping," my mother snapped.

"Think of it this way," Matthew offered. "If the boat sinks, at least we'd all go down together."

I started to cry.

"Oh for God's sakes," my mother said as I blubbered. "Ed, do something."

"I'm doing everything I can."

They all looked at one another, my father rowing against the current, my brother in the middle, my mother with her arms now folded angrily across her chest.

"Just jump!" they all said at once.

"Do it for me." My mother held out her arms to me again. "Do it because you love me."

I closed my eyes and willed myself to jump. It was an act of faith, and all I had to do was trust that my mother would catch me. But my legs felt like they belonged to someone else the way I couldn't stop them from shaking.

"One, two, three," she counted.

I opened my eyes. I was still on the dock.

"Oh, thanks a lot," my mother said. "Now I know how you really feel." Then she turned to my father. "Just return the damn thing. We'll do something else."

"But it's already paid for!" my dad said. The only thing he loved more than my mother was his money.

She stared at him hard. "Seriously?" she said. "Nice." She half stood, wobbling as the boat rocked and creaked with her movement, forcing my father and Matthew to grip the sides for dear life.

"Mom, wait," Matthew said. "We can figure out a way to get Cassie."

"Forget it," she said, lowering herself off the side of the boat and swimming to the ladder at the far end of the dock. She climbed up, came over to where I was standing, glared at me and then turned expectantly toward my father, waiting to see what he would do. It was clear she expected him to go and return the boat despite his protests, but instead he just dug in his oars and the boat slipped away. My mother and I stood there for a while in silence, watching them shrink into the distance, Matthew waving to us as they went.

"It's okay," my mother said to me finally, her eyes still on the water. "I didn't love my mother either."

"But I do love you!" I cried.

She turned her back to me and headed for the shore.

For the next few hours my mother sat on a plot of sand and stared out at the water, waiting for Matthew's return the way a prisoner might keep a longing watch over the outside world through a small cell window. She swatted at the big green horseflies that surrounded us. She sighed repeatedly and looked at her watch. Even in her agitation, she was beautiful, her pale knees tucked small to her chest, her sand-colored hair glistening like the bounce of sun off the ocean.

I set to combing the beach in small circles around her, approaching every now and again with broken shells I'd collected. But each time my advances were met by her angry profile, I retreated to my pacing. It must have been over an hour before I came upon a shell so pristine, I gasped when I saw it. It was white and tan and looked like a small tornado. I ran back to my mother. I had never seen anything like it.

"Ooh, it's perfect," she said, brightening. She put it first to her ear and then to mine. "It has the ocean inside. Can you hear it?"

I shook my head.

"They say the farther away you are from the beach, the louder it sounds. That way it's always with you and you can always find your way back."

I put my hand over hers and pressed the shell harder against my ear, wanting to hear what my mother heard, to have access to the same magic she did. I thought that if I could hear it too, there would be something special between us that no one else shared and then I would matter to her like Matthew did.

"Hear it now?" she said.

I looked up into her face and smiled. "Yes," I lied.

That evening, my father left the house abruptly and then reappeared in the doorway a short while later with a foolish grin on his face, holding two large, see-through bags.

"Guess what we're having for dinner," he said, and there was so much pride on his face, you'd have thought he had scooped them from the bottom of the ocean himself, and then using only his teeth. "LOBSTER!" He stood there for what seemed a long time, the lobsters wiggling as he hoisted the plastic bags in the air as if he were flagging down an airplane. When no one said anything, his arms dropped, but slowly, as if someone had stuck a pin in them. "I know they're your favorite, Bev."

"That's nice of you," my mother said with a tight smile. I could tell she was still pissed about the boat, but at least she was trying. "I hope you asked someone how to cook them."

This was enough positive feedback to send my father into new heights of loud cheerfulness. He turned to Matthew and me. "Apparently your mother doesn't realize you have a master chef in the house. Watch and learn, kids," he said as Matthew poked at the bag and started naming the lobsters as though they were his pets.

My father put a pot full of water on the stove and then yanked the rubber bands from the claws of the first lobster.

"Murderer," Matthew whispered as my father dropped the first lobster into the pot.

My father gave him a look and then dropped in two more.

"Serial killer!" Matthew shouted, making my mother laugh.

My father dunked the last lobster in with such an overdramatic flourish that my mother wondered aloud if my father might not fit in the pot as well. She and Matthew giggled at this as they strolled out of the room.

My father sighed. He'd been sighing a lot lately, and when he did, he put his whole body into it. His whole body was a sigh. "They just don't know true talent when they see it, do they, Miss Cass?"

When I noticed he was waiting for a response, I shook my head no in agreement.

"That's right," he told me. "See, you understand me."

Instantly, I regretted my collusion. I did not like being considered an ally of my father. It seemed a dangerous role to take on in light of how my mother treated him. I felt as if I had been recruited, against my will, onto the losing team.

I was about to make my own exit when I saw the top of the pot jiggling up and down ever so slightly. I turned back to my father, who, with his head now in the refrigerator, whistling as he searched for butter, saw nothing. The lid moved again. And then it appeared. From out of the depths. A dark wet claw emerging like a hand from a grave in a horror movie.

It groped blindly, searching for escape and then clipped itself upon the rim of the pot and pulled behind it another menacing claw and two angry bulging eyes staring right at me. I wanted to run. I wanted to point to my father and say, "He did it!" But I couldn't move.

It stopped there, wearing the lid on the back of its head like a beret. Then in a flurry of spindly movement, the lobster extracted itself from the pot and scampered to the edge of the stove.

Stunned, I looked at my father and saw that he was setting the table for a dinner that was presently escaping. When I turned back, the second lobster was climbing out. And then the third and fourth. They pitched over the edge of the counter to the floor. Their claws snapped threateningly above their buglike little faces.

"Holy shit!" my father said, turning.

"Holy shit!" Matthew echoed as he strolled back in through the swinging kitchen door.

My mother wandered in. "Holy shit!" she screamed, and pushed me in front of her as a shield.

"Run free, little sea creatures!" Matthew yelled with delight as we all watched my father chase the lobsters around the kitchen, grabbing at their backs and then pulling away when they snapped at his hands.

In an instant the entire house had spiraled into madness. My mother's screams met my brother's entreaties and the lobsters' smacking claws and swelled into a wild, ear-splitting chorus of chaos. My father looked around helplessly. He was breathless with humiliation and effort, and his face was as red as the lobsters would have been had he succeeded in cooking them.

"Jesus Christ," my mother said with disgust.

It was Matthew who finally managed to round them all up. He must have taken pity on my father, because at some point he gave up his Save the Lobster campaign and took charge of the situation. With the expertise of an old fisherman, he moved a steady, fearless hand toward each creature and clasped his strong little fingers around their backs.

The room became strangely quiet, like the still, reverent hush after a snowfall as we watched my brother capture the last lobster and put it in the pot. We were witnessing, after all, a moment of great significance, a moment far more important than the event itself: It was the moment my nine-year-old brother took over the role of man of the house. It was a changing of the guard made final in one singular act, and we all seemed to know it whether or not we could have named it as such.

"Well, that does it then!" my father said with a too-big smile. "Guess I should have boiled the water first, ha ha! But I've taken care of it now." Then realizing the water was still not at a boiling point, he quickly but nonchalantly reached back his hand to hold down the lid. He kept it there until we heard the lobsters' screams echoing within the stainless steel walls, and then long after the screams had ceased.

I stood in the corner and wept.

My father tried to explain that the lobsters were not actually screaming and that the air escaping from their shells was the real cause of those piercing cries. But the distinction made no difference to me. I was hearing the sounds of death, of a life that had fought for itself and lost. I only ate the corn.

Tension was palpable throughout dinner, and Matthew and I tried to break it by hurling peas at each other every time my mother turned away from us to glower at my father.

"By the way, Ed," she said, eating quickly, as if she couldn't get away from him fast enough, "I think Matthew should sleep in my room tonight. I'm concerned he might sleepwalk."

"He hasn't sleepwalked in years," my father said, his jaw clenched.

I looked at Matthew, who, in turn, began walking around the room with his arms outstretched and his eyes closed, bumping into the refrigerator and stove.

"That's not fair!" I said, angry that she was taking my brother away from me, angrier still that it was always Matthew she wanted to be with. "What about me?"

"You can sleep with your father. Forgive me if I don't want to find my son's bloated body washed up on the rocks tomorrow morning."

My brother paused, opened his eyes wide and then collapsed in a dead man's float on the floor.

My parents continued to argue over my brother's body while I marched right past them and dramatically dumped the magic shell I'd been carrying around all night—the one with the ocean inside it—straight into the trash can. I watched as the perfect shell chipped against the bottom, and I felt a disproportionate sadness and regret about it, as if it had been me that had broken. When nobody paid me any mind, I made a big production of storming off to my bed, punishing my family with my absence.

A short time later, my father came and stood near the side of the bed where I sat staring out the window, clutching Betty in my arms. The sky was black and without stars.

He cleared his throat.

He sighed.

I kept my face to the window. The silence sat between us like an uncomfortable bystander.

He moved closer and placed beside me the shell I had so ceremoniously dumped.

"I think you dropped this," he said finally.

"I don't want it," I told the window.

"But you said it was magic! You spent half the night holding it!"

"It didn't work," I said.

"What didn't work?"

I turned to look at him, searching his face for the possibility of understanding.

"Just throw it away," I said finally. "It's stupid."

"I don't think it's stupid," he said.

I wanted to smile, to give him the illusion that his efforts had succeeded. I knew he was trying, he was always trying. But it was her that I wanted. Her that we both wanted. I yanked the blankets all the way over me and did not uncover my head until the sound of his defeated footsteps shuffled away from me.

Minutes later, in the hall, my parents continued their argument.

"I'm your husband, goddamn it. Quit acting like you're married to Matthew and not me!"

"He's more of a man than you are, that's for sure."

I pulled the covers over my face again just as my father stormed back into my room. The last thing I heard before drifting off was the sound of a sigh that could have been my father or could have been the rain that started falling outside my window.

It rained the rest of the week.

We left Maine two nights early and the weather cleared just as we hit the freeway. My mother made me sit up front with my father while she sat in back with Matthew.

I dozed in and out of a light sleep, the one-eyed sleep of dolphins, listening to the engine of the Blue Bomb rattle like cans beneath the quiet sighs of my father.

Occasionally I sat up to watch panels of light from passing trucks streak across the windshield and disappear. My mother and Matthew slept deeply behind me; both could sleep through anything. It was my father and I who were restless custodians of night, joined in a molecular fear of the darkness and what it might bring.

After seemingly endless hours of driving, my father finally pulled over, woke up my mother and broke the news. He had gotten us lost, for, of all things, missing a sign. In the backseat my mother wept as if she'd lost a child. Matthew tried to calm her but she was inconsolable, wildly, frighteningly so as if the trip itself had robbed the last of her hope.

"I don't know where I am, Matty," she sobbed, rocking back and forth. "I don't know where home is."

A few months later, my father took a new job that required him to be out of the country for weeks at a time. He didn't want to take it, but my mother insisted. I remember the day we dropped him off at the airport for that first business trip, how I kept thinking a bus was going to hit us as we parked there on the side of the terminal. It was like I could hear the wheels of something big and unstoppable rumbling toward me—a terrible, irreversible crash. It was only a few months later, through no coincidence at all, that Great-Aunt Dora showed up.

thirteen

I DON'T KNOW how long I've been lying in my bed, entrenched in memory, descending into a thick, heavy unconsciousness, when suddenly, a sickening shiver runs through me and I swim up from the blackness, fighting against its pull. It takes me a moment to place myself in time, to recognize my dorm room and remember where I am. With great effort I manage to sit up, and immediately cough a gross amount of blood into my hands. I have to get help. Right now. I go to stand and find myself facedown in a sea of thin blue carpet.

I can't get up. The pain in my ribs is so bad, it blurs my vision. The door looms at a terrible distance. I eye it with the certainty that if I don't get out now, I will fossilize here. Slowly, I crawl toward it, have to pause and gather strength before I can reach up to the knob and successfully turn it. I fall back dizzy and light-headed.

It takes another lifetime to move into the hall. Dimly, I understand that this is all very bizarre and certainly not the best way to introduce myself to the community. I knock on the door opposite mine so weakly that I wonder if I've made any sound at all. Finally it opens and there is the girl who dropped the picture frame on the first day of school, her thick blond hair haloed by the light behind her. She looks out, confused, and then glances down and puts her hand to her mouth.

"Hospital," I say, surprising myself with how much effort it takes to get the word out.

"Holy shit," she says, and then she is helping me to my feet, letting me put all my weight against her as she half carries me down the hall. She is round and soft and smells of gum. Soon we are in her car and she is looking at me saying, "Oh my God, you're green!" and I am trying to apologize for it all, for needing her help, for being so sick, for looking so ugly. She glances at my oversized jeans and old baggy sweatshirt. "Just don't croak on me," she says with her funny Long Island accent. "You're the first girl I've met in this dorm who doesn't look like a sorority chick. You're not a sorority chick, are you?"

"God, no," I manage to say.

"Oh good. I'm Zoey, by the way."

Then the world goes black.

I open my eyes to fluorescent light and the murmur of people moving down a nearby hall. I blink several times. When I look down and find myself in a hospital gown, I am instantly wide awake.

"She lives!"

I look up, surprised to see the blond girl from my hall.

"I wasn't sure you were gonna make it, so I ate your Jell-O," she says with an unapologetic grin. "I'm Zoey, in case you forgot." She plops down in the chair beside my bed and leans in. "By the way,

I think the guy in the next room has the plague, so maybe don't breathe while you're here."

I lift my head to try to glimpse through the curtain, and immediately start coughing. I turn back to Zoey. "You didn't have to stay here with me."

"Um . . . hello? Free Jell-O!"

"How long have you been here?" Her presence is both comfort and threat, knowing that I have burdened her with myself, and for that, there must always be a price.

"Relax! Not that long," she says. "By the way, it's pneumonia. They said you had water in your lungs."

For a moment this makes a peculiar kind of sense, as if whatever foreign and contaminating thing I've always felt inside me has now been named. I imagine the relief of having it snaked out, watching it empty black into a bucket. Then I remember my recent near drowning, how I swallowed half the sea, and am disappointed to realize that my entire life can't be explained with a simple diagnosis, resolved with a week's worth of antibiotics.

"The good news is that it's curable," she says. "The better news is that I bought you cookies from the gift shop." She waves a bag of chocolate chip cookies in my face and then peers closer. "Gotta say, you're looking better already. You were completely green when you showed up at my door. Literally. Like Kermit the Frog green. Oh, and I called your mother."

"What?" I sit up so fast, my ribs shriek with pain. "How?"

"You gave the nurse her number when you checked in. I know my mother would want to know. Anyway, she was very nice. Very worried."

I wonder if it's true, if my mother was worried.

"You can call her if you want," she says, offering me her cell.

"Maybe in a little bit," I lie.

"Ooh, here comes your doctor. Who is hot and also mine, just so we're clear." She sits back with a big grin and fluffs her hair. "How do I look?"

The doctor walks in, brown and handsome, with thick eyebrows and dark, deep-set eyes. He gives me a prescription for antibiotics and lectures me about how I should have seen a doctor sooner, how I need to take better care of myself, how easily I could have died. I nod and nod and nod and then ask him if there's a place in the hospital I can go to smoke. He stares at me.

"I'm going to assume that was a joke," he says. "I know you're smarter than that."

When he leaves, Zoey says, "Okay, so maybe he's a little controlling, but it's only because he cares." She stares after him with exaggerated dreaminess.

"So listen," I say, looking around with a growing unease as I consider how long they might keep me here, imprisoned in this room. "I kind of hate hospitals."

"Say no more," Zoey says. "I'll lead the way."

Back at the dorm, we part ways in front of our respective rooms, where I thank Zoey again for all her help and she gives me the bag of cookies to keep.

"You can come in and hang if you want," she says. "It's just me."

"You don't have a roommate either?"

"No, I transferred here at the last minute. Technically I'm a sophomore, but all the sophomore dorms were filled. You looking for a roommate?"

"Oh no, no," I say quickly. "I'm good." I know I should accept her offer of company, take the opportunity of having a friend here. Instead we both linger for a moment and then say "bye" in unison and watch each other disappear behind our doors. The stale, germy air of my room hits me the second I walk in. It smells like death.

A moment later there is a knock on my door and I fling it open, relieved to see Zoey again, hoping that she has returned to insist that I hang out with her. Instead she holds out her cell. "Your mother is on the phone."

"Oh . . . uh . . . okay, thanks," I say, trying not to let my face reveal anything. "Can you tell her I'll call her back on the pay phone?" I don't want Zoey to hear this conversation.

A moment later, I'm in the hallway calling home.

"Cassie!" my mother says when she picks up the line. "Where are you? What happened?" I can't tell if she's worried or angry. "I got a call from some strange girl and—"

"That was Zoey," I say. "And I'm fine." Even as I say this, some stupid part of me wishes she would hear the lie of it, wishes she would say, "Come home and let me take care of you." I know it's the last place I should want to be, and yet the allure of home always holds promise even when it never existed. I stare at myself in the mirrored surface of the pay phone, my face distorted and grotesque in its warped finish, and I hate myself for this moment of need.

"How's everything else? I can still remember how excited I was my first few weeks at Dunton."

"Fine," I say. "Like I just said. So . . . is there anything else you want? 'Cause I have stuff I need to do." I light a cigarette, feel the scorch of it on my raw, aching lungs.

"Actually, yes. I have good news! I'm coming to see you."

"You are? Why?"

For two and a half years my mother stuffed me away in a hospital and could barely bring herself to show up for a visit, and now she wants to see me? I don't get it.

"We can pick up some nice things for your room when I'm there."

"There's no need to come," I say. "And I don't need anything." I think of my bare living space, all the ratty old clothes in my closet.

"Of course there is, Cassie. College is a huge milestone in a young girl's life, and everybody needs their mother for that."

I stare at the phone, wondering who has inhabited my mother's body.

"Oh, and by the way, let's keep this little trip between us. I'll let you know when I'm coming."

I want to ask why a trip to see me would need to be secret, but she's already hung up. I stare at the receiver for a moment and then go back to my room and lie down. It takes a while to fall asleep but when I do, I get pulled into a dark and feverish dream, the same one I've had for years. I wake with a start in a cold sweat, left with a residue of terror and a long-ago name in my head.

fourteen

GREAT-AUNT DORA CAME with November, arriving on a day when the wind was up and the dead leaves were doing gymnastics on the driveway. She was my grandmother's older sister, and the fact that Leigh despised her was likely the very reason that Dora was invited to visit us. I had never met her before but had often heard my grandmother refer to her as "that fat bitch who lives in Queens." Considering that her impending visit had inspired a cleaning frenzy, the likes of which I did not want to experience again, I was inclined to dislike her as well. And yet, standing with my mother and Matthew on the doorstep that day with the autumn sun in our faces, I was also eager to meet this aunt who was so great that *Great* preceded her name and who lived in a place called Queens.

When Dora made her way out of the cab and stood to announce, "I'm here!" she was not at all what I expected. In contrast to my grandmother's cold beauty, Dora was round and smiley with a puff of gray hair as soft and fuzzy as dryer lint. She wore a floral house-dress and white orthopedic sneakers, and though she was quite old, she was also sturdy and quick the way she dropped her bags and ran to my mother.

"Bevy," she cried. "My God, it's been too long!" She threw her arms around my mother's slim shoulders and rocked her side to side. Then she stepped back and took my mother's face in her hands, gazing warmly into her eyes. "It's so great to see you. You are as beautiful as ever."

My mother beamed. "I've missed you so much, D," she said. "You look wonderful too. You haven't aged a day."

"Oh please," Dora said, batting her hand at the air. "I'm so old I can hardly remember to breathe. Which reminds me . . . Before I forget . . ." She reached into her big purse and pulled out a small blue box from Tiffany's. "It's just a little thing, but I thought of you when I saw it."

"Oh!" my mother exclaimed. "You didn't have to get me a gift!"

Before my mother could open it, Dora shouted, "Hold on!" and scurried back to her luggage, which sat on the edge of our lawn. "Speaking of gifts . . . I want to show you something!"

"Hey lady," the cabdriver interrupted as he stood scowling in the driveway with his hand out. "I'd love to stick around for the tea party but . . ."

"Oh right, right," Dora said, reaching back into her purse and shoving some bills at him.

He tipped an imaginary hat before jumping back in his taxi and tearing out of our driveway.

"Now what was I doing?" Dora muttered. "Oh yes!" She rummaged around in one bag and then the other until she finally produced a childlike drawing tucked inside a frame. "Do you remember this, Bevy?" She brought it over to my mother. "You made it for me on my fortieth birthday."

My mother took the frame and looked at it as if she might burst into tears. "Oh my God, I must have been, what, five? You kept it all this time?"

"Of course I did!" Dora said. "It's one of my most treasured possessions. You were an artist even then. I keep it right on my nightstand."

My mother hugged her for a long time, clutching the Tiffany's box in one hand and the drawing in the other. When they finally parted, Dora stepped back and looked at our house. "Oh, Bevy, this is where you *live*?"

I cringed. This was a sore spot for my mother, the source of her greatest shame, and the very reason we had been so frantically cleaning and gardening all day. But then Dora looked at my mother with such sympathy and understanding that once again I thought my mother might cry.

"Isn't it awful?" my mother said.

The two of them stood side by side now, gazing up at our small, mustard-yellow house with blue shutters.

"I'm just trying to understand the color scheme," Dora said, rubbing her hand on her chin.

My mother looked at her grimly. "There was a sale on paint," she said.

They turned to each other gravely and then burst out laughing.

"Oh, Bevy," Dora said when she had composed herself. "I can only imagine how much my witch of a sister is enjoying this. You're like Snow White living in a trailer!"

"I am!" my mother said. "That's exactly how I feel!" Then calm and happy as if she had been relieved of this terrible burden, my mother said, "Now, before I give you the grand tour of the rest of this dump, let me introduce you to my kids. This is Matthew." She put her hands proprietarily on my brother's shoulders. "Isn't he just the most gorgeous child alive?"

Dora looked Matthew over, squinting in the sun that stood low and bright in front of her. "Oh, *gorgeous* doesn't even begin to describe . . . He's the spitting image of you, Bevy."

My mother glowed at the compliment. She crossed the lawn to grab Dora's bags and then, as if suddenly remembering, she called back over her shoulder, "And that's Cassie."

Dora stepped toward me, bent down and stuck her big smiley face in mine. "Well, hello there," she said. "Why haven't you given your Great-Auntie Dora a kiss?"

I smiled back at her but passed on the kiss. She was ancient and smelled like baby powder.

She drew back with a sigh. "If that's how it's going to be, I guess you don't want the candy I brought you." She made a sad face.

Clearly she had no idea who she was talking to. I stepped forward, held my breath and squeezed my eyes tight. Her cheek skin was rough and dry, like kissing a paper towel.

"Much better!" Dora said, standing erect.

I held out my hand like the cabbie but she didn't seem to notice.

My mother returned with Dora's bags in tow. "That was a good idea the cabdriver had about the tea. Why don't we have some?"

The two began moving into the house so I called, "Aunt Dora, wait!"

She turned.

"What about the candy?" I said, big smile on my face.

"What candy?"

"The candy you said you brought me."

Dora looked perplexed. "I don't remember saying anything about candy."

"Yes, you did!"

She turned to my mother. "That one sure has a big imagination, doesn't she?" she said, bemused. "Well, she's absolutely right, I should've brought the kids some candy."

"She's lying!" I said.

My mother's eyes went wide with embarrassment and she shot an apologetic glance at Dora. Then she marched over and bent down to my level. "What has gotten into you?" she hissed. "I've raised you better than to act like this."

"But—"

"No buts. Now get inside," she said, slapping me on the back of my legs.

Dora was to stay for two weeks, and although my mother loved having her and was happier than I had ever seen her, to me it felt like her time with us was not so much a visit as a hostile takeover. For the first week and a half I could not approach my mother without Dora hovering around like a linebacker, blocking me at every pass. "Run along," she'd say to me as she massaged my mother's feet or helped her with the dishes or folded the laundry while my mother napped on the couch. "Leave your poor, exhausted mother alone."

With Matthew, Dora was different. She did not prevent his

passage to my mother because there was no need. Matthew did not seek out my mother as I did, but was instead sought by her. He could stay away for hours because he carried my mother inside him. But my ties to her were looser, a thinner thread that did not bear up under too much distance. This, in Dora's opinion, was a problem.

"It's downright oppressive the way she always wants to be near you!" Dora said to my mother one day as the three of us sat in the kitchen. "An adult needs her space, for God's sake! Go out and have a shopping spree, have lunch with a friend. I'll stay here and care for her."

"That does sound nice," my mother said, stirring her tea.

"No, it doesn't," I said, stirring mine.

But it was clear that my mother had taken Dora's words to heart, the way you can't help but do with advice given by a mother figure. A short time later, she slipped her keys into her hand and announced she would be back in a few hours.

"Where are you going?" I followed her to the car.

"Out," she said, climbing into the driver's seat.

"Can I come?"

"No."

"Why?"

"Adults need space sometimes, Cassie."

"But I don't want you to go," I said.

"You'll be fine. Dora is here if you need anything."

"But I hate Dora!" I cried. It was true. I hated Dora for sending my mother away. And for forgetting her promise about the candy—quite possibly the worst two crimes a person could commit against me.

"What is it with you?" my mother said. She closed the door and then rolled down the window, her face tight and tired. "Dora has been nothing but an angel to me, and if you loved me as much as you say you do, you'd make an effort to be friends. Wouldn't you?"

"But—"

"Wouldn't you?"

"But—"

"It's a yes-or-no question."

I nodded yes.

Sometimes I didn't understand how I could be so terrible.

My mother rolled up the window and then backed out of the driveway. I watched her go, my longing stretched toward the car like a rubber band, snapping back with a sting as she disappeared around the bend.

I turned to see Matthew and the neighborhood gang chasing each other in the backyard, clamoring with the sounds of kids at play. They were in the midst of a game of tag and my body stirred to watch them run, wanting to be a part of the rush and the wind and the thrill of the hunt. But then I thought of my mother, and headed toward the back door with a sigh.

The house was quiet when I entered, and still carried the trail of my mother's perfume. Dora was in the upstairs bathroom, and since I had often seen her bring enough newspapers in there to start a paper route, I knew it might be a while. I went to my room and waited on my bed, passing time by playing dress-up with Betty and my other dolls, all of whom were getting a stern lecture on behaving themselves. I was lost in the world of pretend until I heard a singsong voice say, "Caasssieeee."

"Hi, Aunt Dora," I said, smiling as big as I could.

She stepped into my room, fanned herself, pushed open a window. "Stuffy in here."

The sounds of Matthew and the neighborhood gang drifted into the room. They must have started playing hide-and-seek because someone shouted, "You're it!" and another shouted, "Hide!"

Dora examined my bookshelf. A soft breeze floated through my window, a soupy wind of autumn and our neighbors' barking dog, the sounds of boys in play.

"My grandchildren love books. I read to them all the time."

"I love books too!" I said.

"That's nice. But I only read to good little girls."

"I'm good!"

She raised an eyebrow and turned back to the bookshelf. She looked like a nurse in her white housedress and orthopedic sneakers. "I don't know about that. You haven't been nice to me at all."

I could hear my mother's voice in my head again telling me to be nice to Dora. "I'm sorry," I said. I wanted to be nice. I wanted to be good.

She turned to the window and pressed her lips together as if considering my apology. Outside, the neighbor screamed for her barking dog to shut up.

I waited for Dora's forgiveness. It was more than the story. I needed her to like me so my mother wouldn't be mad at me anymore.

"You promise you'll be nice from now on?"

I nodded vigorously.

"Okay, then," Dora said. She pulled out a thin book of nursery rhymes, sat beside me and smoothed out the creases of her dress. I sat up straighter and smoothed out the creases of my own dress as well, a blue jumper with a rooster on the front that was my favorite. I felt like I had won something as she opened the book and began to flip through it.

"Oh, that's a good one!" I said, pointing my finger across her lap, and "That one has an old lady who lives in a shoe!" and "That one's my favorite!" and "Look at the frog!"

I was never able to play it cool like Matthew, who was accustomed to such singular attention.

"Here we go," Dora said finally, draping her arm around me and clearing her throat. "This is a good one."

"Georgie Porgie puddin' and pie . . ."

I don't remember Dora leaving my bedroom, only that I was alone again and that time had somehow elapsed without my being conscious of its passing.

The sun fell through my window in an absurdly bright and discordant yellow pool. The book of nursery rhymes lay tossed open on the floor like wreckage floating up from a bad dream. I sat with my legs dangling over the side of the bed, fixed there as if lost and waiting for somebody to find me. A vast and lonely sadness encompassed me, a sadness so pure and borderless, without thoughts to contain it, that it was less a feeling than its own bleak universe, so far removed from everything else that when the sporadic shouting voices of Matthew and the neighborhood kids punched again through the window on a breeze, the distance between us seemed so great that I never dreamed I could just walk outside and find them there.

My Betty doll sat on my bed, looking at me, her shiny black eyes full of shiny black fear. I picked her up and squeezed her to my chest. I rocked her in my arms and sang "Jimmy Crack Corn" the way Matthew had always sung it for me when I was sad or scared. I sang it quietly, so quietly that it was more like mouthing the words, and I sang it over and over again without stop or pause, until the song became a spell, until the spell erased the day, until the day had been only this song and nothing more.

When my mother came home, she poked her head in my doorway. She looked strange to me, as if she was someone I had not seen in a long, long time.

"Were you a good girl for Dora?" she asked.

I nodded yes, but the sadness found its edges and gathered into the shape of arms that groped desperately inside my chest, reaching as if through prison bars, unable to break free. I felt there was something I wanted to tell my mother, but I couldn't remember what it was.

Later that evening I found my mother sitting outside on the front steps. I plopped down beside her, eager to be close, to feel her warm body beside mine.

"Dora's gone," she said glumly, staring out toward the street. She put her hand to her neck and fondled the necklace that had been Dora's gift—a delicate sterling silver heart on a chain. "You just missed her taxi. I tried to convince her to stay longer, but she wanted to be with her grandchildren for Thanksgiving."

＊

Suddenly my mother reached over and hugged me.

"Oh, Cassie," she sobbed into my hair. "I'm gonna miss her so much. She's my best friend in the world."

She clutched me hard against her just as I had longed for her to do, but all at once I felt smothered and trapped. I squirmed out of her grip. Her tears stopped. She looked at me with surprise. I stood up and went back inside.

fifteen

IN THE HOSPITAL, when I had one of my nightmares, I could wander out into the hall, take rare comfort in the presence of the night nurses who were more lenient, letting us stay up past curfew and watch late-night TV if we couldn't sleep. But in the isolation of my dorm room, even after I turn on the lights, the ghosts remain. I want to call James again, to hear the familiar sound of his voice, to talk to someone who knows me. I want to ask what he thinks about that strange call with my mother, her plan to visit. But I can't keep calling the hospital, can't keep looking to James to make me feel better. To do so would be a step backward, proof that I can't make it on my own.

I stare at the door and imagine Zoey sleeping soundly just across the hall—close, and yet not close enough to feel the protection of another. I wonder if I should have accepted her offer to move in.

In the morning, I hear her leave her room, presumably to go to class. It's been over two weeks now and I still haven't gone to any of mine, but when I imagine the stress of getting ready and then walking out among all those strangers and trying to find my classes on the sprawling campus, I tell myself I'm still not well enough, pull the covers over my head and go back to sleep.

At around 3:00 P.M. there is a knock on my door.

"You in there?" Zoey says.

I have no makeup on, so I tell her through the door that I'm not ready to see anyone yet but that I'll stop by in a little bit. I can tell by the way she says "okay" that she thinks it's weird that I won't just open the door.

When I'm dressed and ready, I find her door wide open, music floating from her room into the hallway. I knock on the frame.

"Come in, Kermy," she says.

"Kermy?"

"Do you prefer Kermit?"

It takes me a second. Then I remember her saying how green I looked when I first showed up at her door. "Oh right, the frog. Ha."

In contrast to the barrenness of my room, Zoey's walls are plastered so thickly with pictures that not a speck of paint seeps through. There are curtains on the windows, and a pink-and-white-checked quilt covers her bed. There's a phone and a hot pot and a small TV set, making the place feel as homey as a bedroom. I imagine Zoey and her mother shopping for all this stuff, picking out all the things that would make her feel safe and comforted in her new life.

Zoey is sitting on her bed, hunched over and appearing to do surgery on a cactus plant. She holds up a broken cactus arm. "I accidentally put too much water in," she says, "and this part rotted."

"Can't you just throw that piece away?"

She shrugs. "I could. But I like fixing things. Besides," she says, digging her finger into the soil of a second small pot and placing the broken cactus arm into it, "they're resilient little guys. It just needs to be replanted and it'll start to grow again."

"Cool," I say.

She puts the newly planted cactus on her windowsill and smiles. Everything about her is colorful, from her school-bus-yellow hair to her bright red mouth. She is a human version of Ms. Pac-Man, eater of ghosts. I eye the empty bed across the room from hers.

"Don't just stand there. Come in. How are you feeling?"

"Better," I say and then start coughing, which makes her laugh and wince at the same time. "Thanks so much again."

I move deeper into the room, taking in the proximity of the bed to the door, to the window, to the other bed, marking my exits. I examine the pictures on her wall and on her dresser. "That's your mom, right?" I pick up a framed photo of the two of them at Christmas, leaning into each other and laughing, wearing hideous matching Christmas sweaters. "You guys look alike."

Zoey nods. "Thanks! She's the best."

"Yeah, mine too," I say with a big lying smile. I turn back to the photo, trace the image with my fingertips.

"Time for a music change," Zoey says as I sit down on the bed across from her. "Whaddaya want to hear?"

I shrug. "Anything."

"Anything? Great! I've got hours of my mom and me doing karaoke . . ."

"Except that."

"No?" She stares at me with mock shock. "Okay, your loss. How about Taylor Swift?"

"Not much of a country fan."

"Seriously? Who doesn't love T-Swizzle? This does not bode well for us. How about—"

"Yes!" I say, before I even know what it is.

"Going old school. Guns N' Roses."

Yikes.

She raises her hands in victory and then, because I am closest to her laptop, she points at me. "Fire it up, Kermit!"

I search through her files until I find the band, then pause and turn to her. "Must that really be my nickname?"

"You don't like Kermit?"

"I guess I just always hoped for something a little . . . cooler."

"Like?"

"I dunno. Maybe Ace or something."

She bursts out laughing. "A cooler nickname like . . . Ace?"

"Never mind."

"Oh no." She is absolutely cracking up. "I'll call you Ace if you want."

I click on the first song and turn up the volume so I can drown out the self-mockery taking place in my head. *Ace? Ace?! What kind of loser comes up with Ace?*

We listen to a few songs, chatting over the music.

"So, do you have a boyfriend?" she asks, and even though I know it's not what she's saying, what I hear is, "Does anyone love you? Does anyone find you worthy of love?"

I hate that I hear that. "Guys are a pain in my ass," I lie. Then I think of the actual boyfriend prospects I've had over the past two and a half years and determine it's not entirely untrue. Dating a guy who hears voices and thinks there are policemen in his top desk drawer, for instance, probably would be a bit of a pain in the ass.

"I wish I felt that way. I love boys." She sighs and falls back on her bed.

We are about a third of the way through the album when Zoey declares the next song her favorite and orders me to turn it up before it starts. As the previous song bleeds out, she sits perfectly still and waits. Then as if keyed into some soundless cue, she raises one hand dramatically above her shoulder and at the very same moment that the music starts, she strikes down on the imaginary chord of an invisible guitar. The song is slow and pretty at first, and Zoey moves her body like stirred water, her arms undulating in small circles above her head, her torso following in a wider arc.

As the music becomes faster and more maniacal, she jumps up onto her bed and slams her body wildly against the air as her mouth works itself silently around the lyrics. The song hits a musical interlude and she shouts, "Oh yeah," and laughs and returns to the air guitar, her blond hair flying while her fingers work the chords, all of it exaggerated for my amusement.

I can feel myself watching her with my mouth open, astonished by her lack of self-consciousness, her ease with her body, her expectation of acceptance.

She opens her eyes and laughs, clearly enjoying my undivided and awed attention. "You're not going to leave me onstage all by myself here, are you?"

I lean back coolly on my elbows. "That's exactly my plan actually."

"You're no fun," she says and closes her eyes and goes back to jamming like a lunatic.

I light a cigarette and Zoey's eyes flash open. "Dude, you can't smoke in here! You'll set off the fire alarm!"

"Oh shit, I forgot!" I say as I scan the room frantically for a place to put it out. Two seconds into a new friendship and I've already ruined it with my cluelessness.

"Open the window at least," Zoey says.

I go and open the window and stick my head out as much to hide my humiliation as the smoke. I wonder if I should just leave, if she wants me to. But when I turn around, I see Zoey already back in musician mode, dancing with her eyes closed. I think about her saying I was no fun and now I am torn. I want to make up for my stupidity, want so much for her to like me, but I don't know how to *be fun*, how to relax without revealing more than I want to, without revealing myself. I sigh and start to play the drums in my lap, feeling safely hidden from her closed eyes. After a while I close my own eyes and let the music take me a little bit more.

"What's going on over there, Ace?"

I open my eyes and see Zoey now donned in full rock-star gear, her hair wrapped in a bandanna, T-shirt sleeves rolled to her shoulders, dark shades covering her eyes. She is paused mid–air guitar and looking at me like I'm the one who's crazy.

"I'm playing the drums!" I say.

"Oh, thank God! I thought you were having a seizure!"

I shove my hands between my knees, feel my face get hot. Zoey sees my embarrassment, but it just makes her laugh harder.

"Awww," she says, looking at me like I'm a broken cactus plant. Then she proceeds to mimic me, thrashing about like a fish in a boat. I bring my knees to my chest and hide behind them. The more embarrassed I get, the more she exaggerates her imitation until I can't help but laugh. Zoey joins me, and before I know it we are both beside ourselves, curled up on our respective beds and laughing hysterically.

This idea that a flaw can be funny is new to me. I turn it over like something shiny.

"Maybe I should take drums and you can have this." She throws me the sunglasses and the imaginary guitar. "Go on. Let's see whatchya got."

"I think I'd rather just be the audience. I can light my lighter and throw underwear at the stage."

"Ace! Ace! Ace!" she chants.

I laugh and say, "Please stop," but the chants just get louder, coupled with fist pumps and encouraging nods. Reluctantly, and if only to silence her, I put the glasses on and then wiggle my fingers out in front of me, trying to imitate her moves. Immediately her teeth clench, her nose scrunches up and she shakes her head.

"No?"

"You look like you're playing the harp." She falls on her back, laughing all over again.

"That's it! I'm quitting this bullshit band." I pretend to throw my harp–air guitar on the ground and kick it.

She sits up, eyes wide with an idea. "I know! The sax."

"The air saxophone?"

She shrugs. "You got a better idea?"

"Do they even have a saxophonist in Guns N' Roses?"

"They do now."

I sigh, stack my hands below me, purse my lips and blow.

"There ya go!" she says and gives me a thumbs-up. I raise an eyebrow, and we once again collapse on our sides in hysterics. Still, we manage to play through the rest of the album. Zoey slides to the floor and tortures the chords of her guitar while I sit on the bed and blow air into my sax. Every once in a while in the midst of this, it occurs to me that I am having a silly college experience with a new friend, and I want to go call James and tell him about it, knowing how much he'll appreciate it, how proud he'll be of me, that there is life after death row, just as he always promised.

Someone knocks on the door then, shouts for us to keep it down, and I think of how just over two weeks ago I was all by myself listening to the sounds of others' laughter.

"I'm exhausted," Zoey says finally. "This rock-star life is tough on the body."

It's only then that I notice it has gotten dark outside. I stand abruptly, certain this is my cue. "Yeah, I should go." I move to the door, already dreading the return to my room, like stepping out from a warm hearth into a snowstorm.

"What time's your first class?" Zoey says.

"Don't know. Haven't been to any of them yet."

"Are you kidding? None?" She looks at me with concern. "We need to fix that!"

I shrug. Anxiety kicks up like dust, making the air thick to breathe.

"Tomorrow?" she asks, just as I am walking out.

I pretend I didn't hear her.

In the hallway, I can feel all that light leaking out of me. I push open the door to my room. The whiteness is a vacuum. The ghosts of memory await me.

sixteen

IT WAS AROUND the time that Dora left that I started having trouble sleeping. There were monsters in my room, under my bed and behind my furniture, throwing their great big shadows across my walls. I clutched Betty tightly as I listened to their creaks of movement and felt their hungry, pulsating energy.

One night when my terror was especially great, I called hoarsely to my mother, hoping she would come and deal with the monsters, soothe my fears. But she was with Matthew in his room, the two of them talking and laughing together, and if she heard me, she did not acknowledge me. The sound of my voice hanging unanswered in the air sent new charges of fear through me. I had identified myself to the night, I had announced my location and my aloneness, inviting danger, drawing it to me by daring to exist. I became very still, my antennas tuned to the shadows, and every now and again to the sounds of my mother and Matthew laughing together just down the hall. I wanted so much for her to come into my room and sit on the edge of my bed and talk and giggle with me the way she always did with him.

I pulled the covers over my head and got into a small ball beneath them, but my nightgown kept annoying me to no end, riding up my body every time I moved, scratching at me with its lace hem. I thought that if I were a boy, like Matthew, I wouldn't have to wear nightgowns that never stayed in place. If I were a boy like Matthew, I wouldn't be afraid of the dark. If I were a boy like Matthew, my mother would love me. She would stay and laugh with me in my room. I would be safe from monsters.

I summoned my bravery, got out of bed and ran to my door to turn on the light. Then I went to my closet to look for some pajamas. There I saw all the pretty girly dresses I loved so much hanging silently in a row like bodies. In an instant of decision, I tore them from their hangers and stuffed them in a ball behind my Snoopy suitcase.

I took a deep breath and went to my dolls, all but Betty sitting sweetly side by side at the end of my bed. They had kept me good company over the years, had sat with me while I combed their hair, even suffered some well-intentioned but not-so-well-executed haircuts. I had to force myself to hate them. Boys didn't like dolls, and although I knew I could never be a boy, I could refuse my girlhood in my heart. In my heart I could be a boy like Matthew. So I gathered them up and dumped them with the dresses, then thought better of it and stuffed them in my suitcase so I would never have to see them and have an urge to pick them up. Betty was the last one to go in. I turned to her, hardening myself against the loss. "I'm sorry," I whispered. "I can't love you anymore." I shoved her in quickly so I wouldn't have to see the sense of abandonment and betrayal in her face.

It was a great stroke of luck that a few days later at school, my first-grade teacher ran out of girls' costumes for our upcoming Thanksgiving pageant before she could assign one to me. As a result, I spent the next three days dressed like a male Pilgrim with no plan of ever changing my clothes again. I loved the costume more than anything I'd ever worn. In it, I felt strong and free and brave, like I could single-handedly conquer new worlds and face unrelenting hardships with nothing more than my buckled shoes and my black steeple hat. Dora was gone, I was practically a boy, and for the first time in my life, Thanksgiving had meaning.

My mother, inspired by my theatrical attire, was sitting at the kitchen table regaling Matthew and me with her singular experience on the stage as an eight-year-old girl. The play she had been cast in was a modernized version of *Cinderella*, and my mother had been given the role of a partygoer with one line: "Please, sir, would you care to dance?" My mother told us she had put her heart and soul into practicing that line, knowing there were no small parts, only small actors. But just moments before her cue, the actor with whom she was to share the scene vomited into the orchestra pit, and my mother, unwilling to be denied her moment, grabbed the janitor's broom, dragged it onto the stage and proceeded to ask it to dance.

It seemed that the sincerity and commitment with which she delivered this line was too much for the audience, and the roar of laughter that followed left her stunned and staring into the white lights. So pleased was she by this unexpected response that she repeated her line again and again to keep the laughter alive. And it worked. She felt like the star of the show until a small figure in the back of the auditorium stood up, cupped her hands to her mouth and shouted over the laughter, "Somebody get the hook!"

It was her mother.

Matthew and I thought this was just about the funniest story ever told. Immediately we began trying out the line for ourselves. We took turns curtseying to the broom in the kitchen, our small heads bowing shyly as we called out, "Please, sir, would you care to dance?" Each time we looked up to see my mother on the sidelines, playing the part of a crazed director, pacing and scratching her head and wincing in pain.

"No, no, no," she said, shaking her head. "It's about intention. You can't just spit out the words, you have to really connect with the broom. Start over."

Every time we failed to give a proper delivery, my mother demonstrated again. She pretended to be exasperated, but you could see that underneath she was still that enchanted eight-year-old girl standing in the lights, so pleased to have a new but equally delighted audience.

"Show us again!" we cried, and each time she did, we shouted, "Somebody get the hook!" until we were all getting stomachaches from laughter.

This was the mother Matthew saw constantly, the one whose childlike glee and humor could send anyone over the top with merriment, and every time I was included in the fun, I felt like an overfilled balloon, so happy and excited, I could pop clear out of my skin.

We were still in the midst of this play, my mother toddling around the kitchen with the broom, saying, "Please, sir, would you care to dance?" and Matthew and I shouting, "Somebody get the hook!" when my father appeared in the doorway.

"Well, hello there, folks! Happy Thanksgiving!" he boomed expectantly.

My mother hated when my father called us "folks."

"We are not 'folks,'" she told him repeatedly, "we are your family." But there he was, saying "hello, folks," and we all looked up, surprised, because we had forgotten he was coming back.

"Oh perfect," my mother said as the energy of the room flat-lined. "The turkey has arrived."

"That's right," my father said with a smirk. "Gobble, gobble."

Matthew and I giggled, and he winked at us as if we were laughing with him.

"You'll get a lot of meat off these bones," he continued, rubbing his bloated belly. "Ho ho ho!"

We stopped laughing. We didn't want to encourage him.

"At least you won't need to pluck me. Your mother's been skinning me alive for years."

"Okay, Ed," my mother tried.

"Just make sure you fill me up with a lot of stuffing. I'm hungry!"

My father didn't just beat a joke into the ground, he dug it a hole so deep you could send it straight to China.

"Somebody get the hook," Matthew said.

My father, chuckling singularly, turned to me. I glanced over at my mother to make sure she wasn't looking and then gave him a half smile just to put an end to it, certain that if someone did not give him some sign of approval, he would go on like this for days. The room became quiet then, all of us standing there in silence with my father in the doorway still waiting for the homecoming parade to appear.

"I have good news, folks," he said. "I have just been informed that I am the leading candidate to be the next assistant vice president of Robust Plastic Bags Incorporated!"

His eyes darted to my mother and our own eyes followed them. Middle class was the place she had hung her unhappiness, and my father was the prison warden who kept her there. Now it seemed as though we were possibly moving toward the life she was born to, meant for, and we all waited breathlessly, my father with his good news and his eyes saying *love me.*

My mother turned her back, took a dishrag from the sink and began wiping the counter.

"Wait," Matthew said. "What does that mean exactly?"

"It means," my mother said, scrubbing furiously at a stain, "don't get your hopes up. I've heard it before."

I looked at my father, and his smile was high and tight like he was holding himself up with it.

"Okay, kids, let's get dressed," my mother said, tossing the dishrag over the faucet and wiping her hands on her skirt. "We have to be at your grandmother's for dinner in an hour."

Matthew groaned.

"I know," my mother said miserably. "But we have nowhere else to go."

My mother came into my room a short time later, her blond hair brushed shiny and back off her face, her pantsuit drifting over heels that clicked like little hammers against the hardwood floor. Her perfume flooded my room, all ripe fruit and cheerful flowers, a garden wafting from her wrists. I loved seeing her decorated like a parade float, a celebration. I wanted to eat her, to swallow her whole and hold her inside me, to fill myself up with her beauty. Increasingly, I was becoming aware of our physical differences: me with my thin, mousy brown hair and the newly dark hollows under my eyes, the child who looked nothing at all like her mother, who was an insult to her loveliness.

"You look so pretty," I gasped as she click-click-clicked over to my bed. But my mother was all business, prepared and contained in her pantsuit, the playfulness of the morning locked up inside her belt. Only her mouth was twitching, a slight tic at the left side of her smile, flickering on and off like a dying lightbulb.

"I laid this out for you," she said, picking up the frilly yellow dress that had been left on my comforter. "I had to iron it because I found all your dresses in a heap at the bottom of your closet. Any idea how that might have happened?"

I put on my most innocent face. "No."

She gave me a look and held out the dress.

"I want to wear this," I said, referring to the black-and-white Pilgrim costume I was still proudly sporting.

"You can't wear that silly little getup. Now come here and let me put this on you."

"I can't climb trees in a dress," I said, backing away from her. This wasn't really true but I didn't know how to explain the real reason I couldn't bring myself to put it on.

"You won't be climbing trees. You'll be eating turkey."

"It makes me itch."

"You don't have to wear it for long."

"Matthew doesn't have to wear a dress!"

"Well, you are not Matthew. You are a girl. And girls wear dresses."

"But I don't want to be a girl," I finally confessed, moving back toward her, asking her to understand what I didn't know how to say.

She looked taken aback. "What's wrong with girls? Jesus, you're starting to sound like my mother."

"Well, how come you're not wearing a dress then?"

She grabbed my wrist and pulled me toward her. "Stop trying to make my life difficult. Now lift up."

She tried to raise my arms to remove the top of my costume, but I clenched them firmly against my sides. The thought of being stripped down and forced into that dress made my insides scream.

She slumped down onto my bed and sighed. "I don't know what's gotten into you lately," she said. "You refused to hug me when Dora left. You don't want to wear the nice dress I bought for you. I don't know why you're so rejecting." Tears came to her eyes. "All my life, I dreamed about having a daughter. How much she would love me and how I would dress her up like a pretty little doll." She looked at me sadly, her eyes reaching for sympathy. "I just don't know why you won't be the daughter I wanted."

I stepped back from her with new determination. She stood abruptly and marched to the door.

"Put the damn dress on," she said.

As soon as she left, I hurled the stupid yellow dress at the door. But without my mother to witness this act of rage, it didn't feel satisfying. I scanned my room, looking for something I could destroy. Finally I opened my suitcase. I stared down at all the dolls I had stuffed inside. All at once I genuinely despised their lifeless eyes, their stiff bodies poised like dead people. I gathered them up, and one by one, I pulled off their heads. Their plastic faces popped off like bottle caps. I could hear my mother just down the stairs, and I stepped out onto the landing with the decapitated bodies in my arms. I launched them over the railing in a heap. "Put them in dresses," I told her. "I'm wearing this!"

I am a Pilgrim, not a doll. And I have a face.

It was my father who finally managed to wrangle me into wearing the dress.

"You're upsetting your mother," he said, moving into my room and placing a handful of headless dolls on my bureau.

I lunged onto my bed and buried my face in my pillow. "She's upsetting me!"

My father sighed. He was a man stricken in the face of emotion. He cried only once that I knew of, during a trip to Washington, D.C., a visit to the Jefferson Memorial. He wept as he read me a quotation from the Declaration of Independence: "'We hold these truths to be self-evident: that all men are created equal . . .'" It was the *We* that got him. He choked on it, had to cough it out like something stuck. The idea of *We* imprinted on a plaque made my father cry. But the day-to-day emotions of others left him baffled and helpless as a tipped cow.

"I'll give you a dollar if you wear it," he said finally.

I lifted my head off the pillow and wiped my tears with the back of my hand. "Let me see it first."

Of course the offer was merely pretense and I would ultimately have to wear the dress regardless. But my father was giving me the opportunity to feel some sense of control over circumstances that neither of us had the power to do anything about.

He extracted the bill from his wallet—crisp and green—and I paused as if considering. He waved it enticingly in front of me, but it was not until the bill was sitting light as a leaf in my hand that I said, "Deal."

It was a moment marked only by temporary joy, because even then, I intuitively understood that the cost of being a girl in my house was much, much higher.

seventeen

BACK IN MY dorm room, I glance at my schedule for the first time, thinking about what Zoey said, about how shocked she was that I've missed so much school. My next class is at 9:00 A.M. tomorrow. I shove the schedule into the drawer where I don't have to see it, and then turn off the lights and jump into bed and stare into the empty, looming darkness above me. I try to keep perfectly still just as I did when I was a kid, as if to move would invite the ghosts. I imagine them there, under my bed and behind the dresser, throwing their great big shadows across the wall like plant life swaying to and fro at the bottom of the ocean. Waiting for me to go to sleep so they can haunt my nightmares.

Across the hall, Zoey's music continues to play, so warm and inviting against the silence of my room. I think of the person I was just a short while ago when we were hanging out—a silly college student, a rock star, maybe even someone a little bit happy. Someone with a friend. Before I can stop myself I jump out of bed.

A moment later, I am standing at Zoey's door, and she is looking at me curiously. I take a deep breath and start coughing again.

"So hey," I say when my lungs have settled. "My English class is at nine tomorrow. I think I'm gonna go."

"Excellent!" she says. "We can walk together. I have Statistics then."

"Great!" I say. "Well, not the Statistics part, obviously . . ." Then I continue to stand there awkwardly.

"Was there something else?" she says.

"No, nope, that's it." I start to go back to my room and then stop and make myself turn around. "Well . . . actually, um . . . I was just wondering if you might want a roommate so bad you'd settle for a sick one?"

As soon as the words are out of my mouth, I start to regret them. I don't know how I'll manage the constant presence of another person, how I'll keep my secrets hidden, keep the old me from leaking out.

"Wow, you sure know how to sell yourself," Zoey says.

"So . . . that's a no then?"

"Oh stop!" she says. "I'd love a roommate. Go get your stuff."

In the morning, my alarm clock wakes me with a start from the first good night's sleep I've had in weeks. Across the room Zoey sits up, glances at the time—6:00 A.M.—then at me like I'm nuts and falls right back to sleep.

"Sorry," I whisper to her. Today is a big day and I need a few hours to get ready. After a quick shower, I try on my entire closet, which isn't much, decide I hate everything and put on the least shabby thing I own.

I unpack my makeup and sit in front of the floor-length mirror to begin the slow process of applying my face. Every stroke of color has to be just right, every hair in place, every imperfection covered up.

Five minutes before we are due to leave, Zoey's alarm clock goes off, blaring rock music and scaring the shit out of me. She gets up, brushes her teeth in the bathroom, sticks a comb quickly and pointlessly through her hair, steps into her flip-flops and is ready to go.

I apply one final coat of mascara.

"Ready," I say. I take one last look in the mirror in the hopes that I might hold on to the solid image I see there once I look away.

We head out amidst a day that is clear-skied and early-autumn breezy. When we get to the quad, Zoey spots two of her friends from class. She calls to them and they stop and wait.

"I'll catch up with you later," she says to me. "We usually have lunch at The Rat if you want to meet us."

"Okay," I say. "Um . . . where is it?"

She laughs and shakes her head. "How about I meet you here around noon and we can walk over together."

"Okay, sounds good." I watch her run off toward her other friends, the three of them greeting one another with big hugs. "Wait!" I shout after her, realizing I forgot to ask her how to get to the English department. But it's too late. Zoey has disappeared inside the building.

I stand alone in the courtyard as groups of students pass me on the lawn, seeming so effortlessly at home with books tucked confidently under their arms and friends by their side. I imagine my mother was like them when she was in school here: popular and full of laughter, navigating her way through this world so easily.

A couple of girls in cute outfits and ponytails approach. I move toward them in the hope that they can point me in the direction of the English department. One of them looks over at me. I smile and then open my mouth to speak but she gives me the once-over and looks away. In that instant of her dismissal, I am ugly again, suddenly aware of myself in my outdated, oversized clothes.

I push my shoulders back and keep walking, my heart already working to repair the tiny fracture, whether real or imagined. Two guys pass by and look at me in that way like they think I'm pretty, and I feel a sense of vindication, and somewhere just behind that, a sense of emptiness.

The campus clears as students disperse inside. I stand helplessly in the middle of the courtyard.

"You lost?" someone suddenly says behind me. The unexpected kindness makes my throat ache. I turn to see a guy in surf shorts and flip-flops. He has happy eyes and light brown hair that is slightly wet and sticking out in all directions. Something happens in the space of air between us, like the wind has stopped there. Embarrassed, I look away.

"Nope," I say like an idiot. "I'm fine."

He crosses over to me.

"May I?" He takes the schedule hanging uselessly from my hand. "English Lit. That's my class too. We're in Johnson Hall. Over there on the left."

"Right. I knew that."

"I'm Chris."

"Cassie O'Malley," I say with ridiculous formality as I extend my hand.

He looks down at my hand with surprise and then shakes it. "I saw you on the first day by the girls' freshman dorm."

"You saw me?" The idea is alarming to me, both being seen unaware and being seen at all. Immediately my guard is up.

"You were wearing winter clothes but had sand on your feet." He laughs at the image.

"Oh yeah. I'd just come from the ocean."

"From the ocean, huh? What are you, a mermaid?"

He smiles, and something fast and electrical shoots up me. Startled, I step back. "What are you, a dork?"

There is a moment of shock for us both, and then he looks down at my schedule and hands it to me.

I struggle for a joke or an apology. Instead I pull out a cigarette and light it, cueing him to leave.

"Well, I guess I'll see you in there," he says and heads toward the building. At the door he pauses and looks back and holds me in his gaze for a long beat before he disappears inside.

eighteen

WITH THE COURTYARD now empty of people, I plop down on a bench and finish my cigarette. I'm going to be late for class, but I'm too busy trying to manage my humiliation to care. I gently remind myself that I've had no practice talking to guys who are cute and completely sane, but all that does is remind me that I'm an ex–mental patient with a fucked-up past, which reminds me that no guy would ever like me anyway. Because come on, if you can't even make your own parents like you, what hope is there for anyone else?

I think of my mother and all her exciting college romances, and I imagine how different she must have been around guys, how cool and self-assured and normal she must have acted. I remember the first time she told me about Dunton. I was around ten at the time, and I had followed her into her art room, where the sharp smells of paint and turpentine surrounded us. I'd always loved to watch her there, sitting at an easel above an old drop cloth. She was still then, and I could sit inside her stillness, feel the frantic batting wings inside me quiet.

That day she was painting the deep end of an ocean with a white ladder descending, and her brushstrokes were little waves that lapped at the canvas with care. I had brought my markers in and sat just inside the door, keeping one eye on my drawing and the other on my mother sitting in a slow peaceful trance at her easel, brushing blue.

She had her back to me and I didn't think she knew I was there until she raised her head from her work. "Do you ever feel like you're disappearing?" she said.

She turned and searched my eyes, and for a moment I felt so understood and loved because that was exactly how I felt, how I had felt for so long that I could not remember when it started or a time when I felt solid. It seemed to me as if my brother, Matthew, was real in the way that love made the Velveteen Rabbit real, whereas only the act of being his shadow had kept me from being erased. And now I thought my mother finally saw it, saw that I too needed to be painted in, made into something visible. So I nodded yes, *yes, I have felt like I was disappearing,* but she had already turned away.

She stood up and went to the window. She took a deep, slow inhale and let it out with a sigh. She said that the light outside and the smell of fall approaching reminded her of college. "I was so happy there," she said.

"Why?" I asked, because I wanted her to be happy here, not there, and I needed to know what made the difference.

And then all at once she was telling me of her life at Dunton, and so vivid was her detail that I quickly forgot myself in her memories. I could almost see the faded brick buildings of the university and smell the ripened leaves blowing at her back as she darted through autumnal days youthful and free, clutching books filled with the promise of discovery. She talked of being homecoming queen and riding a parade float past streets of screaming fans who threw confetti that fell on her like colored snow. She told me about all her many boyfriends, the one who buttoned up her coat on a cold day at a football game, the one who walked across the entire campus in a thunderstorm to bring her soup when she was sick, the one who kissed her for so many hours straight that she wondered later if it was really possible to go that long without breathing. And as she spoke, the flush of young love seemed resurrected on her face and in the lilting of her voice so that the room became electrified with her memories.

I sat perfectly still and listened. I loved that she was talking to me and me alone.

"Oh, I wish I were young again," she said, staring out the window. "My whole life was ahead of me then. There was so much . . . potential. So much hope."

She put her hands on the screen. I wanted to follow her there, to see what she saw. It *was* possible, I thought, as I waited for her to speak again, to go for such a long time without breathing.

"You know," she said finally, "I never loved your father. In fact, I wanted to throw up the first time he kissed me. Isn't that awful?"

I looked down at my hands, to escape both her words and the weight of the betrayal I was committing in listening to her speak about my father that way. But I was bound to him only by pity; I was bound to my mother by something much stronger, something I could feel, even then, tightening around me. I was bound to her by pain.

"I wish I could go back in time and . . . shake myself for marrying him. I don't know what I was thinking . . . or running from.

My parents, probably. And your father was so eager and in love with me, I think I just felt like 'Here is a man who will never leave me.' But it's not enough, is it? I guess I kept hoping he could be what I needed, even after it was clear there was no hope for that."

I didn't say anything. It made me too sad to think about needing something you could never get, about there being no hope.

She turned to me then. "Tell me something," she said. Her eyes searched my face, feverishly bright. Even from a distance, I could see her need, feel it. I watched her, feeling pinned to the floor as if absorbing the weight of her regret through the atmosphere. "I deserve to be happy, don't I?"

The question shocked me, the idea that there could be any doubt. "Yes, Mom! Of course!" I nodded furiously, as if convincing her would fix everything, as if the sheer urgency of my want for her to be happy again would make her so.

"You know what?" she said. "You're right. You are absolutely right." She got up and shut the window as if to put an exclamation point on some internal decision she had made. She seemed completely light again, full of hope. "You're a good girl. Thanks for being my confidant. I know what I need to do."

She walked past me and patted me on the head. "Don't say anything about this to Matty, okay? It would upset him."

"Okay," I said. "I won't."

She smiled down at me in the way I had wanted her to for so long, and I was sure I had finally found my way into my mother's love. So I didn't understand, as I lay on the art room floor like the sheet that captured her spills, why I suddenly felt like throwing up.

Two days later, my mother discovered she was pregnant with Gavin.

I stub out my cigarette, go inside and head straight to the bathroom to reapply my lipstick and to tell myself that I don't care what that stupid surfer boy thinks of me. Already I'm exhausted, like I'm holding my breath underwater, and all I want to do is run back to my dorm room and shut the door so I can breathe again.

Twenty minutes after the hour I sneak into class and take the first open seat near the door.

"You're late," someone says, and I turn to see Chris sitting catty-corner in front of me. He smiles and the rest of the room fades for a second, leaving me with only a deafening self-consciousness. I push my seat back and the chair makes a loud, embarrassing screech. The whole class turns.

"Where are your books?" he whispers.

"Bookstore," I say, and he laughs.

He tears a piece of paper from his notebook and hands it to me so I have something to write on.

"Thanks," I say. My face is burning.

The teacher, a small round man with a few strands of hair slicked over his bald head, drones on at the front of the class. I try to focus, but it takes so much work just to sit here and not flee, so much mental energy to keep track of each person in the room, to keep my face and body angled in a way that I imagine looks pretty, to be so perfectly in control of myself and my surroundings that nothing gets in and nothing leaks out.

I look around at everyone scribbling like crazy into their

notebooks and I wonder how they have the energy to care about poetry when just surviving takes so much effort. To make matters worse, every few minutes I catch Chris staring at me and my nerves start jangling and my heart pounds loud and fast, beating beyond my chest and into my fingers, my stomach, my ears.

"What?" I mouth.

He puts his hands out and scrunches up his shoulders as if to say, "What?" back.

I face forward, pretend I have no peripheral vision, force myself to listen to the teacher over the surge of blood in my ears. He is quoting "Prufrock": "'I should have been a pair of ragged claws.'"

Chris turns around again.

"Seriously," I hiss. "Why do you keep looking at me?"

He shrugs and the skin on his neck turns red. "I dunno," he says. "Maybe I like your face."

And even though I have spent an enormous amount of energy trying to make myself pretty so people will like me, his words are like seawater to the shipwrecked: I'm tempted to drink them in, and at the same time, they feel dangerously deceptive. Because it's not true, it's not possible, it's not my face he likes, it's the makeup I'm covering it with.

So I go ahead and give him the finger.

nineteen

I DASH OUT of class the moment it is dismissed to avoid further impulsive acts that will cause me to look bat-shit crazy and stand in the cover of a shaded tree waiting for Zoey. A happy couple walks by, holding hands as if it's the easiest thing in the world to be somebody who can be with somebody else. I light a cigarette just to appear occupied and at last Zoey arrives, looking fresh and young and collegiate in her bouncy ponytail and university T-shirt. She is so happy to see me, a big Labrador, like we've been apart for years instead of hours. It's mystifying.

"How was class?" she says.

"I don't know. I wasn't paying attention."

"You can't afford to not pay attention! You're already so far behind!"

"Screw it," I say as I stamp out my half-finished cigarette. "It's all such a bore." I start walking fast, like I'm being chased, and she scrambles on her short legs to keep up. I want to tell her about Chris, but it's too embarrassing.

"Hold up," she says. She motions to a building at the top of the hill. "Can we stop over there first? I need to talk with one of my teachers real quick. Two seconds, I swear."

I look up. It's the Department of Psychology.

"This isn't a setup, is it?" I smile to cover the sudden irrational anxiety, the memory of ropes on my wrists, the sound of the hospital's blaring alarm.

She laughs. She has no idea.

We climb the hill and enter the building's empty corridor. "You can wait there," she says, pointing to an open room lined with chairs and a table with some magazines on it.

Above the door are the words "Counseling Center."

"No!" I say, but she is already starting down the hall.

She turns, looks at me quizzically. "What's the matter?"

I stand stupidly for a moment. "Nothing, never mind."

"Two seconds, I promise," she says, and then adds with a grin, "Watch out for the crazies."

"Right. Right. The crazies."

There is no one in the waiting room or at the reception desk. I take a seat on a pale yellow couch, pick up a campus quarterly and bury my face in it, flipping through pictures of students smiling so big, it looks like it hurts. I arch my neck and glance at my watch repeatedly in order to appear like someone who is waiting for a friend rather than one in need of "help." My nerves have not settled since I left class, and every time I think of Chris saying that he likes my face, they reactivate like I'm being chased by a bear. When I revisit the part where I give him the finger, I want to disintegrate into the couch. I move between these two states—panic and self-hatred—until some woman pokes her head out of an adjoining door and looks at me. She has large round glasses, brown hair, pale skin. There is kindness in her face.

"Are you here to see me?" she says.

"No!" I say too loudly.

"Oops, my mistake." She smiles and turns and disappears behind the door.

I go back to my magazine and my self-loathing. A few minutes later, she pokes her head out again.

"Still not here to see you," I say with a smile.

She nods, steps farther out the door to get a better look at the room. She is clearly waiting for someone who is also clearly not here. She goes back inside.

I check my watch, wish Zoey would come back.

Five minutes later, the woman pokes her head out a third time and I have to climb over my obvious paranoia that Zoey really has set me up, that I'm the person this woman is looking for.

"I don't think they're coming," I offer.

She nods in agreement.

"Rude," I say.

She shrugs and smiles. "It can be hard for people to admit they need help."

"What isn't hard?" I say with a laugh.

She tilts her head and studies me with a soft look on her face. Then she gives me a wink and goes back into her office, and for one strange second, I feel like following her. Instead, I decide I can't stand to wait another minute in this place, so I get up and start back to my dorm, leaving Zoey behind. I am almost at my dormitory when I see my mother standing out front with a man I do not know.

twenty

I STOP DEAD in my tracks at the sight of my mother, my whole body braced like I'm caught in the crosshairs of a sniper's gun. I don't know why she is here, who this guy is, what I should do. The last time I saw her was on a rare hospital visit where she sat on the very edge of the couch like it was dirty and bragged about Matthew and glanced repeatedly from her watch to the exit. I consider turning around and running, but just at that moment she spots me.

"Cassie!" she calls out. Her smile is spontaneous and wide, her arm lifting toward the sun to wave at me as if I'm someone she is thrilled to see. I start cautiously toward her.

"What are you doing here?" I say when I reach her. Her hair, streaked with bright highlights, is pulled back, elegant and sleek.

"I told you I was coming!"

"You said you would call first."

"Well, surprise!" she says, and glances up at the guy beside her with a nervous laugh. For a second I think she is actually going to hug me, and I tense up, not just because I don't want it, but because my body feels instinctively confused by it. She places her arm lightly on my back instead. I move away.

"Pete, this is my lovely daughter, Cassie," she says, and then turns and beams at me. I wonder when I became her lovely daughter and why no one informed me of this sudden change.

Pete looks around my mother's age, tall and tan with hair the color of tinsel. He shakes my hand quickly, does not quite meet my eyes.

"Pete and I were just reliving our glory days. We can hardly believe how little everything has changed."

"You went to school here too?" I say for the sake of being polite.

"Pete is a very distinguished alumnus," my mother jumps in. "Also a very large benefactor." She looks up at him and beams. "He wrote your letter of recommendation. I believe you have him to thank for getting you in here."

"Oh," I say. "Thanks."

I suppose I should feel grateful, but right now I just feel uncomfortable.

He nods distractedly and then turns to my mother. "I should let you two catch up." To me, he adds, "It was nice to meet you, Cassie."

"Tonight then?" my mother says.

He glances quickly at me and gives her a small nod. She watches him go and the light in her face dims as if she's stepped into shade. Then she turns back to me, and the light returns at half-mast.

"Oh, it's just so perfect seeing you here," she says, taking me in. "It brings everything right back. I was thinking we could do a little shopping. Pete and I saw a bunch of cute shops on Main Street and I'm dying to check them out."

I stare at her, trying to make sense of why she is acting so weirdly happy to see me. I'm sure it's just another game she's playing, but I can't figure out the purpose of it.

"No, thanks," I say. "I have another class to go to. Maybe if you'd called first like you said you would . . ."

She squints at me, a small frown, which passes quickly. "Don't be silly. I'm paying for this school and I can take you out for the day if I want to."

I'm desperate for new clothes, but I remind myself that I don't want or need anything from her. "I can't lose another day. I missed a bunch when I was sick."

"Oh, you're a smart girl," she says. "You'll catch up." She puts her hand on my back and leads me toward the car. "Besides, I've got your father's credit cards, so it's going to be a really good day for you."

I look down at my dated clothes again, remember the way I felt when that girl looked at me quickly and then away like I was nothing.

Screw it, I think. *I'll get some stuff and then bail.*

As soon as we get into the car, my mother stops and looks at me again. "I've been doing a lot of thinking lately," she says. "Ever since Matthew up and went to school halfway across the country . . . and Gavin is growing up so quickly . . . you can't imagine how empty the house feels. And now you're here and it got me remembering my own time in college—the best years of my life—and I was thinking how nice it would be to relive those times through my daughter's eyes. My mother was never interested in my experiences. I was the only girl in my sorority whose mother didn't come to graduation. She was in Miami. Never even sent a card. She's dying now, you know. I don't know if I mentioned that on the phone. Breast cancer. Stage four."

"No," I say. "You didn't mention it." I think of Leigh, wonder if it's bad that I feel no sadness at all about this news.

"She's going to die without ever having really known me," she says, choked. She starts the engine and pulls out of the campus parking lot. Then she turns to me. "I don't want that to be us. I want to try again. Do you think we could do that? I never wanted things to be this way, you know."

I let the silence be my response. Then I turn on the radio. She turns it off.

"Cassie?"

"What do you want me to say? That I forgive you for having me locked up in a mental hospital?"

"I did what I—"

"That I can just forget about it and start over?" Even as the righteous anger in me speaks, I can hear the tightness of tears at the back of my throat. I hate that she can hear it too. I don't want to give her that.

"I was trying to protect you," she says. "To protect all of us."

"Oh, bullshit!"

"What was I supposed to do? You were so angry—"

"I wasn't angry! I was in pain! I wanted you to love me!"

"It was impossible to reach you."

"You didn't even try! You lied to have me locked up!"

"I know it must have been awful to feel like we abandoned you."

My throat swells with the truth of this.

"I knew that once you got control over yourself, life would be so much better for you, for all of us. And we could start over."

I stare out the window. Houses and trees whirl by as we pass them. Every time I think I have a sense of where I am, my mother takes another turn that disorients me, makes it harder to trace my way back, and I am left dependent on her sense of direction rather than my own. I think about what she said. It's true that I had gotten a little out of control, that I had done desperate things in an attempt to get her love and attention. But that didn't justify what she did. Did it?

"I feel like we've missed out on so much mother-daughter stuff," she says. "And that's very sad to me."

I glance over and see tears forming in pools beneath her eyes. The expression on her face is so open and intimate that I can only meet her gaze for a moment before I have to look away.

"I always dreamed that you and I would have the relationship that I never got to have with my mother," she says. "I don't even know where it went wrong anymore. But so much time has passed now."

I wrap my arms around myself, trying to keep everything locked in, trying to keep everything locked out. I fight to hold on to what I know, to what she did. I hear James in my head saying, "Don't do it. Don't trust her." But her tears and her words are so confusing, proving that she loves me, which is, after all, all I've ever wanted from her.

"Anyway," she says, wiping her eyes. "I can see that you don't want to talk about it, so enough. Let's just try to have a nice day, okay?"

"Fine," I say, keeping my eye on the prize of new clothes.

"So . . . what did you think of Pete?"

I shrug, pick at my fingernails. "Whatever. He seemed okay."

She watches my face. Her own is suddenly youthful and glowing, a strangely quick shift in her mood. A giddy sort of grin appears to be fighting to break free. I can almost see the college girl still in her.

"What?" I say.

Her eyes widen with delicious mischief. "Well, I finally took your advice." She pauses for dramatic effect. "I'm having an affair."

I stare at her. "I advised you to have an affair?"

"You don't remember?" She looks wounded. "I asked you once, when you were much younger, if I deserved to be happy. You were adamant that I did." Her smile is wide and prompting.

"Well, yeah, but I didn't mean—"

"You know your father was never the one for me. Even on our wedding day it was all I could do to keep from running out of the church."

My head feels thick and pressurized. I fumble in my purse for a cigarette, roll down the window and light up.

"I don't know why I didn't. Why I was so afraid to be alone. But you were so right—"

"But I never said—!"

"And now I'm so happy. Pete's the only man I've ever really loved."

And now I remember which boyfriend Pete was: the one she had kissed for so many hours that she wondered how it was possible to go that long without breathing.

"I knew he was still heavily involved with the school, so when that nurse mentioned you wanted to go to college, I thought, *Here is my chance to finally be happy.* So I picked up the phone and called him."

141

"That's why you got me in here? So you could start an affair?"

"No! Of course not!" she says. "How can you say that? I did it for you. This was just a bonus. Anyway, it turned out he was somewhat newly divorced. So I drove up last week and got a hotel room."

I turn to her, take this in. "You were here last week?"

When I was so sick?

"Just for a few nights." Her eyes are shining, her happiness so big that it takes over everything else. My own thoughts become slippery, impossible to hold. "I'm telling you, it was as if no time had passed. Can you believe it? We're taking it slowly, of course. But I'm thinking eventually I can move here, maybe get an apartment nearby. Wouldn't that be fun?" She stops and her eyes mist over. "You know, I owe it all to you, Cassie. I really don't think I realized when you were growing up how much you really saw me."

I stare at the dashboard, trying to keep my resolve. And yet it feels true, this sense of being attuned to my mother in a deeper way than my brothers were. To hear her say it feels like a seemingly hopeless battle has finally been won. She finally sees me, recognizes that I was the one who really knew her, that only I understood her despair with my father and her clawing sense of loss in having a mother who could not mother.

"It's proof, isn't it," she says, "that second chances are possible?"

"I guess," I say, surprised to find some small part of me wanting to believe—despite everything that has happened, despite memory, which even at this moment taps insistently, warningly at my shoulder—that there could be a second chance for us, too.

twenty-one

IT'S THE THOUGHT of second chances that takes me back in time to an afternoon several months before my mother was due with Gavin. I had just come home from school when she called to me from the room where she had once done her art. The last time I had been in this room, the last time I had been alone with her at all was the day she told me she didn't love my father. Now all of her beloved brushes and paints had been tearfully stored away in the attic, replaced with a crib and a changing table and a rug with trains on it. I went over to where she sat rocking in a creaky chair. There she surprised me by putting my hand on her stomach so I could feel the baby move, its feet tapping at her insides like a goldfish bumping its nose against the glass of its bowl.

"Maybe things will change once the baby's born," she said.

I looked up. I had forgotten how blue her eyes were.

"I think they will. Don't you?" she asked.

"I don't know," I said, because I saw too much, because I was never that good at pretending.

Her eyes widened with surprise and then something else. She pushed my hand off her belly. "Maybe you don't want things to be different."

"What?"

"Is that it?"

"No!"

"I don't know," she said, her face darkening as her thoughts gathered momentum. "Maybe you don't really want me to be happy. Maybe all that crap about me deserving happiness was just a way to turn me against your father. That way you can have him all to yourself."

"What are you talking about?" My mind twisted to understand what I'd said to make her turn on me so quickly. "I don't even like Dad!" This wasn't fair or even true, but in the moment it felt true, like the mere suggestion that I would want him all to myself filled me with disgust toward him. I wanted her to see how wrong she was, to know that my allegiance was with her.

"I suppose it's normal for a daughter to want to replace her mother in some way. I'm just kind of surprised I didn't see it before. To think you actually had me considering leaving him."

I stared at her, too confused and stunned to speak.

She stood up and went downstairs.

It was not long after that, not long after the baby was born and nothing changed at all, that my mother stopped looking at me altogether. She was busy taking care of Gavin, of course, and Matthew as always captured much of her attention, but whatever she had left she withheld from me, the way one walks past the reaching hand of the homeless as if there isn't a human being sitting there. I had made the mistake of telling the truth, and the truth was the enemy, the truth was the one thing my mother could not bear to see.

♦ ♦ ♦

Something happened to me after that, right after Gavin was born and my mother stopped looking at me. It was more than the sense of disappearing I had become accustomed to feeling. It was when I discovered that there are two kinds of death. There is ceasing to exist, usually accompanied by a funeral and loved ones in mourning. And then there is emotional death born out of necessity and measured solely by the absence of grief it causes: the turning off the lights of oneself in order to shut down the feelings of being alive. Eventually I just checked out of the world altogether, leaving behind only my body, like a snail abandoning its shell. Sometimes I would catch myself in the mirror, surprised to see someone staring back at me, a stranger whose face I struggled to connect as my own, whose body was visible and intact despite the feeling that I moved through the world as a ghost.

Nobody noticed that I was gone. Everybody went on, in fact, as if I had never been there at all. Life continued, and I watched it like a television show through the window of a stranger's house. I was outside. I watched.

Most people are afraid of death. They shield their eyes, pretend it's not there. But sometimes, unwittingly, they bump up against it. And when they do, they get angry.

Like my mother, for instance. Most of the time she looked over my head or turned her back, but sometimes when I caught her off guard, she looked startled to see me there, as anyone would upon seeing a ghost.

In these moments she would rear back at the sight of me and then grow taut with sudden fury. "Goddamn it," she'd say. "Stop skulking around here like a zombie. You're making me feel like a bad mother."

Nobody likes to be haunted.

As for Matthew, he was in middle school by then and so might not have noticed me even if I had been fully present. Most days he would saunter into the den after a day out with his friends and, in typical older brother fashion, change the channel right in the middle of my favorite TV shows. It was nothing new, really. The only difference was that I didn't bother to protest anymore. I just sat there and let him do it and didn't say a word about it because I wasn't really in the room anyway. For the most part, he seemed happy with this arrangement, but every once in a while he would take sudden notice of me sitting there so quiet and shut down, and he would lunge forward and wrestle with me, something we used to do when we were younger. Only now when he threw me into a headlock, or pretended to pile drive me into the carpet, or maneuvered me onto the floor and sat on my back, there was an added element to it, a too-hard twist of the arm, a too-deep knee into my ribs. It was anger disguised as fun, torture devised to get a reaction, and maybe that's all he really wanted: some kind of response, some indication of life, like a dog shaking a dead animal in its jaws.

But when I finally gave in and screamed bloody murder, my mother would come running into the den and say, "Stop all that yelling! You're giving me a headache." She'd look at me with my face in the carpet and Matthew sitting on my back and say, "Quit bothering your brother."

"Exactly!" Matthew would say, smiling smugly, victorious. "Quit bothering me."

He was getting the message loud and clear.

That was when I pretty much moved into the basement. I began to spend all my time there because there was a TV that no one else cared to watch because our basement was so cold and damp and made of concrete. But I didn't mind. Everything sort of had that feel to it anyway, no matter where I was.

That's the weirdest thing about being cut off from life. Everything gets washed out or muted or recedes into the background except for other people's laughter. Other people's laughter gets very loud and jarring. It penetrates. It is a reminder that other people live.

It was pretty quiet in the basement except for the laughter that seeped down from upstairs when my mother and Matthew would watch television together in the den. That was very loud and it made me feel lonely.

But there was one good thing, one reason to slip upstairs sometimes and visit the world. There was Gavin. Gavin with his small body and eyes as round and blue as the Earth, who would rest, without judgment, in the crook of my arm. Gavin, who was immune to the opinions of others. Gavin, who, years later, would watch my parents tie me up and drag me away to a mental hospital with tears in his eyes, knowing it was all a lie.

twenty-two

I AM JERKED back into the present when my mother overshoots a parking spot and hits a curb.

"Oops," she says. "Good thing it's a rental!"

We have arrived on the quaint and beachy Main Street, which is lined with small boutiques and outdoor cafés where students and beach bums and the last of the summer people gather. Many of the shops are geared toward college-aged girls like me, with Dunton sweatshirts in the window beside mannequins in cute jeans and flowing tops. I start toward one of those stores, but my mother steers us to the small shop next door.

"Ooh, look at that adorable skirt!" she says, stepping up to the window. The clothes on display seem more geared for her age group. "Let's go in there."

"I'm not going to like anything in there," I say.

"You can't keep dressing like a bag lady," she says. "You're in college now. Besides, I'm the one with the credit cards, remember?"

We enter the store and my whole body tightens as she beelines for the dress rack. She still refuses to accept that I don't wear dresses. She still refuses to accept me as I am. I can feel the rage bubbling up.

"I haven't worn a dress since I was, like, seven!" I say. But as soon as the words are out of my mouth, I know they aren't quite true. That in fact, I can remember very clearly the last time I was made to wear a dress.

I was fourteen, it was late August and so hot that the air felt boiled. School was just about to start and I was resentful that I had to spend one of the last days of summer stuck inside a stuffy church that smelled like lemons and old people.

The dress was way too tight from all the weight I'd been gaining, and I found it hard to breathe between the squeeze of fabric against my skin and the sharp sounds of my mother weeping uncontrollably over Great-Aunt Dora.

The service began. The low metallic sound of the organ played. The pallbearers walked up the aisle, and Dora's coffin passed by me so close I could almost reach out my hand and tap on its wood. An image flashed in my mind of her trapped and panicked and suffocating inside. At that moment, something came loose in me and broke free, kicked out involuntarily.

I turned to Gavin, who had just turned four. "Dora's in there," I blurted out gleefully. "She's stuck forever in that box."

As soon as the words were out of my mouth, the loose thing retreated like a worm back into a fruit, and I didn't know what had made me say that or why it had seemed so important. I watched Gavin, small in his suit, and waited for his reaction, but he just looked at me with eyes wide and blue as sky. Then Matthew leaned forward from the other side of him and punched me in the leg.

"What the hell?" he said.

"What happened?" my mother asked, leaning over.

I stared at Matthew, willing his silence with my eyes, asking him to see me, to cut me a break, to not throw me under the bus just this once. He stared back at me, studying my face. I was sure he had received my message, that he understood, that he would keep silent.

Then he turned to my mother and repeated what I'd said, and I realized in that moment that I had lost Matthew to my mother, that he had been lost to me for some time, only I hadn't let myself believe it.

My mother looked at me, eyes full of shock before they turned to anger. "Dora was like a mother to me. You must really despise me to say something like that!"

"No!" I said. "That's not true!" But because I could not even explain to myself why I'd said such a horrible thing, I looked down at my lap and wondered what the hell was wrong with me.

Now my mother piles an armful of dresses and blouses and skirts into my arms. "Just indulge me for once," she says. "If you don't like them, then we'll talk."

"Whatever," I say. The sooner I can get this shit over with, the sooner we can go to the other store, and the sooner I can get what I need and go back to my dorm.

I head to the fitting room and throw on the black low-cut blouse and pencil skirt she has picked out first. The clothes hug my body and something about the intention behind the outfit makes me queasy, makes me want to cover myself up as fast as possible. I yank the blouse upward toward my neck and step out. I put my arms out and look at her miserably.

"It's gross," I say. "Can we go now?"

"Oh my God!" she says. "You look gorgeous!"

"What?"

She steps back to take in the whole of me, her eyes shiny with approval. It shouldn't matter. I shouldn't care.

"I'm so jealous of your figure," she says. "I wish I could wear clothes like this." She steps forward and adjusts the blouse back to its original position. "It's supposed to hang like that. You want to show off your cleavage."

I turn and look at myself in the mirror, trying to see me as she does right now. I'm surprised to see that I actually do have a pretty good figure, that I never noticed it until my mother pointed it out. Still.

"It's a little grown up, don't you think?" I say. "I'm sure there is better stuff next door."

"No, it's perfect. Trust me." She steps back and looks again. "Absolutely gorgeous!" she says, and somehow when she says it, it feels like it could be true.

"I don't know . . ." I say. But even as I try to resist her power, my mother's is still the only opinion that matters, the only person who can say with authority that the ugly, unlovable thing in me is now gone.

I try on three more outfits and several pairs of shoes.

"Isn't this fun?" my mother says. "This is what I always wanted—a daughter who would let me dress her up."

Yeah, I think, *just what you always wanted—for me to be someone else.*

But then she says, "I can't even decide. You look so amazing in everything! Let's get them all!" and I wonder if maybe I'm being too hard on her, that if I could just find it in myself to forgive her, maybe we really could find a new beginning.

We bring the clothes as well as two new pairs of shoes up to the salesgirl, a tall smiley redhead who looks a few years older than me. "Lucky you," she says when we pile the clothes onto the counter. "I wish my mom would take me on a shopping spree!"

My mother laughs happily, enjoying the role.

We leave the store with three huge bags in tow.

"What a perfect day this has been!" she says as we climb back into the car. "I'm so glad we can finally be gal pals!"

I catch myself thinking that the day did end up being kind of nice, and quickly swallow the instinct to say so. Instead I look out the window, guarded again.

We reach the campus and she pulls into a parking spot. "I really did have so much fun with you," she says, and she sounds so sincere that it really feels like the mother I knew has been replaced with the mother I always dreamed of having.

"Well, thanks for the stuff," I say. I get out of the car and am about to head toward the dorm when I stop, reconsider. "Do you maybe want to see my room? And meet my roommate, Zoey?"

She looks at the clock on the dashboard and grimaces. "I'd love to, but I have to get back to the hotel. Pete is taking me to Le Chateau tonight. I hear it's *très romantique*."

"Oh." I look down at the shopping bags at my feet. "No problem, whatever."

"Maybe sometime later in the week."

"How long are you going to be here?"

"I'll call you," she says.

I give her mine and Zoey's room phone number and she punches it into her cell phone.

"Great. Oh, and I told your father I was staying with you, so he might ask me for the number. If he calls for any reason, cover for me, okay?"

Then she pulls away and is gone.

twenty-three

MY SHOPPING BAGS bounce against my legs as I dash up the stairs to my room, nearly colliding with two girls who live at the end of our hall—theater majors, I'm guessing, by the fact that they blast *Les Misérables* on a nearly endless loop in their room. I'm hoping Zoey is back from her classes so I can show her all the loot my mother bought me.

I battle through the door with all my stuff and find her lying on her bed with a Norton anthology in her hands and an open box of crackers and crumbs beside her. The TV is on, but muted.

"Hey!" I say, and raise the shopping bags gleefully in the air.

Something is wrong. It takes Zoey a moment too long to look at me.

"Where were you?" she says, turning back to the TV. "I looked everywhere for you."

I freeze. In the shock of my mother's arrival, I forgot that I left Zoey back at the psych building. *Shit.* At once I know I'm in the wrong here and also that I can't let her see that, see that she has the upper hand. My own inability to anticipate her anger infuriates me. I know better than to ever let my guard down with anyone. I move toward the closet with my shopping bags. "I took off," I say coldly. "I didn't feel like waiting around."

"But we were supposed to have lunch together. I wanted you to meet some of my friends."

"Yeah," I snap. "And then you left me sitting in the stupid counseling center for, like, a year."

I stare into my closet and take stock of all my belongings. I calculate how fast I can pack up my clothes, my toiletries, my bedding. I do a mental run-through of the key code to my original dorm room to make sure I still remember it, thankful I never notified housing of my change. Already I'm picturing myself back there, within those white walls, all that silence. I tell myself I don't care, that it's better this way. I know how this story ends.

"You're right. It did take longer than I thought," Zoey says quietly.

I stand in the closet, holding my breath. I'm not quite sure what's happening.

"What?"

"I said you're right. I didn't mean to keep you waiting. I'm sorry."

The words are so foreign and shocking that my brain is unable to process them right away. I will myself to look at her, but I can't quite trust it or get a handle on what I'm supposed to do here. I've never heard anyone say, "I'm sorry," or at least not in a real way, not in the heat of a fight. Part of me just wants to step outside of the moment and ask, "How did you *do* that?" because it's so incomprehensible that someone would leave themselves open like that. I want to turn around, confess that *I'm* the one who should be sorry, but I can't make the words come out, can't let myself be that vulnerable. Instead I say, "Forget it. I just don't like waiting around for people."

"You were probably smart to bail anyway," she says. "Molly and Piper spent the whole time talking about current events like I care and refused to check out cute boys with me. Plus I'm pretty sure the mystery meat of the day was fried catcher's mitt."

I turn and laugh, so relieved I want to cry. I hate myself for twisting things.

"So, I'm going to a beach party tonight if you want to come."

I start to say no—the idea of being around so many people seems daunting or at least exhausting—but then I wonder how many more times I can do that before Zoey decides her other friends are more fun than me. "I guess I should start meeting people," I say.

"Yes, you should! What's in the bags?"

"My mother was here. She took me shopping." There is relief in being able to say this, to be just like every other kid here whose parents come to visit.

"What? I didn't get to meet her?"

"Next time. She had to split."

I hold up my new outfits one at a time while I clue her in on my mother's affair so she'll know what to do if my father calls.

"Wait," Zoey says. "She wants you to lie for her?"

My whole body braces.

"She shouldn't ask that of you, Cass."

"You don't get it," I say. "She needs this. She needs me."

"You're right," she says. "I don't get that."

She stares at me with concern, and a small seed of distrust sprouts in me. Of course Zoey with her perfect life wouldn't understand that sometimes being needed is enough. Or, at the very least, it's better than nothing at all.

twenty-four

IT'S ABOUT AN hour before sunset when Zoey and I arrive at the beach party. The light is champagne and the water sparkles. In the near distance is the staticky distorted sound of a radio turned too loud and at least a hundred students gathered in a large dense circle, partying.

"Are you sure I'm invited?" I say.

"It's a *beach party*," she says. "Everyone's invited. Plus, I know the girls who organized it." She kicks off her sandals, loops them through her fingers and starts down the sand. Her hair is picked up by the wind, creating a wistful picture as she moves. The air smells of fire and ocean and late September. Of endings and beginnings.

A group of girls shout, "Zoey!" as we approach and she waves to them and then whispers to me that she needs a beer before she can deal. We head toward the keg where a ruddy-faced football player is doing a keg stand while others around him cheer, "Go! Go! Go!" A few feet away, a group of girls sing really loudly and very badly to a song on the radio. They sway and stumble. Everyone seems so young and open, so easily amused. It's completely alien to me, this innocence. I watch them with envy, hating myself for not being able to be like them.

"Hey there." Someone nudges me.

I turn to see the surfer boy, Chris, and jump back in such an extreme way that he says, "Sorry, I didn't mean to scare you!"

"Hi!" I say in a ridiculously high-pitched voice. I try again, flat and cool this time. "What's up?" Out of the corner of my eye I see Zoey watching me with a shit-eating grin on her face. She obviously suspects something.

"Hi, there," she says, stepping forward. "I'm Zoey."

"I'm Chris," he says, and shakes her hand warmly.

"So you are," Zoey says and gives me a wink that Chris catches. I want to kill her.

"This is Murph," Chris says, elbowing his friend, who's in the midst of shotgunning a beer. Murph stops and burps and nods in our general direction.

"Hi, Murph," Zoey says, twirling her fingers through her hair. "Do you know where a girl like me can get a drink like that?"

"Follow me," he says, and leads her deeper into the party.

"Wait! Where are you going?" I call after her. She turns and waves at me, nods in an obvious way toward Chris and then disappears into the crowd, hugging and waving to people as she goes. I want to call, "Don't leave me here. I don't know how to do this!" Instead, I turn to Chris. "Where are they going?"

"I think your friend wants us to be alone." He traces sand with his shoe, then looks up and smiles, embarrassed.

"That's weird," I say, and look away.

I go to light a cigarette and he cups his hands around mine to shield the wind. I lean in, feel the heat of both the flame and his nearness. Our eyes meet. The cigarette catches.

"You shouldn't smoke," he says.

"You shouldn't lecture." I turn my face and blow smoke in the opposite direction.

"I'll stop if you stop."

I roll my eyes and he grins. I look toward the ocean, envision myself out there beyond the breakers, fighting to stay afloat.

"Waves look good," he says.

"So go surf then. There's still light."

"How do you know I surf? Have you been stalking me?"

"No! *God!*" I say. "I just assumed by the way you dress."

"I'm kidding! I do surf, but why would I do that now? You're here."

"I don't need you to entertain me."

"That's not what I meant." His face, in profile, hardens.

I don't want to be this cold, defensive person and yet here I am, being exactly that. Chris pulls two beers out of a cooler near his feet, cracks one open and hands it to me. A thin blond girl runs past us and vomits a short way down the beach.

"Lovely," I say, and we both turn away and laugh.

"Wanna walk somewhere less . . . uh . . . ?"

"Pukish?" I search the crowd, all those strangers' faces, Zoey nowhere in sight. "Okay, I guess."

We move toward the water. The sun is dropping, setting the surfers against a pink sky. They look like seals, playful and fearless as they tumble off the tails of waves. Even the wipeouts seem like a part of the fun, as if the surfers never anticipate anything but a soft bottom.

"I've always wanted to learn," I say as one of the surfers leaves the water and passes us. "You're not afraid of sharks?"

"They say you have less chance of being eaten by a shark than—"

"—of being struck by lightning. Yeah, I've heard that. Which is also why I don't stand outside in a thunderstorm with a metal pole."

"There are bigger things in life to be afraid of," he says.

"Really? Than being eaten? Like what?"

"I don't know." He looks toward the water, then back to me. "Like missing out because you're too afraid to try, for starters."

"That's deep," I say, and roll my eyes.

He turns to me, a quick glance, but it contains something I've never seen before, a way I've never been looked at. It is not even sexual so much as hopeful. A hopeful, innocent wanting.

"What happened to all the seashells?" I say quickly, staring down at the sand. "Didn't it seem like there were more of them around when we were kids? Or did we just look harder then?"

I'm talking fast and I can hear that my own voice sounds unnatural. Something in me has been stirred by his glance. Both a happiness and a fleeting urge to cry—to bawl, really. "My mother used to say you could hear the ocean in a shell, but I could never hear it. I always thought there was something wrong with me that I couldn't."

"Wait here," he says abruptly, and starts down the beach, leaving me wondering why I brought my mother into this moment and ruined things.

His head is bowed as he moves toward an area strewn with seaweed. There is a small tattoo on the back of his ankle, which I decide is stupid, just like he is stupid, just like I am stupid, just like this whole thing is stupid.

I go and climb the lifeguard chair to show him that I won't do what he tells me to. From above, I watch him in his madras shorts and striped shirt, so boyishly mismatched that my heart yearns and leaps before I have a chance to shut it closed again.

I finish my beer and then he is climbing up to me, stopping on the last ladder rung so that we are face-to-face. His eyes are liquid brown and grow shiny and soft as he looks at me. In his hand is a shell just like the one I found in Maine, and he smiles and puts it to my ear so earnest and sweet that a tiny bell pings in my chest and my stomach drops. Then he cups my other ear protectively, blocking out the external noise. His hand is big and hot. His body is close enough that I can smell his soap. My heart beats so hard, it feels like waves slamming into the sand.

"Hear it?"

"No." My legs are shaking. I have never been this close to a boy before, not without a shield of platonic indifference between us. I wonder if this is how my mother felt when she was first with Pete.

"Nothing?"

"It's really faint. And I don't believe it's the ocean." My voice is half swallowed. I'm trying so hard to be normal, but I'm leaking pure terror.

His free hand moves down my neck, and my spine tingles. His eyes watch me. "I've heard it's the sound of your own blood pumping," he says.

"So I'm hearing myself?" I wish suddenly for a mirror. I want to make sure everything is in place, that there's no avenue for him to see past the made-up face before him and find the unlovable ex–mental patient underneath.

"Yep. And you sound like the ocean," he says, smiling. He presses his forehead lightly against mine, takes my wrist into his hand and rubs the veins along it.

"Where do you think Zoey is?" I say too loudly, pulling back.

Chris doesn't answer, but nods to himself and gets quiet. He sits down beside me, only farther away than before, and looks out at the sea. I finally spot Zoey a short ways down the beach lying with Murph. They are kissing, and I make fun of them for it so that Chris doesn't think I want to kiss him, even though I sort of do. I keep chattering, filling up the distance I've created with meaningless babble, pausing only to drink a second beer in the six-pack that Chris has brought. The beer hits all at once, killing the anxiety, making me floaty and relaxed.

The sky has turned dark without my noticing, and the moon leaves a stripe of pearl light on the water. The rest of the ocean looks like a black undulating version of the sky, ancient and alive. It occurs to me that I am on the beach with a cute boy at night in a lifeguard chair, the kind of thing that happens to other girls, the kind of thing I never imagined possible for me. With my fear drowned in alcohol and Chris sitting at a safe distance from me, the urge to kiss him returns and grows stronger, but I don't know how to make it happen. I inch closer, let my shoulder press against his, leaning, daring. He doesn't respond, and I know it's because he doesn't like me anymore, that he got too close, saw too much, saw that I wasn't really pretty.

"Are you drunk?" he says.

"No. Why?" I pull away, sobering instantly.

"Because," he says, laughing, "you're sort of acting like you like me all of a sudden."

It feels like an accusation, like I've revealed something terrible and foolishly misguided. "Uh, wrong," I say. "On both counts."

In the distance I hear voices moving toward us, a quiet murmuring, and then Zoey's boozy cackle.

"Zoey!" I jump to my feet.

She and Murph are black shapes in the darkness, barely visible until they are almost under the lifeguard chair.

"Oh, look at you two lovebirds up there," Zoey slurs.

"As if," I say, and toss an empty beer can at her feet.

"Not nice." She waves her finger at me and then picks up the can and shakes it to see if there is any beer left in it to drink.

I climb down the chair, almost losing my balance as I near the bottom. Chris catches my arm and I shake free of him and go to Zoey. She grabs my shoulders and tilts toward me, almost pushing me over as she does.

"Did you kiss him?" she whisper-shouts as if the boys aren't standing right beside us. Her breath is so full of alcohol, it burns my nose.

"Ew, no," I say, humiliated.

Chris bends his face to the sand as if I have hurt him, and I immediately want to take it back. I'm such an asshole sometimes.

"I'm sure the feeling was mutual," I add quickly.

"No, it wasn't," Chris says, and our eyes meet, and the world does that thing where it stops for a second again and there is only him and me.

"I kissed Murph," Zoey continues to whisper loudly. She is staggering even as she is trying to stand still. "It wasn't that great."

"Hey!" Murph says.

"I'd probably do it again if I was drunk enough, though."

Murph gives a thumbs-up. "Works for me!" he says. "I'm gonna see if I can score some more beer."

Chris and I help Zoey to Chris's old beat-up convertible, but despite our efforts, she falls three times en route. On the drive home she tries several times to stand up, only to have Chris lean back to help me pull her down. At our dorm, he helps me assist Zoey up the stairs, and then she breaks free of us and runs to our room. We watch her make several tries with the keypad, and then she enters and quickly shuts the door behind her, deliberately leaving Chris and me alone in the hallway. We hear the door lock from the inside and the sound of Zoey cracking herself up. Chris and I laugh too at the awkwardness of the moment. Our eyes meet again.

"I guess I'll see you in class," I say.

He nods, makes a move to go. Stops. "You want to hang out this weekend? I promise I won't try to kiss you."

Before I can answer, the door swings wide open and Zoey kicks me hard in the foot.

"Okay," I squeak through the pain.

Chris laughs but appears slightly alarmed by it all. "How about Sunday? Pick you up at noon?"

"She'll be there," Zoey says, and then yanks me inside and closes the door on him before I can change my mind.

We listen as his footsteps disappear down the hall, and then she turns to me and sings, "You have a daaaate!"

I must be drunker than I thought, because I run to the bathroom, drop to my knees and grip the bowl.

twenty-five

IN THE MORNING Zoey and I have a strenuous debate over which one of us is more hung over. I insist that Zoey must be better off since she actually made it to her 9:00 A.M. class. She contends that my skipping class cannot be an accurate gage of post-party trauma since I do it all the time anyway. It's a difficult point to refute so I am perfectly thrilled when the phone rings and saves me from losing this argument. I glance at the caller ID. It's my mother. I pick up.

"Tell her you have a date!" Zoey shouts.

"You have a date?" my mother says, squealing with excitement.

She is happy for me. I matter to her. I am more than just an alibi.

"Um . . . yeah," I say. I hesitate, consider how much I want to share with her, decide it's worth a try to let her in just a little bit. "On Sunday. With this guy Chris."

"Ooh, maybe he'll be your Pete," she says. "Wouldn't that be wonderful?"

I can't tell if the tightening in my stomach means it would be wonderful or awful. Excitement and anxiety always get mixed up for me, the wires constantly crossing. I wish I could just go on a stupid date like everybody else without feeling like it's a life-or-death situation.

"Do you know what you're going to wear? Men love tight."

I hadn't even thought about clothes yet. Ugh. I have no idea how to dress for a date. "Maybe you can help me pick something out?" I say, in another small attempt to give this new mother-daughter relationship a shot.

"Wish I could! Unfortunately, Sunday is my last day with Pete."

"Oh," I say. I think about asking what about tonight. Or tomorrow. But I don't. Instead I just hold my breath for a good ten seconds to suffocate the sense of disappointment and rejection so it doesn't spill out. After all, I alone know how long she has dreamed of this, how long she stayed trapped in the wrong marriage, trying to convince herself it wasn't so bad. I alone know the depths of misery she reached when she did not have the love she wanted.

I was just fourteen when my mother told me she was going to die. I was in my first month of high school at the time, still trying to adjust to the enormous new building, the intimidating teachers, and my fellow students, who had all seemed to grow into themselves over the summer while I was still trying to get as much distance from myself as possible. All around me, tight, exclusive cliques were forming, and I remember feeling as if I were in a giant gym class, where instead of being picked last for a team, I wasn't picked at all, had somewhere along the way taken myself out of the game, and now I didn't even know the rules.

In class, girls I had once been friends with leaned across my desk to pass notes to each other and chatted around me about parties they had been to over the weekend. In the hallways, kids shouted greetings to each other over my head. At lunch, I sat alone, certain that no one would want to talk to me, certain that even if they did, I wouldn't know what to say. I had been cut off from life for so long.

I kept my focus on the teachers and my schoolwork and waited for the hour when I could go home and disappear into the basement, into the safe haven of TV land, where I could be with other people and it didn't hurt that they didn't look at me in return.

One afternoon, I arrived home to find my mother lying on the couch in the den with the shades drawn. Ever since Dora's death, she'd seemed changed. Her boisterous laughter, which had carried through the house when she talked to Dora on the phone or chatted with Matthew, had been replaced with silence. The light in her eyes seemed permanently dimmed. Her beauty seemed to have abandoned her.

Dora had died of a heart attack, but it was my mother's heart that seemed broken. It made me angry sometimes. I don't know why.

I tiptoed past the room my mother was in so as not to disturb her as I made my way toward the basement. The house was quiet as a shadow.

"Cassie, come in here," she said. I paused, my heart thumping faster. She so rarely addressed me that my name sounded strange and unfamiliar coming from her mouth. I figured I must be in trouble for something, so I only took a few steps inside the room, ready to flee when necessary. Even though she had summoned me, she looked surprised to see me standing there, as anyone would upon seeing a ghost.

"You've gained more weight," she said.

"I know," I said. I hated my body and had tried to diet but I just couldn't stop eating, stuffing myself to sedation, filling and refilling that hollow place where a self should be.

"Well, don't just stand there. Come over here. I need to tell you something."

I went and stood in front of her.

She took a deep, pained breath before she spoke. "I'm sure you've noticed the twitch I've developed in my face."

I had not noticed, but now the left side of her mouth jerked subtly toward her left eye as if to prove itself.

"I've been reading about it on the Internet, and it's not good."

"What is it?"

She paused, started to say something, choked on the words. My legs felt watery, boneless.

"Brain tumor," she said finally.

"A *brain tumor*?" I said.

"That's what the symptoms suggest."

She began to sob. "Oh, Cassie," she said. "I can't believe this is happening to me. Why is this happening to me?" Her eyes searched my face. "And of course, your stupid father is off in Europe! And I have to deal with this alone." Her lips trembled. She wiped a tear. "I should have divorced him when I was still healthy. Now I'm stuck." She grabbed my hand and squeezed it.

I wanted to pull away. A hazy atmosphere seemed to wrap itself around my thoughts, making my own brain feel blurry.

"Don't you see?" she cried, and her emotions hurtled through the air as if she had tossed them at me with a bucket. "It's too late. My life is over and now I don't know what to do!"

"Maybe you should see a doctor," I said. "I mean, there are probably other things it could be besides a brain tumor."

She dropped my hand. "Oh, forget it. What do you know?" She pushed herself upright and brushed away a few hairs that were sticking to her wet cheeks. She looked newly composed and determined, like a young girl who has just bravely accepted that her date has stood her up.

"Anyway," she said. Then she smoothed down her blouse and folded her hands primly in her lap. "I want you to know that I have decided to kill myself."

I stared at her.

"Believe me," she said. "It's better this way." She gave me a small, courageous smile. "Someday, when you grow up, you'll understand. You'll know that I did it for you kids. So that you won't have to care for an invalid mother."

She watched me impassively as I took this in. Then a strange, satisfied look came over her face. Suddenly our feelings were reversed. Now I was the one who felt sick. I was the one searching her face, scared and alone and wanting something. And somehow, I understood that this wasn't by accident. I wanted to scream that I would not understand, that it wasn't fair for her to do this to me. I knew that I should tell her that I loved her and didn't want her to die, but in that moment, I did not love her. And so the words would not come.

"You don't have anything to say to that?" she said. "I don't know why I expected any different." She lay back and draped her arm across her eyes again. "You're probably happy about it."

Now, years later, I'm determined to prove to my mother what I could not, no matter how hard I tried, prove to her then—that I did want her to be happy, that I had loved her more than anything. If only I could have made her see that, see *me*, then maybe things would have been different. She would have loved me back. She would have been a good mother to me. I am sure of it. So instead of asking, "What about tonight or tomorrow?" I say, "Don't worry about it. Enjoy your time with Pete."

"I'll be back to visit soon," she says, "and I promise I'll make it up to you. I'm so proud of how great you're doing! I don't tell you that enough."

I hang up and sit down with Zoey to the cold remains of a large pizza we ordered late last night when there is a knock on our door. It's the girl who lives next to us announcing that there is a call for me on the pay phone.

Zoey and I freeze midbite and look at each other wide-eyed and spooked. Who would be calling me on the pay phone?

"Maybe it's Chris!" Zoey whispers as if somehow he can hear her.

Neither of us moves. We continue to stare at each other like deer in headlights until the absurdity of our paralysis sets us giggling.

Finally curiosity gets the better of me and I get up and start down the hall. Zoey follows. The pay-phone receiver dangles in the now empty hallway, waiting for me. I pause and then pick it up.

"Hello?"

"Is this Cassie O'Malley?"

"Yes," I say warily.

"Hi, Cassie, this is Janice from Dean Wilson's office." By the tone of her voice, I immediately assume someone, perhaps even multiple people, are dead. I wait.

"I've been looking over your file, and according to our records you have barely attended any classes in the three weeks that you've been here."

"Oh . . . ah . . ." To Zoey I mouth, "dean's office" and roll my eyes.

Instead of laughing, she looks worried.

"Your attendance record is so bad, in fact, that we wondered if you're still enrolled."

"Uh . . . yep, pretty sure I am."

"Well, failing to attend classes is not acceptable. Dunton has a reputation and standards we intend to uphold, Cassie," she continues. "High standards. Showing up for class is the first among them."

"Right. Sure."

"Dean Wilson takes these matters quite seriously. If you can't provide acceptable reasons for your absences, we will have no choice but to initiate a disciplinary hearing before the Academic Conduct Committee."

"Uh-huh," I say. "Well, thanks for the heads-up."

I hang up the phone and repeat the conversation to Zoey.

"Oh shit," she says. She looks pale and alarmed, having never learned that in order for authority to work, you have to actually care.

"Don't worry," I say as I start back to our room. Then I echo my mother's words. "I'm a smart girl. I'll catch up."

"Are you serious?" Zoey says, following me. "Cassie, it doesn't matter—they can expel you for absences alone."

"Oh, come on."

"Didn't you read the student handbook or the orientation packet?"

The hilarity of this notion is cut short by a sudden slam of panic. "They can?"

I light a cigarette, try to calm myself. "Well, if they do, they do," I say finally, trying to summon my own indifference. The only problem is that I actually do care, and it's only now that I've screwed everything up that I realize just how much. After all, where the hell would I go? What would I do? To get kicked out of school would mean never seeing Zoey . . . or Chris. And worse, it would prove to my mother, whose love and approval I have finally achieved, that I really am the irredeemable fuckup she once perceived me to be.

Zoey kicks into crisis-management mode. "It's okay," she says with a determined look on her face. "Everything is fixable. We just need to come up with an excuse."

We sit, staring at each other.

"Like . . . ?"

"Cramps?" she offers weakly.

"I think that only works in gym class."

Zoey bolts upright like she's just discovered fire. "What about the doctor in the ER? Couldn't he write you a note for the pneumonia at least?"

"After we skipped out of there like a couple of criminals? They're probably still trying to track me down! Besides, how do I explain all the classes I've missed since I've been well?"

"Right. Shit." She continues to worry her lip while I feel myself deflating with the hopelessness of the situation. "What about someone else? Know any other doctors who would be willing? Like a family friend or something?"

I immediately think of the hospital, the first hospital, the mental one. "I know some doctors."

"Any who would lie for you?"

"The doctors I know are more likely to believe lies than to tell them," I say.

Zoey looks at me, understandably confused.

Then an idea hits me, and I know what I have to do.

twenty-six

AS I CONSIDER the details of my emergency plan to stay at Dunton, I can't help but recognize the irony of my situation. There was a time in my life when I was a perfect student, would never have dreamed of cutting class or skipping an assignment or, as I'm doing now, failing out. The world of school was one of consistency, a place where the rules were clear-cut and easy to follow. Despite the isolation I felt from other students, school was the only place where it seemed like I had any control, where all I had to do to earn my coveted A for Adult Approval was study hard and pay attention.

But after my mother threatened suicide, all of that changed. She was always with me after that. Even when I was away from her at school, she was there in my mind. In dark daydreams I'd imagine myself finding her on the kitchen floor, wonder what her dead body would look like, whom I would call. I spent my classroom hours rehearsing her death in my mind as if I could prepare myself for it, steeling against a future I felt no control over. I never considered telling anyone else what she told me. It did not even occur to me that I had a choice.

Sometimes I would actually wish for it to happen, imagining

the compassion and pity I would receive as the "girl with the dead mother." Then, as self-punishment, I would force myself to picture her corpse in the coffin until the image was so upsetting, and the grief so real, that when the school bell rang, I came up from the story slightly dazed as if woken by an alarm clock in the middle of the night. It was because of this, because of my head being elsewhere, that I ended up being late to English class one day during freshman year and was issued my very first detention. At the time, it seemed like the world had ended. My last refuge, the last place where I was considered good, had been contaminated.

I walked into the detention hall like I was heading to the gallows. Only one other student was in the room, a boy named Wade Mattell. Wade was one of the popular kids, tall with a long face and eyes so pale they looked like rain. He was slouched at a desk in the back, spinning a basketball on his fingertip.

At the front was Mr. Dobbs, a gym teacher with two bucked front teeth that jutted out in opposite directions from beneath his thatchlike mustache. The entire school called him The Walrus, though not actually to his face. From where I stood, The Walrus appeared to be sleeping. I walked over and cleared my throat.

"Hi," I said tentatively. "I've never had detention before. It was just an accident that I was late. I'm usually always on time. And, um . . . I'm not sure what I'm supposed to be doing."

Dobbs didn't even open his eyes. "Grab a seat and be quiet, please," he said.

"Yeah, sit down and shut up," Wade called from the back of the room. "Can't you see The Walrus needs his beauty rest?"

I froze, trying to convince myself that I had not just heard what

I thought I had. I had never in my life heard a student be so disrespectful to a teacher.

Mr. Dobbs shot forward, eyes open wide. "What was that, Mr. Mattell?"

I took a step back.

"I was just telling her to sit down, sir," Wade said sweetly as he spun the ball on his fingertip. "Like you wanted her to."

Dobbs gave him a stare that could melt wire and then closed his eyes again. I went and took a seat as far away from Wade as possible so I wouldn't be associated with such a delinquent.

For the next twenty minutes, we all sat in a tedious silence, the universe realigned now that Dobbs seemed back in charge of the room. Then, from the back, came a soft, low moaning sound. I glanced at Mr. Dobbs, but he seemed not to have heard it. Minutes passed, and I wondered if I had imagined it. Then the sound came again. This time, a longer and louder groan. Dobbs looked up and eyed Wade, but the moment he did, the noise stopped. They observed each other in a kind of death-match staring contest until Wade finally shrugged and looked away. Mr. Dobbs watched him for a few more beats and then returned to his nap.

The instant Dobbs closed his eyes again, Wade let out a noise that sounded like a cross between a crying seal and a braying donkey. It was so loud that it seemed like the whole room shook with it. And that's when I realized with horror what the sound was.

A walrus call.

Oh my God.

Dobbs jumped to his feet.

I sank down as low as I could in my chair.

"If I hear that sound one more time," Dobbs said, charging toward Wade, "I will have you suspended until you graduate!"

I peeked behind me, praying Wade would shut the hell up.

Instead he looked up innocently at Mr. Dobbs. "What sound?" Wade asked. He didn't seem the least bit afraid. To my dismay, he turned to me. "Did you hear something?"

I looked up at Mr. Dobbs, who was staring at me so intently, he appeared to be boring the word *yes* into my forehead. I turned back to Wade, who watched me with a slight smile on his face as if he was curious to see what I would do, enjoying making me squirm. I glanced again at Dobbs, who stood with his arms across his chest, confident in his power and authority over me.

I took a deep breath. "No," I said quietly. "I didn't hear anything at all." I may have been a kiss-ass, but I wasn't stupid.

Dobbs glared at me, so red-faced and angry, he looked like he might spontaneously combust. Then the bell rang and I bolted out of the room.

I walked home slowly, dragging the day behind me like a broken parachute. Not only was I friendless but I had now made an enemy of a teacher too. Behind me I began to hear the rhythmic smack of a basketball against the sidewalk. I was pretty sure it was Wade, but I didn't want to turn around and look.

"Hey!" he shouted, and since there appeared to be no one else within a two-block radius, I realized he could only be talking to me. Thus I did the only thing I could think to do: I ducked around the corner and then ran away from him so fast that my own shadow had to catch up. I had no idea what he wanted, but being that he was one of the "cool kids" and I was fat and unpopular, I was pretty sure he was just going to be mean.

As I neared home, the dark daydreams of my mother intruded again. I pictured coming upon a carnival of ambulances and police cars parked in front of our house, the neighbors gathered in small hushed groups on the sidewalk. Or worse, that no one would be there at all. That I would be the one to find her.

I turned up our driveway to find the back door wide open. Instantly, I knew something was off. I could feel it as a lack of feeling, the way an empty house has a sense of absence about it. I entered through the kitchen. My footsteps were made louder by the silence. I tiptoed toward the den and poked my head inside the door. Empty. I crept up the stairs and peered quickly into each of the four bedrooms. Nothing. Nothing. Nothing. A bright panic flared over my gloom like blooms of plankton in a night sea. I went down to the basement. I thought of horror movies.

There were two rooms in the cellar: the one with the television where I spent most of my time by myself, and the creepier room with the laundry machines. The room with the television was vacant. I pushed the other door open quietly, slowly.

My mother was not dead but standing motionless in the middle of the room. A basket of clean laundry sat near her feet as if she had meant to retrieve it only to forget in the process.

Her whole body was perfectly still except for her mouth, which twitched toward her left eye. She did not seem to see me. She just stood there staring fixedly at the laundry machines with the same startled horror I'd seen on her face when she looked at my father's old yellow boat. As if she'd just woken up and found herself in the wrong life.

"Hi," I said so she would know I was there.

She turned and her expression did not change but intensified.

We stared at each other across a space that seemed made of barbed wire. I became aware of myself standing there, could see through her eyes the depressed droop of my mouth, the too-long pant cuffs dragged and torn beneath my shoes, the hair in my eyes, the weight, all the weight.

But I saw too that she was my mother and that I was her daughter, and I thought that if only I could confess right then and there how unhappy I was, how alone and friendless and scared I was that she was going to die, the distance between us could finally be breached. So I stood there and stood there, trying to force the words out of my mouth. I didn't understand my own reluctance.

"What the hell is wrong with you?" she said, stepping toward me. She reached out and smacked me across the cheek. "I'm sick of having to see that miserable face of yours."

I stumbled backward in surprise. She came after me again. The second time was harder but hurt less.

"From now on, every time I see that pathetic look, I'm gonna smack it right off!" She paused to examine the effects of her actions and, failing to find what she was looking for, hit me several more times in a row very quickly like a frenzied bird flapping its wings. "Smile," she said as she struck. "Smile! Dammit! Smile!"

I wanted to point out that it was impossible to smile when she was smacking me in the face, but by the time I thought to say it, she was already on her way upstairs.

Besides, my smile would have been a lie, and no matter how much my mother wanted me to be, I still wasn't good at pretending.

"And lose those god-awful jeans," she yelled. "You look like a beggar."

I looked down at myself. I felt like a beggar.

A short time later I heard her singing happily, as if her life was everything she ever wanted.

It was that night that I decided to kill myself. That night I stared at myself in the mirror, at my face so easy to hit, and I realized that the person my mother really wanted to die was me.

twenty-seven

MY FIRST ATTEMPT at suicide was to suffocate myself with a pillow, which, as it turns out, is an impossible way to off your-self. But being only fourteen at the time, I just kept thinking that if I really wanted to die, I could override that internal tireless lifeguard who kept resuscitating me.

After a good hour of trying, I was left with a new sense of failure and a headache, which led me to my mother's medicine cabinet in the hall for something to kill the pain. As soon as I saw it, I couldn't believe I hadn't thought of it sooner—one hundred aspirin and the promise of "fast pain relief."

I fell asleep clutching the bottle. I was too tired to try again, and it was enough just to have it wrapped in my fingers, smooth and round and comforting, like holding someone's hand.

Morning came the way it always did, crashing into the reprieve of unconsciousness. I remembered the aspirin with relief, felt around in the sheets until I found it, got up, got dressed, put the bottle in my jacket and left for school.

The day was swimming-pool blue with a bright sun sitting

high. It was the kind of day—inviting, warm, vibrant—where people seemed thrilled just to be alive. It made me wonder if a lot more people killed themselves on days like this just to turn down the volume of the sun. The sun that ordered, "Be happy!" That screamed, "Wipe that miserable scowl off your face." That slapped, "Your life is perfect! There is nothing wrong with your life!"

"Good-bye, flowers," I said solemnly as I walked to school. "Good-bye, trees."

I was going to take the aspirin at lunchtime and be dead before the closing bell.

"Good-bye, sidewalk," I said. "Good-bye, plane flying overhead. Good-bye, grass."

It was all terribly theatrical. But by God, if no one else was going to recognize the tragedy of my impending death, then I would just have to step up to the plate. Besides, indulging in the aspirin-clutching drama of *No One Loves Me and I Want to Die* created a distance from the soft-tissue truth of no one loves me and I want to die. It put everything Out There. Away from me. Like shedding tears after a loss, which, though a tangible expression, is not the real grief. The real grief is quieter, sits like a muffled, unmovable howl in a place that no one can reach.

It made me think of Madeline Dupine.

I never knew Madeline personally. Back in elementary school she had been in Matthew's sixth-grade class, but he didn't really know her either. She was an outcast. Kids thought she was weird. One day Madeline showed up in class with her long brown hair hacked off as if with a knife. Another day there were bruises on her face and arms. Then one day she didn't show up at all. Instead she stayed home and killed herself. She was eleven maybe, twelve at the most.

The story behind the story quickly filtered out. The live-in housekeeper came forward. She reported that she'd witnessed Madeline's parents beating her. That sometimes at night, they had forced Madeline to stand outside in the freezing snow in her pajamas. Occasionally the housekeeper had tried to sneak a blanket to her. Neighbors emerged to verify the housekeeper's story. They too had seen Madeline standing outside in the snow. They had thought it was odd, suspect. But no one had helped her.

She must have appeared a figment, paper thin and white under a streetlamp. That's how I pictured her. A paper cutout of a girl with big, round eyes, snow falling in illuminated white puffs on her chopped-up hair. Translucent under the glare of passing headlights, invisible to the warm houses drawing curtains against a cold night. Easy to overlook, because nobody likes to be haunted.

But when she killed herself, Madeline came to life for the first time. She pointed her finger at the world. She forced people to open their curtains and see her. To touch her skin and feel how cold she was. She bore witness to her own pain because no one else would. She exposed the secrets that created it. She exacted revenge. And everyone was sorry. Everyone was filled with regret. They loved Madeline in death as they had not loved her in life. Kids who never even talked to her laid claim to being her best friend. Because people seem to want the attention of being associated in some way with a tragedy. Because death raises the import of the life it takes, especially a young life.

At the time it was just a sad story, but now I wanted to be like

Madeline. She seemed brave. I even envied her bruises and her chopped-up hair, because those were visible proofs of her parents' hatred, something other people could see. Her suicide seemed to me like a final act of self-love, an act of self-preservation even. Because Madeline had taken her power back. But mostly, what stood out was that her last howl had been heard, that in the end she had gotten the love she wanted. And even if that love had come too late, it seemed better than never having it at all.

I sat through my classes that morning watching life happen as if from behind a one-way mirror. All around me kids talked and passed notes to each other, oblivious to what I was about to do. I felt like jumping up on the desk and screaming, "I'm going to die today!" Instead I sat through the drone of teachers and stared at the clock as it ticked off my final minutes on Earth.

At lunchtime, I headed slowly for the cafeteria.

The room was packed. The light was pouring through the windows in a way that was both ordinary and somehow brighter. The din of the students seemed celebratory, every smile, every laugh amplified as if someone had turned up the color on all that was happy, all that was alive and untouched by grief. I watched myself move invisibly through the crowd, operating on a different speed, on a different plane—one-dimensional, made of paper.

Lately I had been buying a sandwich and a candy bar and taking them into a bathroom stall rather than eat by myself in front of everyone. This time, I picked up a tray and pushed it down the line, picking out everything I'd ever wanted to get: Jell-O, chocolate pudding, French fries, ice cream, an extra-large soda.

I moved toward an empty table in the middle of the lunchroom.

Other tables quickly filled with groups of friends, shouting at each other as they unpacked homemade lunches or made jokes about the slop on their plates. I sat down and put the aspirin bottle on the corner of my tray. My throat swelled as I stared into my French fries. Two girls passed by me and paused as if they might sit down. I looked up hopefully, but another girl waved to them from a table in the back and they moved away.

I opened the bottle, lifted it high in the air and poured the aspirin onto the table. I glanced around to see if anyone noticed and saw a boy on the football team looking over at me. He nudged his friend, and the two of them stopped eating and stared at me with eyes wide and curious like children at the circus.

Do it, their eyes seemed to say. *Entertain us.*

Tears fell unchecked into my ice cream dish. A table of girls began singing "Happy Birthday" to one of their friends. The song became a mockery. *Do it. Kill yourself.*

I began counting pills, lining them up like a path of white stones. I picked up the first aspirin and stared at it. I wondered how long it would take and if it would hurt and what it would feel like to be dead. I wondered if my mother would finally be happy.

Around me, more kids started to notice and whisper. When I met their gazes, they looked away. I put a pill in my mouth. The sadness of that first swallow was a surprise, so pure and bottomless, the mourning not of myself but of what life could be and was not. I thought again of Madeline Dupine, and I saw now how suicide was *not* the romantic act of self-love and bravery that I had believed it to be. Instead it was an act of total despair, an act not followed by the love I imagined finally receiving but by nothingness, the black void of nonexistence. But I couldn't think of another way out.

I took a second aspirin and then a third. One of the football players said something to the other, who laughed in my direction and then stood to get a better look. I wiped my tears with my sleeve and told myself I didn't care, that soon it wouldn't matter. I scooped the rest of the aspirin up in a handful. I tried not to be afraid.

Whispers seemed to spring from all corners of the cafeteria. *Do it,* their excitement said, building on itself, a growing pressure. *Kill yourself.*

I brought the pills to my mouth and closed my eyes, imagining how soon this would all disappear, pinholing into darkness like the last seconds of an old movie.

Do it, do it, do it, their stares seemed to urge.

And then suddenly one person, one voice said, "Don't."

I looked up.

It was Wade Mattell.

"Let's get out of here," Wade said.

We were standing in the hallway outside the cafeteria where he had escorted me away from all the rubberneckers. He took the aspirin bottle from my hand, walked over to the trash and emptied its contents.

"You mean, just leave school?" I said. "Won't we get in trouble?"

"So what?" he said, and I laughed because all at once I realized it was true. *So what?* I had just come *this* close to killing myself. There was nothing left to lose.

We didn't even bother sneaking, just strolled right out the front door. I remember both the shock and freedom of that, of seeing how flimsy the rules of adults were, how they required my complicity, how anytime I wanted, I could bust them wide open.

As I walked beside Wade, his nearness made me so self-conscious that I kept my eyes on the ground in the hopes that he might not notice that I was fat and ugly as long as I didn't look at him. We wandered the streets aimlessly to the rhythm of his basketball hitting the pavement. Every once in a while he would dribble the ball in circles around me and then feign a free throw over my head.

"So . . ." he said finally. "Wanna watch me play basketball?"

He kept his eyes on the ball. His lashes were long and light.

"Okay," I said.

We started toward the local playground. The air was cool and crisp, the afternoon sun nesting on the colored leaves. Occasionally we brushed against each other by accident and drew quickly away like opposing magnets.

"I hate girls," he said suddenly.

"Oh," I replied nonchalantly, because I liked walking beside him and I was reluctant to point out the obvious.

When we reached the basketball courts, Wade pointed me toward a grassy area where I could sit and watch. He looked suddenly happy and childlike, nothing like the sullen, insubordinate kid from detention. I took a seat as he began to dribble at an impressive speed.

"It's the fourth quarter," he said in an announcer's voice. "The score is tied with three seconds remaining. Wade Mattell has the ball. He dodges left, then right, then left again." Wade dodged imaginary players. "The crowd is on their feet."

He pointed to me. I stood.

"Mattell goes in for a layup!" His long, lean body charged the basket, lunging into the air. "He shoots . . ."

The ball left his hand and hit the rim. For a moment it hung there, suspended and circling. We held our breaths and watched. Our focus was pure, unified, time-stopping. A total merge. And then . . . swish!

"He scores! And the crowd goes wild."

Wade pointed dramatically at me and I gave a little self-conscious clap.

"And the crowd goes *wild*!" he tried again, and this time I clapped as hard as I could and hollered at the top of my lungs. Wade took a victory lap around the court, his arms in the air, mouth agape in wonder at his own achievement. I sat back down and laughed.

"Okay, it's the fourth quarter . . ." he said, starting all over again.

Later, when it got too dark to see the ball and my voice was hoarse from emulating a thousand cheering fans, Wade came over and lay down on the grass beside me.

"I'm going to be the greatest basketball player in the world," he said.

Before I could answer, he sat up and glared at me. "What? You don't believe me."

"No, I do!"

"Okay." He collapsed onto his back again. "Good."

We stayed there, gazing up at the sky for a long time, and I was surprised by how comfortable I was lying next to one of the most popular boys at school as if it were a natural, everyday occurrence.

The grass was slightly damp and cool, and the night was deep with stars. There was something almost religious about lying on the solid floor of the Earth and staring up into that vastness. I thought of how far away the morning seemed, how inconceivable that only hours before, I had wanted to kill myself. I thought of Madeline again and how sad it was that she never got to see how quickly life could turn, how it could get better when you least expected it. I remembered the look of care in Wade's face when he took the pills from my hand, and I wanted so much to say thank you, but it was the kind of thank-you that meant so much, I couldn't get the words out.

"My mother hates me," I said instead. I don't know why I said it, it just popped out of me like a cork, and yet, I wasn't all that surprised to hear myself utter the words. Somehow, secrets didn't seem like they needed to be secrets with Wade. I peeked over at him to see his reaction. I wanted him to feel sorry for me.

He pulled a pack of matches from his pocket and began to light them one by one, allowing for a quick flicker of light like a firefly before blowing them out. It seemed as if he hadn't heard me, or worse, didn't care.

I turned forward again, my own face burning with shame at my confession. We lay there in silence for a long time.

"Screw her," Wade said quietly, seemingly out of nowhere. This time he let the match in his hand burn down to his fingers before tossing it into the damp grass.

"Screw who?"

"Your stupid mother. Who cares about her?"

"I do."

"Why?"

"Because she's my mother."

"She's a bitch."

"But you don't even know her."

"I don't have to know her. It's obvious."

I didn't know what to make of that. It seemed a mean thing to say and it certainly wasn't the pity I was looking for, and yet, strangely, I was elated.

We stared back up at the sky.

"You should come out here late at night sometime," he said then.

"Why?"

"I dunno. Just because. I do it all the time once my parents are asleep."

"Maybe," I said, though I was sure I wouldn't dare.

He stood abruptly. "I gotta go eat."

"Okay," I said. Then I stood and watched Wade run off into the night, leaving behind a fat, lonely girl, half a book of matches and a small light of hope. I stuffed the matches in my pocket—a keepsake—and started for home, wondering as always, if I would find my mother dead.

As it turned out, my mother was once again not dead, but alive and well and, moments after I arrived, filling the doorway of my room.

"I got a phone call today," she said, watching me. "From your guidance counselor. I'm assuming you know why he called."

I tried to make my face blank. "Nope," I lied, because I was sure it was about my cutting school with Wade.

She came over to me and frowned thoughtfully. "A student told him that you were trying to kill yourself in the cafeteria." She tilted her head and peered at me with an unreadable expression on her face. "That's not true, is it?"

I was shocked, wondered who had told, had no idea how to answer that question. On the one hand, I was still convinced that everything between my mother and me was a misunderstanding, that if I could just make her see me for who I really was, she wouldn't be angry anymore, she would love me, she would love me as much as she loved Matthew. Sure, it hadn't happened yet, but I was always going to be that kid holding a lottery card in her heart, believing, despite the odds, that my number would someday be picked. And yet, the thought of looking in her eyes and admitting how alone and worthless I felt was so shameful that it was all I could do just to fight back the tears.

"Well?" she said.

I nodded so slightly, I wasn't even sure my head moved.

"Is that a yes?"

I nodded again, so wide open in that moment that I had to close my eyes to avoid her gaze.

"You. Stupid. Asshole," she said. I looked up in surprise. Her hand came down across my face.

My head stayed sideways where she slapped it, my hand automatically on my cheek. I was shocked in the same way I had been the first time she hit me, shocked directly in the place where that hope for her love still lived.

But this time I thought of Wade's words, and it was like some internal valve shut off and another one opened. I turned to meet my mother's eyes, and when I did, the expression in my face must have matched the look in hers.

"You're the one who gave me the idea," I said, "so I guess that makes you a stupid asshole too." Then, without thinking, or perhaps with more thought than I'd ever had, I drew up my hand and slapped her back.

The sound of my palm against her face was a cracking whip, so loud it seemed to stop time for a second. I watched her wobble backward, watched the outline of my hand bloom across her cheek, and I was struck by a realization I never would have thought possible: I was stronger than my mother. I was the stronger one.

My mother steadied herself and brought her hand to her face, eyes hot with fury.

"How dare you!" she said, and there was so much righteousness to her outrage, so much authoritative certainty, that for a second I wondered, *My God, how dare I?* But I made my rage louder. I let it drown out all but its own roar. I stood tall, firm, huge with it.

"No, Mom," I said. "How dare *you*." And somewhere deep inside where the tiny light of the life force burns, these were the words that felt truer.

Her eyes widened. They were wide with the shock of how big I had gotten. Like in all this time that she had been feeding me her rage and despair, depositing it into me like coins into a slot, she had never stopped to consider what might happen to all that hate. And now that she was face-to-face with it, I could almost see the dawning awareness that she had created this, and that this which she had created was now bigger than her. It was bigger than both of us, but especially my mother, because I was used to carrying it.

She stood there speechless as the truth hit her. She appeared defenseless. She looked almost sorry, like she saw me and saw herself for the first time. And that was what I needed so desperately: for her to see me, her child, her daughter, and not the hate she had assigned to me. For that I could let it all go, forgive everything and ask to be forgiven in return.

But then her eyes changed. I watched it happen. I watched the shade drop down, and the moment that it did, a slow, pitying smile spread across her face.

"You're a very sick girl," she said. Her tone turned soft and compassionate like a nurse. "Very, very sick."

"I'm sick because I defended myself? Because I'm tired of you treating me this way?"

She shook her head sadly and walked to the door. At the entrance she paused. "I feel sorry for you," she said. "It must be terrible to be so misguided. I'm actually surprised you didn't go through with your little suicide plan." She turned on her heels and started down the hall.

"You would have loved that, wouldn't you?" I called after her.

Then I went and sat down on my bed and thought that I should cry, but the tears would not come. Instead, I felt only a hardening over everything soft, like a newborn hermit crab acquiring its shell. I knew I had crossed some invisible line between the innocence and compliance of childhood and the rebellion of adolescence, and with that I had exchanged despair for not giving a shit.

I sat on my bed and pulled Wade's pack of matches from my

pocket, and just as he had done, I lit them one by one, letting the quick flicker of flame ignite my own before blowing them out. A few moments later my mother walked by, talking to my dad on her cell phone about me, making it sound like I was the one who had hit her first, like I was the only one who had done any hitting at all. I gave her the finger as she passed, and she put her hand over the phone so my dad couldn't hear, held up her own middle finger and hissed, "Right back at you, you little brat."

I waited until she was asleep and then I slipped out my bedroom window and went back to the basketball courts to find Wade. As soon as I got there, I understood why he came there late at night. With the whole neighborhood quiet and sleeping, it felt like Wade and I were the only people in the world.

It became a habit then to sneak out at night, to take ownership of the universe for a little while when there was no one else around to stop us. Sometimes we just lay on the grass and talked. Other times we rang the doorbells of nearby houses and ran, charged by the symbolic victory of waking some adults up. Nothing made us happier than hearing one of the kid-hating neighbors we targeted screaming from their window, vowing to call the cops. To our ears, the voices of adults had become as meaningless as a birdcall. Their threats no longer had power. We just liked to run.

And so we ran through those nights with the cops on our heels but never upon us. We ran until I felt myself exploding into my youth, being lifted out of my stagnating swamp of a life and thrust into the moving world with the thrilling force of a fast ride in a convertible. We ran until running was the bond between us, and I knew that in Wade I had a true friend. It was the kind of thing that could make a girl forget all about her shitty home life, that could make a fat, lonely girl think that in some way, her lottery number had been picked after all.

I didn't care that my grades were plummeting because I was too tired during class to pay attention, and when the teachers said, "What about your future?" I rolled my eyes at them. The only people who have room to worry about the future are those who aren't fighting just to survive the present.

For the first time in my life I felt both at home in the world and free.

I had no idea what was coming.

twenty-eight

THREE HOURS AFTER the phone call from the dean's office, I am ready to put Operation Stay in School into motion. I am dressed to the nines—perfect makeup, perfect hair, the steady click of my new heels announcing that I'm fine even as I head off to convince someone that I'm not. I'm still hungover from the beach party, made worse by the stale pizza, the anxiety about school, and the prospect of an actual date on Sunday, and naturally, the place I'm headed is at the top of the steepest hill on campus.

I have no idea if my plan is going to work. All I want is to stop and lie down on the grass next to the sidewalk, wake up in another body, another life. It seems like that should be possible—to drop one life like a school course and pick up another. At the very least, I'd like to get the hell out of this history class I keep getting stuck in: Fuckup 101, which, like all history, repeats itself.

I reach the top of the hill and open the door, which is so heavy, it moans with my effort, and then head into the familiar waiting room. This time there is a guy sitting at the reception desk. He checks my name on the appointment schedule and hands me a questionnaire to fill out.

I sit down on the scratchy yellow couch and look at the questions before me. I am old hat at this particular psychological assessment quiz. Back in the loony bin, James had stolen one out of the nursing station for us to entertain ourselves with. He would pretend he was Dr. Meeks, leaning back in his chair and firing off the questions at me like I was under interrogation. Then no matter how sanely I answered them, he would declare me "certifiably, categorically, without question . . . cuckoo for Cocoa Puffs!" and we'd cackle our heads off like the lunatics they tried to make us think we were.

I smile, remembering. I miss James. I'd love to talk to him about everything that's going on, but every time I think of it, Zoey is around. Besides, I know I need to stand on my own two feet and not lean on the crutch of the hospital or anyone in it. It'll be different when James is out, when he's not part of the system I'm trying to break free from. Then we can chat all the time. Hopefully even see each other.

I look down at the test in my hands and locate all the questions that would reveal symptoms of depression. Deliberately, I check off yes to each one even though I don't actually think I'm depressed.

Do you feel unmotivated? Check.

Do you feel overwhelmed? Check.

Do you feel a lack of interest toward school or work? Check.

The accuracy of my responses to these questions is starting to make me a little defensive. Doesn't everybody feel this way?

I laugh when I see the next one:

Do you ever find yourself somewhere and not know how you got there?

That was always James's favorite question. He'd say, "What do they mean by 'somewhere'? Somewhere like the grocery store or somewhere like . . . Maine?" But today, for me, the question seems clear. Today I have arrived in yet another doctor's office, and I don't quite know how I landed in this moment.

I finish the test, double-check that I haven't answered yes to any questions that might indicate I am suicidal or homicidal, crack my knuckles and massage my hands. I am nervous that someone I know will see me sitting here, even though I know exactly two people on campus.

I rehearse my planned speech in my head. My stomach tosses and I tell myself that there is nothing to be afraid of, that I am just here to get a note. But after the mental hospital my body has been well trained to be wary of a place like this.

The door across from me opens and the same woman from last time steps out with her brown curly hair and her kind face. She appears to recognize me. "Not here to see me, I assume?"

"Actually . . ." I stand up.

A look of surprise and then she smiles. "I'm Liz. Come on in."

She opens the door and I follow her through it.

Liz's office is small and dark with stained wood, like the interior of a tree. The only light comes through a small window with a view of the ocean. I sit. The couch is comfortable, invitingly squishy. I perch myself at the utmost edge, straight as a square ruler.

Liz watches me as I take in the dimensions of the room, the distance from the couch to the door and from the couch to the window, marking my exits. There is a yellow ashtray on her desk, shaped like the sun with beams of light sticking out of it. It gives me the slightest sense of kinship and ease.

"You smoke?" I say, pointing.

"I quit," she says. "Haven't been able to quit the ashtray for some reason, though."

"I thought you people weren't supposed to have unhealthy attachments."

"Us people?"

"Shrinks. You're a shrink, right?"

"You see shrinks as different from other people?"

I shrug.

"You don't like them?"

"I don't like people who claim they are 'here to help.'"

"Do you want to tell me about that?"

"Why? So you can help?"

She smiles. "Well, you're right. It is an unhealthy attachment." She picks up the ashtray and looks at it. "You know what?" She looks back at me and then tosses it in the garbage beside her desk. She rubs her hands together. "Oooh, that felt good. Thank you for that."

I am totally unnerved by this, by her willingness to let me have an effect on her behavior. "You'll just take it out once I'm gone," I say.

"I sure hope not," she says with a twinkle in her eyes. "I guess we'll have to wait and see what I do."

"I don't really care what you do," I say, and it comes out harsher than I mean it.

"Okay."

I turn to the window. The ocean is just beyond the highway, a wide stripe of blue catching flecks of silver light. I stare without seeing, reverting easily into the shut-down state I am accustomed to entering whenever I find myself in a therapist's office. I can actually feel the pull of air around me as I enclose myself within it, zip myself up like a plastic lunch bag. Her gaze follows mine to the window but neither of us says anything. I had a whole speech planned. Now my mind is blank.

"So . . . you've come in talking about negative attachments," she says finally. "Is that why you're here?"

"No," I say too loudly. I force myself to look at her, to summon the speech. "I'm having a bit of a problem with school. Basically, I'm failing out."

"Well, that does sound like a bit of a problem," she says.

I expect judgment, but I can't find any in her face. It's hard to assess her age, although I suddenly want to know.

"I was sick with pneumonia first. And then I think I got . . . depressed." I work my mouth into a grim line, letting my shoulders droop the way I have seen in the shuffling patients returning from their morning meds. Part of me wants to laugh at my little act, do a tap dance across the room: *I'm fine I'm fine I'm fine.* Instead I continue, "Not like I want to die or anything." It is important to establish this line. To make sure I give her nothing she can use against me.

"It's just—"

"Everything seems hard."

I sit forward suddenly because she has surprised me. Just as quickly, I lean back, cross one arm over the other. "Why do you say that?"

"Because you told me that the last time you were here. Out in the waiting room." She tilts her head. "I guess you wanted me to know."

"That was a joke. God, you people take everything so literally."

"So everything is not hard, then?"

"Look, I just need a note, okay? I've missed too many classes and I'm worried they're going to kick me out. Can you please hook me up so I don't have to waste any more of your time?"

"You think you're wasting my time?"

"I just need a note."

"A note."

"Yep."

"Well, we can come back to that. But first why don't you talk to me a little bit about why you think you might be depressed."

I sigh, exasperated. "What difference does it make?"

"Humor me."

I can see this scheme isn't going to be as easy as I'd hoped, so I pull out my trump card. "Here's the deal," I say. "I just got out of a mental hospital right before I came here, so I've already been through all this therapy shit." Of course, she doesn't need to know that I was never an active participant in any of the therapy they tried to force on me. Still, it's a relief in some way to mention the hospital out loud, to not have to conceal it from at least one person here.

She nods calmly at this news, and maybe it's my imagination but I could swear I catch the slightest flicker of surprise in her eyes. This gives me comfort and makes me kind of like her. So far she doesn't seem to think I'm crazy.

"Do you want to tell me about why you were there?"

"You wouldn't believe me."

"Try me," she says. "Start from the beginning."

I pause for a moment, calculate the risk in telling, quickly decide there is none. Everything I say to her is confidential, and it's just easier to get it over with, get my note and get out. It doesn't matter if she believes me or not.

"I don't remember everything," I say, though I'm not sure why I say that or if it's even true, only that I have a vague sense that pieces are missing. But I launch into what I do remember, starting all the way back to the first time I drowned. There is no emotion attached to the words I say. No experience weighs more than another. There is only the nagging feeling that I am leaving something out, something large and shadowy, like the words are a trickle of water around a bigger clog.

When Liz says the hour is almost up, it's like I'm coming out of a dream, so surprised am I to see the light in the room has changed, to see my own hands in my lap, to see the clock on her desk marking the hour. I realize I didn't even get to the details of how my mother had me committed, the other words tumbling out first like caged animals finding an open door. And yet even without that, the look on Liz's face is shocking to me. It is not the pity I hoped for. It is not the disbelief I expected. It is something I've never seen before, and it startles me. She is staring at me with what looks like admiration. I lean back. My throat gets scratchy and I clear it.

"No wonder you're suffering," she says. "It's amazing you survived at all."

"I'm not suffering," I say, forgetting my lie. I shift in my seat, sit upright, and look out at the spread of water against the sky, the blue breaking beneath blue. "The past is the past. I'm over it. I'm a different person now."

She watches me but says nothing.

"So the note?" I say.

"Yes, the note. Would it fix things?"

"What do you mean? Of course it would."

"So you'll start going to class and catch up on your work?"

A dull pain launches itself behind my eyes. I hadn't thought beyond getting the excuse. Now I picture the piles of makeup homework, all the new assignments on top of that, the daily attendance in class. I realize with great clarity how impossibly far from me it all seems—this normalcy, this ability to function as an independent, responsible person in the world. It's like I'm still waiting for my childhood to happen before I can get to my adulthood, and the vast expanse of territory between the two seems insurmountable. How do you get here without ever having started there?

"You're right. I can't do it."

"Is that what you heard me say? That you can't?"

"You didn't need to. It's true. I'll never catch up." The room is suddenly too cramped, the couch too squishy. All I want is a cigarette.

"Of course it's a lot to take on," she says. "So why don't we see if we can break it down a little? What's one thing you can do today?"

"I can't do anything. I don't even have my books."

"Can you get your books today?"

I imagine going to the bookstore. Just finding it seems daunting, everything so much work. But I tell myself it's just the bookstore, no promises of anything more than that, so I say yes, I can do that, because Liz seems to think that I can. "But then what?"

"Why don't you come back on Monday. Would nine A.M. work? Then we'll figure out the next step."

"You want me to come back?"

"I want to hel—" She catches herself. "I want you to stay in school."

"My mother might be in town next week, so I don't know what my schedule will be." I don't know why I choose this excuse or if it's even true.

"Your mother?" she says with barely contained surprise.

"Oh yeah, we're actually kind of okay now. I'm trying to put all that stuff she did behind me."

I expect her to be impressed by this. Instead her brow furrows slightly. "Oh?" she says in a way that seems like she wants me to say more.

Before she has a chance to ask me anything else, I stand to go. She hands me the appointment card and I stuff it into my bag. All I want is to get out of there; I have absolutely no intention of coming back. As nice as she seems, I've had quite enough of therapists.

It is only after I'm out the door and walking down the hall that I realize I never got the note.

twenty-nine

ZOEY IS GONE when I finally return to my dorm room with two bags of books that I have no interest in reading. Still, every time I consider saying screw it, I think of the way Liz looked at me with admiration and I am determined to at least try not to screw up. Not that I really care what she thinks, but generally speaking, it's been a long time since an adult believed in me.

At the top of one of my bags is a postcard from James that I retrieved from the mail. It's a hand-drawn cartoon of a guy on a desert island far, far away from his family, who is sketched in at the opposite end of the page. In the middle is a doctor in a rowboat calling, "Good news! Your crazy has gone into remission!"

It takes me a second to get the joke and then I laugh out loud. On the flip side it says, "Can you believe they're letting me out of here soon? Miss you. Maybe I'll come for a visit."

The thought of seeing James again inspires me further to try to stay in school. I want to show him that I'm doing okay, that it really is possible to survive on the outside.

Within an hour, I am half a pack of cigarettes and two chapters into a French textbook, and kicking myself for skipping so many classes.

"Cassie?" Zoey calls, bursting suddenly into the room. She pretends she can't see me through the smoke of my cigarette despite the fact that I have both the windows open. She squints and coughs and thrusts her arms about blindly. "Cassie, where are you?"

She carries on in this dramatic fashion for some time, culminating in the Stop, Drop and Roll, which lands her smiling up at me from the floor at the base of my bed.

"I'm in gay Paree and considering a jump off the Eiffel Tower," I say dryly.

She props herself up on her elbows, registers the book in my hand. "Holy shit, are you *studying*?"

"I'm staring at words—is that the same thing?" I close the book and sigh. "Can you please explain to me why I'm supposed to care whether Pierre buys a croissant or a coffee at the café?"

"Because you want to stay here." She stands up, hands me a cookie wrapped in a napkin that she has stolen from the dining hall. "You do care about your future, right?" She sounds just like one of my high school teachers.

"What future?" I laugh. The next breath seems enough to manage at the moment.

"There's your problem. No vision." She takes the cookie back, splits off half for herself and wolfs it down before I can protest. "And speaking of your future," she says as she gets up and moves to her bed, "your future husband called to confirm your date." She smiles extra broadly, pleased as punch to be delivering this news.

"I hope you canceled for me."

"*Au contraire.* I have assured him you will be there with bells on."

"*Mais je ne want to go pas*," I say, pulling the covers up over myself. "I have nothing to wear."

"Of course you do. You're just scared because you loooove him."

"Why does it have to be a daytime date, though? Such terrible lighting!"

"You are pathologically vain. Has anyone ever suggested psychiatric help?"

"Nope," I say brightly. "Never."

"Curious," she says, and I hurl a pillow at her.

She climbs under the covers, rests her head on the pillow I've just thrown at her, turns off the light next to her bed and flips on the TV. I turn off my own light and lie in the dark, staring wide-eyed at the ceiling.

"Seriously, Zo," I say finally. "Is there any way I can get out of this date? I don't think I can do it."

I look over and find her already fast asleep. I lie awake most of the night, afraid to dream.

thirty

DESPITE MY WILLING it not to, Sunday comes anyway. Chris is picking me up for our date at noon.

It's 11:59.

I pace and sit and stand and pace while Zoey alternates between watching me panic and watching the cartoons playing on the small television on her bookshelf.

I am wearing the new pencil skirt, blouse and heels, although Zoey has delicately hinted they might be too much for a daytime date. I know she is right, but when I look at myself in this outfit that my mother picked out and bought, I feel like an actress playing a version of myself in which I am pretty and together and best of all, untouchable. After all, no one can reject the real me if the real me doesn't show up, right? Even still, I feel a familiar panic creep in.

"I think I'm getting sick," I say, sitting back down again. I cough into my hand. "Maybe I shouldn't go."

Zoey ignores me.

"Seriously, feel my forehead. I'm feverish."

"You're ridiculous. Live a little," she says, like that's the easiest thing in the world to do. "Geez, you'd think you'd never been on a date before."

I laugh as if that's absurd, stand up and start pacing again.

I can tell that Zoey thinks I'm being silly, and it makes me feel like there's something wrong with me for being so nervous.

There is a sudden knock and I quickly estimate the likely success rate of leaping out our two-story window without breaking any bones. I'm pretty sure I could do it, even in heels. Zoey opens the door and there is Chris, freshly scrubbed, hair still wet at the tips, looking slightly embarrassed and so adorable that my heart actually feels squeezed.

"You look pretty," he says, taking me in before he even notices Zoey standing beside him. Realizing his impoliteness, he turns to her, gives her a big hug. She hugs him back with abandon, and I wonder how people do that with such ease, allow someone to get that close.

I smile, grab my bag and make my way toward him. If I speak, I'm afraid I'll throw up. He tries to let me exit first at the same time I'm trying to let him go first and it ends up being all weird and awkward and I wonder why people do this shit and why you don't hear more about first-date-induced heart attacks.

Zoey waves and smiles as we leave, and calls out merrily, "Have fun!"

The outside air is a relief, dilutes the electric aura of anxiety around me. Chris's car is parked just out front, stuffed with surfboards and boy crap and sand on the seats. He opens my door for me and apologizes for the mess as I climb in. He gets into the driver's seat, glances over at me.

"Hi," he says again, all goofy and happy. He puts his hand on my arm and instinctively, I lean away. He does not tell me where we are going, only that it's a surprise.

I hate surprises.

A loud wind swirls around us as we slip out onto the highway, and I am grateful for the way it drowns out my internal rattle. Too soon, we arrive at the end of a dead-end beach street and Chris puts the car in park.

"I've always wanted to go to a deserted parking lot," I say, looking around as he leaps out of the car and moves toward the back. "Is this where you dump the bodies?" I turn just as he grabs the two surfboards, hoists one up and smiles.

"Secret surf spot," he says, pointing in the direction of the ocean. "You said you wanted to learn."

Oh no.

"Actually, I think I said something along the lines of being afraid of sharks." Though, really, sharks seem like the least of my concerns right now.

He laughs. "They won't bother you. They don't like how you taste."

"Tell that to the Discovery Channel. Anyway, I'm not exactly dressed right."

Thank God.

"Two steps ahead of you," he says, so pleased with himself that his shoulders go back and his chest expands. He pulls out two black wetsuits and smiles like a little boy. "Murph works at the surf shop. I got a small and a medium because I wasn't sure."

I look between the two suits. "How about I just watch?"

His arms fall slowly, the suits drooping beneath his hands. "I thought you'd be excited."

"You thought wrong," I say, and then think, *Jesus, I sound like my mother.*

"Oh," he says, and his eyes drop for just a second before he looks back up and smiles. "Okay. Well, we can do something else."

The quick recovery of his disappointment stabs at me. He is trying so hard. He stuffs the boards back in the car, shoulders sagging just slightly, and for a split second I forget myself and all the reasons why there is no way I can do this.

"No," I say. "Let's do it."

Chris turns. "You sure?"

I nod and he smiles.

"You're going to love it," he says. "I swear."

We walk down a winding dirt path lined with bramble that opens onto a small cove, intimate and unpopulated.

"The waves are small so it's a perfect day for learning," Chris says. He is carrying the surfboards, the wetsuits and the towels.

"Terrific," I say, carrying the dread.

Already I'm thinking of how I can get out of this, the roil of panic so great that I'm sure I'm going to throw up. Everything about this will expose me. My hair will get wet. My makeup will wash off. The clothes my mother said made me look pretty will be on the beach while I squeeze myself into some horrid-looking wetsuit. Worst of all, I'm going to fail at this thing I don't know how to do. Chris will see the real me and I will see the reflection of my own worthlessness in his eyes, and the familiarity of that look will kill me.

The ocean is calm and lapping, the sky a wash of vivid blue. I observe it as if from a great distance from myself, intellectualizing the beauty. I try to stay present, but I can feel that my mind has left the premises, is back in my room under the covers.

Chris points to where I can change behind a small concrete building with no windows. I stand in the high grass there and sneak a cigarette, suddenly very tired. In the distance I can see the area of the beach where I almost drowned that first day, the bench where the homeless guys sat now empty.

I stay behind the building so long, I'm sure Chris wonders if I'm walking down the side of the highway with my thumb out. Finally I look at the two wetsuits, step into the thick skin of the smaller one and pray it fits.

It doesn't.

I sigh, stick my feet into the second one and tug it to my waist. The suit smells of neoprene and summer and baked-in sunlight, and when I pull it around my shoulders, the weight of it on my body grounds me, provides a cozy layer of protection that I like. I decide I will paddle halfway out and pretend to see a shark.

Chris is getting the boards waxed up when I come out from behind the building, embarrassed and shy. He looks up and sees me walking stiffly toward him. He wears the widest grin I have ever seen.

He checks the back of my wetsuit to make sure it's zipped tight and then bends down and wraps the surfboard leash around my ankle with a gentle, caring touch. My stomach flips and my face burns and my legs tense with the urge to pull away, to stop my body from feeling these strange, out-of-control things it's feeling.

He stands and hands me my board, which is pink and large, dented and browning in several places, clearly a rental from the surf shop. On its nose are two fish swimming in opposite directions, as if one is swimming toward life, the other away.

"Ready?" he says, and whips off his shirt, revealing a glimpse of tan chest before I have the chance to avert my eyes.

I am not remotely ready. Not at all.

He gives me instructions as we walk to the edge of the sand and I try to listen over the roar of anxiety. The wind tugs at the board under my arm, and I worry that I'm going to drop it. Or worse, that I'll lose it out in the water, and once again get pulled into the undertow, nothing to hold on to.

The instant we hit water, the sea marshals me into the present, the first shock of cold so demanding of my attention. We push the boards flat at our waists as we wade out. A small wave rushes toward us, icy water leaping at my chest like a playful dog, making me laugh giddily almost against my will. Chris smiles at me as if he understands completely.

He tries to help me onto my board, but I tell him I'm fine and can do it myself. Instantly I start wobbling, feel myself make stupid faces as I try to get my balance, let out a small unintentional scream when I almost capsize.

"I can't," I say, just as the board steadies.

"You are," he says.

He climbs onto his own board and we begin to paddle. The water is buttery and pliable as I push my arms through it, the board gliding effortlessly. The sun overhead is warm on my back and head. Small waves of white water crash toward me, narrowing my concentration. The whole thing becomes focus and glide, and every once in a while I realize that I am forgetting to be nervous and self-conscious and sick.

We arrive on the other side of the breakers, and I think again of my latest near drowning, how calm the ocean is now, how things change from day to day, how life moves despite our greatest efforts at resistance, how much it can surprise us.

We rest there for a while, the water rocking us lightly, making small knocking sounds against the boards. Everything is calm and lulling. Then Chris sees something in the distance.

"When I give the word, start paddling," he says. "As soon as you feel the wave beneath you, jump to your feet. You're going to fall. Everybody does their first time. Just try to fall feet first, because the tide is low and it's pretty shallow on the inside."

"Okay," I say. But I am not everybody and I can't let myself fall. Especially not now, in front of another person. My adrenaline moves into overdrive, firing off malfunctioning flight signals, telling me that if I fall one more time in my life, I'll never get back up.

"Here's one," Chris says, and the small harmless wave coming toward me becomes a charging monstrous thing in my mind. Before I can abandon ship and swim for home, Chris gives my board a slight push. "Now paddle!" he shouts.

With no other choice, I start paddling, too hard, too fast. The water slaps my face, cold and hard as a hand.

"Easy, easy," Chris calls, and I slow my arms, try to match the pulse of the ocean moving beneath me until I am in sync with the wave, traveling as one with it, catching the sea.

"Stand up! Stand up!" Chris shouts across the water. And so I do. Automatically and bewilderingly, I jump to my feet and the ocean opens wide to receive me. The sun is low over the cliffs and shimmers pale golden light, and I am soaring on top of the Atlantic, Chris behind me shouting, "Go! Go!" as I do exactly that.

Three seconds later I turn to see Chris throw his arms high into the air in victory, his smile wide with unabashed pride. At just that moment, I lose my balance completely and in the most graceless way possible, plunge into the ocean. I manage to land feet first and am surprised to see that despite my wipeout, Chris is still cheering. I scramble for the board, and as I do, I notice that I am smiling from such a deep place that my smile is just there on my face without my having to put it there. It feels like a discovery, this smile, as if I've pulled it up from the bottom of the seafloor like a piece of smoothed glass or a perfect white shell—something old and forgotten underneath all that water.

Suddenly I don't even care that I fell, because of that brief moment when I stood, and I wonder if this is what other people seem to have that I do not—this courage to fall because they have the memory of standing.

Then I look toward Chris, climb back on my board and do the thing I don't believe I know how to do: I paddle back out.

thirty-one

I COME IN still floating from my day with Chris to find Zoey carefully watering her plants. "Look!" she says, holding up the small pot with the broken cactus arm. "It's growing!"

"Is it?" I say. From where I'm standing, it's hard to tell.

"A little bit! Anyway, I'm dying to hear everything," she says as I check the mirror to make sure there's no mascara down my face or lipstick on my teeth that might retroactively ruin the date I've just had. "But first, your mother called. We're having dinner with her at her hotel." She walks over to her closet and holds up two hangers of clothes. "Which outfit do you like better?"

I point to the first. "I thought this was her last day with Pete."

Zoey reexamines both outfits and chucks the one I picked back into the closet. "Apparently, she thinks we're a better time." She bends down to forage for shoes amid the chaos of strewn clothes and then glances up at me. "What?"

"Nothing! I'm . . . just surprised." I'm still processing that my mother has actually chosen me over Pete, that she has chosen me over anyone, really. I turn over the thought that maybe things really are different now, even as my brain struggles with the adjustment, wants to throw doubts at my hope. I push them away. Tell myself I'm finally getting a chance at normalcy, to be that girl whose mother comes to visit and takes her and her roommate to dinner and shares in her experiences. Still, I'm nervous.

"Anyway, I told her we'd head over as soon as you got back."

"Okay, but I need to rinse off and do my makeup first."

"What do you need makeup for? It's your mother."

Exactly, I think as I disappear into the bathroom with my beauty supplies.

Zoey drives the five minutes to the hotel while I text my mother on Zoey's cell to let her know we're on our way.

"I really hope you like each other," I say as I light a cigarette and take a deep drag to soothe my nerves. "I want this to be perfect."

Zoey looks at me strangely. "I'm sure we will," she says.

I roll down the window and the smell of the night ocean rushes into the car, making me think of walking on waves, of Chris. The wind is in my hair. I smile at my reflection in the side-view mirror.

The restaurant is dark, lit only by candle, with heavy curtains and leather chairs. The coat check smells of expensive perfume, mysterious and adult, and being there with Zoey I am conscious of the two of us standing on the precipice of a widening world, stepping into it, trying it on.

My mother hasn't arrived yet, so we move to the bar.

"Two Diet Cokes, please," I say to the bartender.

"With rum," Zoey adds, and we wait, braced.

The bartender looks entirely bored with us, places two rum and

Diets on the bar and does not ask for ID. Zoey and I exchange sly smiles.

"All right," she says. "Let's hear it. Tell me everything!"

I laugh and look into my drink, pleased and embarrassed. I imagine my mother having a conversation like this all those years ago after her first date with Pete.

"Okay, so first of all, he takes me to this deserted parking lot—"

"Oooh, I like it already!" Zoey says.

I give her a look. "So I'm—"

"Wait! Fast-forward a sec. Did you kiss him or not?"

I take a long slow sip of my drink to draw out the suspense. I consider the truth, which is that I was so chickenshit, I leaped out of Chris's car before he could try, half certain that I inadvertently showed him my underwear as I fled.

"I don't kiss on the first date," I tell her instead.

"Oh, that's, like, your rule?" Zoey says, rolling her eyes at me. "Fair enough." She takes a sip of her drink and scans the crowd. "I also have a rule. No first dates before sex."

My eyes open wide.

"Kidding!" she says. "Well, sort of." Then she laughs so loudly at her own joke that other people turn to look at us. I try to act like I have no idea who this girl is sitting next to me. But when I look over at the bartender and see the curl of disdain at the corner of his lip, I can't help but burst out laughing too. Zoey laughs even harder then, without attempting to muzzle herself, and soon the entire bar is looking over at us. I try to get control of myself, but the more I work to keep a straight face, the more we both collapse in a heap of giggling. I throw my head back, and at that moment, I catch sight of my mother at the door.

"Mom!" I say. My laughter is cut short by her expression. Something is not right. She is staring straight at us but doesn't seem to have registered us yet. The maître d' draws her attention back, and she nods at him in a way that looks like it takes effort. Instinctively, my mind starts racing with all the things I might have done wrong.

"That's your mom?" Zoey says. "Wow, she's so pretty."

Before I can stop her, Zoey bounces over in her typical Labrador style. I follow. "Mrs. O'Malley!" she says too loudly.

My mother visibly winces, but quickly recovers with a polite smile. "You must be Zoey," she says. "So nice to finally meet you." Her voice is quiet and careful as if trying not to set off a bomb.

The maître d' leads us to a table in the corner by a window.

"What's wrong?" I mouth to my mother as the maître d' pulls out Zoey's chair. She shakes her head.

"Enjoy your evening, ladies," the maître d' says.

My mother's smile is strained, cloud-covered. "It's wonderful to have you girls with me tonight," she says, and I feel the relief that whatever has caused her mood, it isn't me.

The waiter comes over, tall and somber, more mortician than server.

"I think I'm going to have some wine. Shall we get a bottle, girls?"

I look at her with surprise.

"I'd love some wine," Zoey says, and I can see that my mother has already won over Zoey with her permissiveness. I wonder if Zoey's mom would be cool enough to let us drink.

My mother turns to me. Her fragility is a tangible thing. I can feel myself holding it like an egg. "You look like you have some color," she says, touching her hand to my cheek. "It's very becoming."

Something about this makes me feel guilty, like I shouldn't be looking rosy while my mother is suffering. "Thanks," I say.

"This is such a nice restaurant," Zoey says. "I've never been in such a nice restaurant, I don't think. And I've heard this hotel is amazing."

I watch my mother's face. She smiles. "Yes, it's lovely. I'll be sorry to leave."

"Well, if your husband is anything like my dad, I bet he's champing at the bit to have you home," Zoey says.

I shoot her a look and watch her realize her mistake too late and turn red. The waiter returns with the bottle.

"Sounds like your parents have a good marriage," my mother says.

"Yes, great!" Zoey says, and then glances over at me. "I mean, good. I mean, they don't fight or anything. At least not in front of me. I guess for all I know they could fight all the time, but of course they protect me from that stuff." She looks at me again and shrinks down in her chair, takes a huge sip of wine.

"And what does your father do?" my mother probes.

"He's a gym teacher."

My mother watches Zoey a moment too long and the light of her attention fades. "Oh," she says, and picks up the menu.

I take a huge gulp of wine and look at Zoey, but she appears not to have noticed the palpable shift.

"Maybe we should make a toast," I say, desperate to switch

gears. They both look at me expectantly, but beyond the suggestion I've got nothing.

"Oooh, I know a fantastic toast!" Zoey says. "My friends and I used to say this all the time at home. It has a swear in it, though." She glances at my mother. "Do you mind if I swear?"

My mother laughs, charmed. "Considering the language my daughter uses with me, I'm immune by now."

It feels like a betrayal that she has said this, like she has gone against some unspoken agreement that we no longer look back, that we erase. "Used to use," I say.

"Okay," Zoey says. She raises her glass and leans in toward us. My mother and I raise our glasses as well. "Here's to the men that we love. Here's to the men that love us. The men that we love are NOT the men that love us, so . . . fuck the men and here's to us."

I glance at my mother. She sits frozen. My stomach drops. I can't believe Zoey said that. An awful silence hangs in the air.

Then my mother bursts out laughing. "I love it!" she squeals. "Say it again."

Zoey says it again and my mother tries to follow along out loud, committing it to memory. They are like two teenagers, and I am torn between gratitude and envy that Zoey has helped my mother find her laugh again.

"Of course that doesn't apply to Cassie these days," Zoey says, winking at me.

"Oh?" My mother raises an eyebrow. "Why's that?"

"She had a hot date today!"

I try to nudge Zoey under the table, but hit the table leg instead.

"Oh, that's right," my mother says. "I can't believe I forgot to ask. How did that go?"

They both turn and stare at me, and my stomach kicks like something is trapped in there.

"We last left the story in a deserted parking lot," Zoey says ominously.

"Start from the beginning," my mother says. "What did you wear?"

I look between the two of them. "Don't we need to decide what we're ordering? What are you getting, Zo?"

"The food can wait!" Zoey says. "Why are you trying to change the subject?"

I glance at Zoey and then to my mother. I feel cornered, don't know what to do. I can't shake the nagging impulse that the timing is wrong and also, that I should hold on to the story, not give it away to my mother.

"We don't have all day!" Zoey says.

"Really," my mother echoes, pulling her chair in as if she's eager to listen.

"Okay, okay," I say, both because I don't know what else to do and because some part of me actually does want to tell my mother about my very first date, to have that moment with her, to make up for all the other rite-of-passage moments that I never got to experience and share with her: first crush, first dance, even first day of college. But more than that, a larger part of me wants her to know it's possible for someone to find me worthy of their attention.

I begin to tell the story, cautiously and quickly, downplaying everything, but Zoey keeps elaborating, jumping in on the parts she was there for, teasing me for being so nervous, describing how cute Chris was when he arrived all freshly showered and scrubbed.

I watch my mother's face. She is nodding and encouraging me to go on and things seem to be going well, so I start adding a little more detail, telling them about the struggle with the wetsuit and the way Chris waxed my board and attached the leash to my ankle. When I get to the part where I stood up and rode the wave and Chris cheered, I start to get carried away with the story, reliving the scary, wonderful thrill of it all. I'm embarrassed by how much I keep smiling, but at the same time it feels really good to be able to tell my mother that someone finds me pretty and appealing and likable, like I finally have some sort of proof to offer up.

"So that's the end?" my mother says. She watches me.

I nod.

"Hmm."

"What?" I say.

"Nothing."

"No, what?" My stomach agitates like white water.

She sighs. "I just thought he would at least take you to lunch or something."

"Oh. No. Nope. But, I mean, we spent the whole day together."

The bread basket arrives and we each take a roll from it. Then my mother looks up at me and shakes her head.

"What?" I say again.

"Just a little advice for you lovely ladies. A man who is truly interested in you will take you somewhere nice. Spend a little money."

My heart sinks.

"Oh, I doubt he has much money, being in college and all," Zoey says. "And he definitely really likes her. You should see how he acts around her. It's very cute."

My mother frowns at Zoey. "Well, of course he acts like that," she says tiredly. "That's the game men play to get you into bed." To me she says, "I just don't want to see you get hurt, Cassie."

I stare down at the bread on my plate. I break it into little pieces, feeling confused and hot with the shame of having let myself believe that Chris liked me in the first place, that a guy would actually like *me*. He seemed so genuinely interested, but what did I really know about him, or about guys at all for that matter? I shouldn't have been so gullible, should have known that he wanted something. "I don't even like him that much," I say. "Not at all really."

"Yes she does," Zoey says to my mother.

"No. I don't," I snap.

I stare at her. There is a hard, uncomfortable silence. My stomach feels like it has been filled with rocks.

"Well, excuse me, I need to go to the little girls' room," Zoey says to break the tension.

She gets up from the table and my mother and I both watch her walk away.

"I hate that term, 'little girls' room,'" my mother says. "It's so low class."

"I thought you would like her," I say, angry on Zoey's behalf. "You were acting like you liked her." I had forgotten how good my mother was at pretending.

"Who said I didn't like her?" she says. Her lower lip quivers like that of a child who has been scolded, and then she bursts into tears.

"Mom," I say.

She puts her face in her hands. Her shoulders heave. "He dumped me," she says. Now that we're alone, her tears come raw and real and unstoppable, uncomplicated by anything other than grief. "He said he thought we were just having a good time." Her breath shudders. "I had all these plans. I actually believed we would get married eventually. Oh God, I'm so ashamed."

"Oh, Mom," I say. I think of all the years she clung to the idea that there was one person out there with whom she had shared real love and now there was no one.

She looks past me and I follow her eyes across the dining room, where Zoey has reappeared. For the first time I notice how cheap and shiny Zoey's blouse looks against the sophisticated lines of the restaurant, how unnaturally yellow her hair is. As she begins walking back toward us, I see that a small sheet of toilet paper is stuck to the bottom of her shoe. I stand up and go to her before she reaches the table.

"What's wrong?" she says, alarmed.

"I'm sorry but I think you better go."

"Was it something I said?"

"No, no. I'll explain later."

When I return to the table, my mother looks at me through sad, swollen eyes. "You're such a good girl," she says.

Zoey is on the phone with a friend when I arrive back at the dorm with food for her. I suspect she has been talking about the night because she clams up quickly and says, "I gotta go, Mol. See ya in class."

I hand her the Styrofoam box. I am depleted, feel like my insides have been dried out.

"I ordered the steak for you. I hope you like it. Her boyfriend dumped her."

"Oh," Zoey says. "I kind of figured that's what it was."

"I feel so bad about sending you home."

"No, no, it's fine."

"It's just, you know, she needed a friend."

"Then why didn't she call one?"

"What?"

I stare at her across a long, tense pause.

"Nothing," she says finally. "Never mind."

I try to shrug it off and then slip inside our small closet to maneuver out of my dress. I know Zoey thinks it's weird that I'm so modest, but the thought of changing in front of another person is horrifying to me.

"Oh, before I forget, your boyfriend rang," Zoey says. "He wants you to call him back if you have a chance."

"I won't," I say, more to myself than to her. I poke my head out. "And he's not my boyfriend. Obviously."

"Cassie!"

"What?" I say, but I can hear the note of concern in her voice.

She looks at me and sighs. "I think Chris really likes you. Just because your mother can't make her relationships work . . ."

"What does my mother have to do with anything? I mean, I get that you don't like her."

"It's not that I don't like her. It's that I like you."

"What's that supposed to mean?" I stare at her, braced against what she might say. I want to scream at Zoey that she has had her mother her whole life and I am only just now getting mine and I can't afford for her to be taken away. "You don't know what she's been through," I say. "Her mother was awful to her."

There is a loaded silence.

"Anyway," I say. "I'm tired. It's been a long day."

I close the closet door again and finish changing.

"Don't forget you have that appointment tomorrow," Zoey says when I come out in my pajamas. "You still gotta get that note."

I see Liz's card on my desk with our appointment time, and I swipe it into the garbage when Zoey isn't looking. The last thing I care about right now is school.

"Good night," Zoey says.

I stare at the wall and pretend I don't hear her.

Soon I am drifting off to sleep, being sucked into a dangerous ocean. Someone is on the sand waving me in. I can't see their face. I try to reach them, but the waves are slamming too hard on the shore, and no matter how hard I swim, the undertow keeps pulling me back.

thirty-two

ZOEY WAKES ME up the next morning by sitting on my bed and poking me like a child. "You have to go to your appointment. I'm not letting you fail out."

I roll over on my stomach, hoping she'll leave me alone, but instead she jumps up and starts singing, "Wake me up before you go-go!" at full and torturous volume. When I open my eyes again, I see that she is also using jazz hands interspersed with finger snapping. I sigh, push the covers off and head to the shower.

"That's my girl!" Zoey calls after me. "I'm going to the library after History. Meet me there when you're done!"

The sun is unlit and the grass still damp with dew as I make my way across the campus. My head is swampy from a restless night's sleep, so it takes me a second to register the sound of my name being called.

I turn.

It's Chris. He starts walking toward me, and in that moment of space before memory kicks in, I am happy. Then I hear my mother's voice assuring me that all he wants is sex.

I turn away like I don't see him and duck inside the nearest building. As I pass by the window, I see him staring at the door I've just disappeared behind, his brow creased in confusion. I move out of his line of sight and wait until I'm sure he's gone before I slip back out and head to the counseling center.

By the time I get there, I'm in a pissed-off mood, a brewing rage coming from somewhere I can't name, at someone I can't see. I don't even know why I've bothered to come back here.

When Liz enters the waiting room, she looks so genuinely happy to see me that I can only assume she perceives it as some notch on her belt that I have actually returned for this session. I grunt a hello and walk past her into the office, put my newly purchased schoolbooks down on the couch beside me. I doubt she'll even notice them.

She quickly pours hot water into a mug, presses a spoon against the steeping tea bag and sits in her leather chair. I take the edge of the couch closest to the door and ignore the concerned look on her face. The single lamp casts a pale, strained light against the gray morning. The room smells of cinnamon.

Liz tilts her head as if to say, "What's wrong?"

I fold my arms across my chest like a petulant five-year-old and refuse to speak. Then, on second thought, I decide to tell her exactly what's wrong. I lean forward.

"Look, I'm sorry to say that your little plan to get me back here didn't work." Then because I realize that I am, in fact, back here, I add, "Or at least it won't work. Like, in the future, it's not going to be working."

"My little plan?" She sets down her tea and furrows her brow in confusion. "What little plan is that?"

For a moment her response makes me doubt myself, but the pull of experience reassures me that I'm right. I am angry with myself for being manipulated into trusting her, suckered into believing I'd get what I needed. The anger feels so voluminous, in fact, so completely out of nowhere that I sit on it lest I look like a crazy person.

I turn to the window. A curtain of fog blocks my view of the ocean.

"Did something happen?"

I don't answer.

"You think I would trick you?"

"Whatever. Look," I say. "No offense or anything, but I was only doing this to get a note. And since clearly no note is forthcoming, I think I'll just go back to my regularly scheduled failing out and expulsion." I grab my books and stand up.

"Wait," she says. "I should have told you when you walked in. I realized last time I forgot to give you a note, so I called the dean instead."

I remain standing, refuse to look at her.

"Do you want to hear what he said? I'm not sure if you're looking for a real answer. Maybe you want to fail out?"

"Why the hell would I want that?" I feel the reins of control slipping.

"You tell me. There must be a reason you keep sabotaging yourself."

I stare at her, say nothing.

She matches my silence.

I hesitate. Consider whether or not I should still leave. My automatic impulse is to say, *Fuck it, fuck you, I don't need your help,* and walk out. But I know that would be "sabotaging myself" and thus proving her right. Instead, I sigh loudly, sit back down and refold my arms across my chest.

"I didn't tell Dean Wilson you were depressed. I just said that you had been sick with pneumonia and were struggling a bit and that you and I were working on getting you back on your feet."

She examines my reaction closely. I squeeze myself tighter, refuse to meet her eyes.

"He said that as long as you and I were working toward this goal, he was willing to hold off on any disciplinary action, but that it would be up to your individual teachers to determine what you would need to do."

The fact that she went to all this trouble for me is so far from what I expected that I'm not sure what to make of it. Only that I can't trust it. And the truth is I'm not even sure I want it anymore. The chance, I mean.

"I believe we can do this. Everything you've told me about your life tells me you're not a quitter. Including the fact that I see you got your books." She smiles with what looks almost like pride.

She noticed.

"So whaddaya say?" she says. "Would you like to keep trying?"

"You want me to keep coming back here?" I can't imagine why she would ever want to see me again. "What, do you have some patient quota you need to meet or something?"

For the first time I notice how little of her there is in the room: a desk, a phone, a small table, a clock.

"You're eighteen years old, Cassie. You certainly don't *have* to do anything."

I lean back into the couch and consider my options, or lack thereof. I wonder what would happen to me if I got kicked out, where I would go, how much it would really matter in the scheme of my life. At the moment, it seems far easier than trying. Then I think of my uncle Billy, who spent his whole adult life as an addict living in his parents' basement. I remember how he used to draw pictures for me, my favorite being a surprised-looking scuba diver swimming in a tank full of sharks. My mother used to say that Billy could have been a cartoonist if only he could get out of the basement, but I always thought Billy's problem was that he couldn't get out of the shark tank.

"What's happening over there?" Liz says.

A memory swims around the edges of my consciousness. I can feel its big, dark shadow just below the surface. I sit up. "Nothing."

"You had a look on your face."

"Just thinking about my uncle Billy."

"What about him?"

"I don't know. Nothing. Look," I say. I'm about to tell her that I can't do this, that I'm not going to come back here and deal with another fucking doctor trying to get inside my head and mess with it. I'll just have to figure out some other way. Then I notice something.

"Hey, no ashtray," I say. I had been sure she was going to retrieve it from the wastebasket as soon as I left the last time.

She smiles at me in that warm, bright way my mother always reserved for Matthew. "I meant to thank you for that, actually. You were right. How can I ask my patients to let go of unhealthy attachments if I can't let go of my own?" She winks at me. "Smart cookie."

I roll my eyes, but she pins me with her stare. Her behavior is disorienting. My brain doesn't know what to do with it.

"If you would like to give this a chance, Cassie, I believe we can work on this together."

I fold my arms tighter and turn to the window. I can't look at her, don't want her to look at me. It all feels like such a risk.

"Fine," I make myself say finally, avoiding her eyes. "I'll talk to my teachers and see you next week. But don't expect much."

I gather my books and stand. At the door, I turn, look back at the table. "You miss it?"

She looks confused and then follows my gaze to the space where the ashtray had been. "Actually, it was harder to look at every day than it was to give up, as it turns out. I guess I reached that point where not changing was tougher than changing, ya know?"

I shrug. Not really.

Liz hands me an appointment card for Wednesday at three and calls "bye, Cassie" as I flee.

I step outside, still lost in thought about my session, when all at once a memory of Uncle Billy comes rushing back to me, like it was just waiting until I was alone to visit.

thirty-three

IT WAS THE Thanksgiving just after Great-Aunt Dora had left our house and I was wearing the dress my mother had insisted I wear, the one that my father had bribed me into putting on. We were at my grandparents' house, where the adults were playing charades in the den, getting more animated with each cocktail, while Matthew and I observed them with the special blend of fascination and horror usually reserved for watching mimes. My mother, who was teamed up with my father and Uncle Billy, was, to no one's surprise, kicking everyone's ass in the game. She had always been excellent at charades.

It was my grandmother's turn. Already three bourbons deep, Leigh staggered to the front of the room and mimed that her chosen idea was a movie. Then she put her hands over her head in a point and opened her mouth wide.

"*Jaws!*" my mother shouted, bouncing in her chair.

My grandmother teetered for a second, her eyes widened with drunken shock.

"That's it, isn't it?" my mother said. "It's *Jaws*, right? I got it on the first guess!" She high-fived Uncle Billy and my father.

Leigh slumped back down beside my grandfather Nick, a small, dapper man with a three-pack-a-day habit and a mean streak, and scowled at my mother.

"Oh, look at Bevy," my grandmother taunted from the couch. "She thinks she's sooo smart. La de da."

My mother's head drew back in wounded surprise. "Maybe I don't 'think' I'm smart, Mother. Maybe I actually am."

My grandfather chimed in, muttering something clearly unkind under his breath.

"What was that, Dad?" my mother demanded.

"Who wants to go shoot some pool?" Uncle Billy said, quickly ushering Matthew and me toward the basement and out of firing range.

The basement where Billy lived was an entirely different landscape from the rest of the house. It was womblike but seedy, the belly of a prostitute. The only light was a poker lamp that dangled over the pool table, drawing smoke and casting a petroleum-jelly haze over the room. The walls were lined with posters of motorcycles and naked girls and the chalkboard where Billy drew cartoons for me.

"Anyone up for a bong hit?" Uncle Billy joked as he gathered the pool cues. We stared at him blankly. "Never mind. Wrong crowd."

I didn't really want to play pool so I plopped down on the floor cross-legged to watch Billy teach Matthew how to play. We were having a great time, Matthew acting all cool and grown up with his pool stick, and Uncle Billy pausing between shots to take hits off his bong and do magic tricks for me. But then Matthew overshot his mark and a pool ball came hurtling directly at my head. I was sure I was about to get beaned hard, so I closed my eyes tight and brought my hands to my face as if that would help. Instead, the ball landed with a soft thud in my lap. I opened my eyes, looked down and laughed with relief. Billy was laughing too as he came over and reached down to retrieve the ball.

All at once, his hand seemed to move toward my body in slow motion, huge and terrifying and dangerous. I stopped laughing. Fear-bats beat against my chest. I looked down at the ball and then up at Billy as his hand drew closer. Our eyes met, mine wide with panic and his full of confusion. I jumped to my feet and ran up the stairs.

"Cassie!" Billy called after me. "Wait! What's wrong?"

But the truth was, I didn't know.

I found my mother seated alone on the couch in the den with her arms folded, the game of charades over, everyone else gathered in the kitchen without her. I sat down beside her just as Billy and Matthew reappeared from the basement. Billy's brow was furrowed and his hands were jammed deep into his pockets as he stood in the doorway, shifting the weight of his body from one leg to the other like a swaying elephant. He took a deep breath, looked at me and then went and sat down abruptly on the other side of my mother. His hands came out of his pockets and appeared over the glass coffee table. His thick, square fingers drummed on it in a minor stampede. He stopped, leaned in to her and cupped his hand over her ear. I heard the sound of my name and my ears perked up like a dog's.

"Turkey time!" Leigh's voice called from the dining room.

Uncle Billy was still whispering to my mother. "I'm worried about her," I heard him say.

"I don't know what you mean by that," my mother said, standing. "And frankly I don't care right now. I'm starving, and I want this damn dinner over with."

We sat down at the formal dining room table. The tension, still in the air from charades, was further enhanced by my father's insistence on saying grace. The only known god in my grandparents' house was a bottle of Jim Beam and a lit cigarette.

"Thank you, dear Lord, for this lovely food our hostess, Leigh, has prepared—"

"Had catered in," my mother said pointedly.

"Ah . . . right . . . um . . . Had catered in," my father stammered, glancing nervously between my mother and Leigh. "And thank you, Lord, for the caterers and this loving family I have been invited into."

My mother coughed at the word *loving*.

My grandmother slurred, "I'll drink to that!"

Beside me, Billy reached over to cut my turkey and to dot a dollop of gravy on my nose.

My grandmother clinked her now half-empty glass with her spoon. "A toast," she said, sloshing her glass of booze to and fro. "To all the people in my life who love me so much and so well!" She pointed her cigarette at each of us and added, "As you should."

"Hear, hear!" almost everyone cheered as they raised their glasses high into the air. Only my mother kept silent, her glass by her side.

"And to my brilliant sons, Paul and Billy," my grandmother continued. "Your father and I are so proud of you darlings." I waited for her to say something nice about my mother too, but instead she ended with, "Okay, everybody, dig in!"

I turned to my mother. Her face was red and blotchy.

"I'd like to make a toast as well," she said suddenly. She stood and raised her glass, the ice cubes in her drink rattling as her hand shook.

Immediately I jerked my milk glass into the air.

"To Darling Dad, who liked to get drunk and beat on his daughter. And to Mommy Dearest for standing by and watching and enjoying it. Here's to you, Mom and Dad."

"That never happened," my grandmother said.

"Like hell it didn't."

I lowered my glass.

My grandfather picked up his own tumbler and lifted it high into the air. "And here's to Bevy," he said with a smile, "who never fails to be a bitch."

"Oh shit," Billy whispered to me.

My mother, infuriated, turned to my father. "Are you going to just sit there and let him talk to me that way?"

My father looked up, surprised. Clearly that had been his plan exactly. "Nick," he said to my grandfather, "please don't speak to my wife like that."

"This is my house and I'll speak any damn way I please," my grandfather said, rising from his chair.

My father looked helplessly to my mother.

"Don't look at me!" she cried. "Do something!"

Billy leaned over and cupped his hand against my ear. "Ten bucks says my old man takes your old man in the first round."

"My dad won't fight Pappy," I said. "Pappy's too old."

Suddenly my father lunged for my grandfather across the table. My grandmother screamed. The mashed potatoes went flying, big white chunks splashing onto my dress.

The two grown men were on the floor and wrestling before anyone else even had time to react. My mother started to cry. Billy and Paul jumped into the fray, trying to pull my father off of their father. Matthew stood up and shouted, "Go, Dad!" I looked on curiously. Nothing shocked me anymore.

"We're leaving," my mother said to no one in particular. "You all suck."

She grabbed Matthew, and the two of them started toward the car. I was scrambling to keep up when Billy came running outside.

"Bevy, wait!"

The three of us stopped and turned.

"I still need to talk to you about . . . you know"—Billy jerked his head in my direction—"what I said I needed to talk to you about before."

"Oh, you have got to be kidding me," my mother said with an angry laugh. She paused to glare at me as if I had somehow orchestrated this, and then turned back to Billy. "That's perfect. That's just . . . What about me, Billy? How about the fact that you should have defended me in there?"

"I know. You're right, okay? But come on, what do you expect? I'm just . . . Billy. You know I screw everything up." He made a sad face.

My mother turned to go.

"Please." Billy grabbed her arm. "I know you're pissed off, but just hear me out, okay? It's important."

"Of course it is," she said, shaking her arm free from his grasp. "Everyone is important but me."

Billy sighed.

My mother folded her arms across her chest. "Make it quick."

"Like I said," Billy started, lowering his voice to a whisper, "I'm just concerned because something happened when we were playing pool in the basement and—"

My mother put a hand up to stop him. "Hold on," she said. She turned to Matthew and me. "Kids, get in the car."

Reluctantly, I climbed into the backseat of the Blue Bomb and then rolled down the window, straining to hear the rest of the conversation about me. Uncle Billy's arms were reaching out pleadingly while my mother's remained tightly wrapped around her chest. They both turned at one point and looked at me. Then all at once, my mother reared back and struck Uncle Billy across the face.

I gasped.

Uncle Billy bowed his head as if he had deserved it.

"This is just like you people!" she shouted loud enough for the whole neighborhood to hear. "You know, I always thought you were different. But you're just like the rest of them. I won't let you do it. I will not let you make me think I'm a bad mother! You just want everybody to be screwed up like you are! Well, screw you! Screw all of you! I'm done with this family."

My mother marched toward the car, got in and slammed the door shut.

My father came running out, his glasses smashed and dangling from one ear like an earring. He climbed into the driver's seat and checked his battered reflection in the mirror.

"Go!" my mother said.

My father started the engine.

I turned back to the window to wave good-bye to my uncle Billy—the pothead who lived in my grandparents' basement—the only one who noticed when I was drowning. He raised his hand but did not wave it. I thought that he looked sad.

"You know you still owe me ten bucks for that bet, kiddo," he shouted as my father pulled away from the curb. Then he gave me a small smile and did a little uppercut jab at the air.

I would not see him again.

thirty-four

I DON'T KNOW what to do with this memory, what to make of it, where to put it. It feels like there is information missing, something important. But all I know is that thinking about my uncle Billy, about that day, has made me sad and confused. I'm so caught up in my head, trying to make sense of things, that as I walk to the library to meet Zoey, I don't see Chris until I'm almost upon him.

He is sitting on the steps of the boys' freshman dorm with some friends, looking easy and full of laughter and at home. I consider turning and running in the opposite direction, but I'm almost in front of them and I don't want to draw attention to myself. Instead, I conjure an invisible cloak around me, pretend I have no peripheral vision and hope to pass by unseen.

"Look at you, crazy girl," he calls, and instantly I freeze. Despite my efforts to escape it, that word, the unfair label, has followed me here. I am sure he has found out about me, about my being locked up.

I pull my chest back, stand tall, stare him down. "What did you just say?"

He looks taken aback, and a few of his friends start ribbing him in low, mocking voices about being in trouble with a girl.

"Just that I almost didn't recognize you!" He jumps up and comes toward me, points to the armload of books I am bringing to the library. "You've actually got books. I never thought I'd see the day."

"Huh?" I say, and then the world, which has narrowed to the slits of my eyes, expands again. "Oh, my *books* . . . Right . . . Crazy . . ."

Still, the adrenaline lingers, unwilling to give the all clear just yet. At the same time, my heart remembers Chris, pushes against my chest as if to get closer to him. Then I remember my mother's words.

"Well, nice to see you." I start walking fast again. He follows.

"Hold on . . ." He scrambles to catch up. "What did you think I meant?" I can feel him looking at me funny, though I'm trying to avoid eye contact.

"I don't know. Nothing." I realize I'm being weird, so I turn and add, "Why are you being weird?"

"Am I?" He puts a hand on my shoulder to stop me and frowns with boyish concern. "I probably am. You make me nervous. Especially when you avoid me."

"I'm not avoiding you." I shake his hand off my shoulder and resume walking.

"Oh really?" he says, and proceeds to imitate me speed-walking with my head down away from him. I can't help but laugh.

He turns and smiles, and I immediately stop laughing. "Well, since you're not avoiding me, you wanna go do something? Grab some pizza? Hang out on the beach? Hang out on a pizza?"

He grins at me in that way that makes my stupid stomach flip and I want nothing more than to say yes, my heart leaping yes. But then I think of my mother again, of what she said, and I remind myself he's probably only after one thing. "I have to study," I say. I adjust my arms as the stack of books threatens to topple.

He catches the binder at the top of my pile. "I could help if you want. At least with the English stuff."

"Why would you do that? You think you're gonna get lucky in the stacks or something?"

"Whoa!" he says, stepping back. "What?" He looks angry or offended. Maybe both.

"Nothing, forget it."

He searches my face, which I can feel has gone red, and then he smiles roguishly. "Not that I'm opposed. I mean . . . if that's your assignment or something, I'm totally willing to sacrifice myself for the cause."

I roll my eyes and then grab my binder back from him. "I really have to get to the library before it closes." I start walking even faster away from him. This time he does not follow.

"Uh, Cassie?" he calls.

I turn.

"It's right there. You just passed it. And the library doesn't close."

I look to where he's pointing and see the huge letters at the top of the building that say LIBRARY.

"Right." I change course too quickly and half my books go flying out of my arms. "Dammit!" I drop to my knees and grab furiously at a few scattered papers that have fallen out of one of my notebooks.

Chris walks over and kneels down beside me.

"I got it." I glare at him and then sink into the grass, feeling so foolish and embarrassed, I could cry. Chris picks up my books and hands them to me. Then, before I can stop myself I say, "Why are you being so nice? What do you want from me?"

He looks shocked. "Nothing! Jeez."

"So then do you have a hero complex or something? You think I'm some charity case, is that it?"

He stares at me.

"Or maybe you just like the chase?"

"Maybe I just like you," he says irritably, as though him liking me should be above question. "And I get it. You don't like me. It's fine."

"No, it's . . ." I look down at the grass, at the scatter of papers, all the mess I've made. "It's just . . . why?"

"Why what? Why do I like you? Is that a serious question?"

I meet his eyes, daring him to answer it.

"Okay," he says. "Well . . ." His whole demeanor shifts, loosens. "Hmm . . ." He looks up at the clouds and taps his finger against his chin. "Thinking. Thinking. There's got to be a reason somewhere . . ."

"Oh, forget it!"

His eyes twinkle. "No, no, just give me a minute."

I start to laugh despite myself.

"Okay, well, for one thing I like making you laugh."

I stop laughing.

"And you're very unpredictable. You definitely keep me on my toes . . ."

I roll my eyes.

"And you're almost sweet when you want to be. Plus, you're sort of an endearing disaster."

"Hey!"

He gestures at the remaining papers on the ground. "You want to debate that?"

I open my mouth and then realize I have no case.

His face gets serious then, his eyes holding me. "And I guess I just like being nice to you. Sometimes I get the feeling that no one has been nice to you your whole life."

I go to speak, but his words have knocked the wind out of me. I wonder if it's possible that he really does like me. That in spite of all my efforts to hide myself, he sees me and likes me anyway. That maybe my mother was wrong about him, about all of it.

He puts his hand on top of mine and this strange, salty whoosh goes through my body like a breaking wave. He bends his face to me, his eyes looking into mine, searching my face. I imagine what he sees: mascara, blush, lipstick, foundation.

"You don't know me," I say.

I collect my mess quickly, stand and march ahead to the library without looking back. I picture Chris behind me, coming to his senses, realizing that I'm just too much.

"So let's get to know each other!" he calls out. "Go to the home-coming dance with me!"

I walk into the library and let the door slam shut behind me.

thirty-five

SAFELY INSIDE THE library, I search for Zoey and, failing to find her, plop my books down at an empty corner table, open the first and proceed to read the opening paragraph at least three times without processing a word.

My ears are ringing and my face feels like it's on fire. My mind is at war with itself, a jumble of incongruent thoughts fighting each other to the death. I have to keep reminding myself that Chris is an undercover jerk who just wants to use me. And even if he's not a jerk, even if he *thinks* he likes me, it's only because he's not seeing the real me. But then Zoey's voice in my head argues that I should trust this, that I shouldn't listen to my mother. And sometimes when I'm with Chris I think she's right—that he does care. But I just can't tell what's real.

It's as if all the same questions I've had for years—quelled for a time in my mother's absence—have just now reemerged, demanding answers: Am I acting crazy or am I just protecting myself? Which threats are real and which are imagined? Whose perception is accurate, my mother's or mine? And at the core of all these questions is the biggest one, the only one really: Am I lovable or unlovable?

I remember how James used to literally yell at me if I dared to doubt myself. James, who insisted every day that I see my own worth beyond my mother's rejecting eyes. But of course, a mother's eyes are the very first mirror we look into, the image that gets imprinted on our souls—whether they gaze back at us with love or with disgust. So I don't know how to differentiate between her perceptions of me and my own when hers were the first I've ever known, so deeply ingrained from the second I hit the world.

I think if I could just find a way to be sure of who was good and who was bad, who was right and who was wrong when I was growing up, then maybe the present wouldn't seem so muddied. The answers had seemed clearer to me before my mother came back into my life acting so maternal, making me question my reality, throwing both my past and my present situation with Chris into confusion. She seems so sincere, and yet this mother bears no resemblance to the one I knew.

As I struggle to reconcile the two versions of her, I find myself dipping back into memory once again, to right before it all went completely to hell.

It started with Christmas. On Christmas Eve, I found a single giant present under the tree with my name on it. Even though it was only one gift to my brothers' many presents, the sight of it there was a complete shock, having prepared myself to have no gifts, no Christmas at all. I even double-checked my name on the little tag to make sure there was no mistake. But it was definitely addressed to me.

It was clearly a peace offering of sorts. The spirit of Christmas had seized my mother, pushing her to bring this long, awful war to an end. And even though I would never admit it out loud, I needed desperately for the war to end. The world was hard without parents. That one single Christmas present felt like nothing less than a rescue plane to the stranded.

I wondered all night what it might be. I couldn't sleep. In the morning, both unable to bear the suspense and wanting to prepare my reaction under such tenuous circumstances, I slipped downstairs before everyone else woke up. Carefully, I peeled away a little tape and pulled back the wrapping paper. I saw canvas and a zipper, but still I couldn't figure out what it was. And then it hit me and I felt the awful thud of collapsed hope.

A suitcase.

The message was undeniable: Pack up your shit. You're not wanted here.

So I stayed away as much as I could, hanging out with Wade—the two of us like orphans—both raising each other and rebelling against a world that had shut us out. When I was at home, I moved through the house like a soldier crossing enemy lines, slipping up to my room as quickly as possible, trying not to get caught in the act of existing. I was not invited to join my family at mealtime but instead snacked on their leftovers or scavenged my food from the cabinets. I did this mostly late at night, sneaking quietly into the kitchen like a mouse in a cat's house to grab whatever I could get my hands on quickly: doughnuts, cookies, candy bars. I began stealing money from my mother's purse to pay for school lunches.

Even when my father was home on the occasional weekend

between trips, I remained cast out. He would try to talk to me, small talk at the door to my room, as if nothing was happening, and sometimes I would hear him attempt to defend me in the unfair tirades my mother would wage about me in full voice from their bedroom. But it didn't make any difference. Eventually he just gave up.

February break came.

On the first night off from school, Wade and I had been at a party of some girl whose parents weren't home until the loud music brought the cops, who broke it up. We piled into the car of Wade's friend Max, a senior, and though it was kind of late, none of us wanted to go home. Max, being older, had a later curfew and Wade seemed to have none at all.

"I have an idea," Wade said.

"I'm down for trouble," Max replied.

"You in?" Wade asked me.

I looked at the clock—almost 11:00 P.M. My mother had never mentioned a curfew to me and I assumed she didn't care enough to give me one, though it seemed like common sense that I couldn't just roll in any time I pleased. Then again, my father was back from his latest trip, which made the thought of being in my house somehow even less appealing. When he was around, my mother's unhappiness ballooned, traveling through the atmosphere, looking for a place to land. And, as usual, I was her misery's favorite spot. No matter what I did, I was going to get shit.

"Well?" Wade said, pulling me out of my thoughts and into the car. "In or out. We don't have all night."

"Screw it," I said. "I'm in."

It was silly, the stuff we did that night. We drove around and stole FOR SALE signs and then put them all over the lawn of the high school. We went to the 7-Eleven and ate microwaved burritos standing by the counter and played a game of catch with a box of condoms across the aisles until the store manager chased us out with a broom while we laughed. We drove to the town's outdoor ice-skating rink and climbed over the fence and slid around on our sneakers until police headlights became a spotlight for our pirouettes. Then we ran like hell, whooping as they chased us, cutting through bushes and over fences to escape them. We ran until we found a tree house to hide in and climbed up and inside, pressed against one another in a pile to keep warm while we waited for the cops to give up. It was luminous to be in that huddle of friendship, turned toward one another in the darkness of adolescence, surrounding one another like glass around a candle. I was happy. I belonged. This is what I remember most about that night: that I was alive. That I was allowed to be. It was the last time I could remember feeling that way. It was the last time I ever wanted to be happy, for what a dangerous feeling happiness was, how much worse a fall from such a great height.

"Let's egg some houses!" Wade said as we trotted back to the car once it was safe.

I laughed. "I gotta go. But feel free to egg mine."

It was almost one in the morning when they dropped me off. The lights were on downstairs.

Not a good sign.

I had hoped my parents might have gone to bed without noticing my absence, which wouldn't have been unusual. I could hear them shouting at each other as I came up the driveway, followed by the completely unhelpful sound of Max's car screeching loud enough to wake the whole neighborhood as he sped away.

I put my key in the back lock, my hands shaking with both cold and dread. My mother appeared at the door. "Well, look what the cat dragged in," she said.

I ignored her and stepped past her into the house. My father was standing by the door to the hall.

"Where the hell were you?" he said.

"Out," I mumbled.

"Out where?"

"Who cares where?" my mother said to him. "It's one in the morning. Stop pussyfooting around her."

"I'm not pussyfooting, Bev. I'm just—"

"Oh right," she said. "What do you care if she tramps all over us? You're off living it up in Europe while I'm stuck here being abused!"

I actually laughed. "Abused?" I turned to my father. "She's the one who won't even speak to me. Except to call me fat. Or hit me in the face."

She pointed her finger at me. "You shut up." Then back to my father: "Do you see how she treats me? She's deliberately trying to hurt me."

"*I'm* trying to hurt *you*?" I said. Everything was so backward, so warped and twisted. I couldn't take it anymore. "I'm going upstairs. Go ahead and ground me. It's not like you actually want me around." I started toward the door.

"Oh great," she spat at my father. "You're just going to let her go? God, Ed, you are *such* a simp!"

My father gritted his teeth. All the sympathy he had for her seemed to drain out of him in an instant. I could almost smell the rage coming off of him like the wet panting of a dog. "I am not a simp!" he said, and for a second he looked like he might lunge for her.

"You're worse than a simp," she said. "You're pathetic."

My father's body trembled as if the charge of his own fury were electrocuting him. Then just when I thought he might finally explode on her after all the years of putdowns and abuse, he turned without warning, stepped forward to block my exit and slammed me against the wall.

"What the hell?" I said, stunned.

I put my hand to the back of my head and we stood there looking at each other inside a pause so tense and serious that I almost felt like laughing. For one passing instant, I thought I saw pleading in his eyes. Then just as quickly, it was gone.

"From now on you are forbidden to see these new friends of yours, do you hear me?" he said.

"You've never even met them!"

"I don't give a goddamn shit. We're your parents, and you'll do whatever we say!"

"Oh, so now you've decided to be my parents? What brought on the sudden change?"

He stepped right up to me, towering over me, and stuck his

enraged face into mine. I refused to show fear, though I felt it.

"You're going to give me some goddamn respect from now on, do you hear me? I'm tired of not being respected in this house!"

"Take that up with her!" I said, pointing at my mother, who stood calm now, watching satisfied as my father and I argued. "She's the one you should be pissed off at! She's the one who treats you like crap! And you just take it out on me!"

My father's eyes glittered with rage. I had hit him where he lived. "Don't you talk to me that way!"

"Fuck you!" I screamed. "You're not a father to me. You don't protect me from her. You don't even live here!"

He turned to look at my mother, and in that split second, I ducked past him and ran up to my room, slamming the door behind me. I sat on my bed and waited, heart pounding as I heard my mother's footsteps climb the stairs. They stopped in front of my room.

"You're done," she hissed through the door. "Do you hear me? Done."

I climbed under the covers and closed my eyes and thought of Wade so I wouldn't cry.

In the morning I awoke to them standing over my bed, my mother, my father and Matthew, with ropes in their hands.

"Earth to Cassie," Zoey says, and waves her hand in front of my face.

I hadn't even noticed her standing there.

She plops herself down across from me.

"Have you been here long?" she says. Then before I can answer she adds, "I don't actually need to study. I'm just here to check out guys. Do you realize the homecoming dance is *next week*?"

I roll my eyes. "Who cares?"

"Umm . . . we do. And we need dates."

"Try again. I'm not going to the stupid homecoming dance."

"Oh please," she says with a dismissive wave of her hand. As if she would ever allow that to happen.

thirty-six

TWO DAYS LATER I somehow find myself in the fitting room of Macy's trying on dresses while Zoey, who has just picked out her semiformal gown, stands on the other side of the door, talking about all the fun we're going to have at the dance.

"I'm seriously not going," I say for the tenth time, but Zoey has failed to accept this fact, which is why I'm standing in my underwear going through the motions of dress shopping. "Why don't you just go with your other friends?" As soon as I say this, I regret it. The last thing I need to do is remind Zoey that she doesn't need me.

"Because they think they're too cool to go."

I poke my head out of the dressing room. "So you're making me go because I'm the least cool?"

She grins. "Exactly."

"Fair enough," I say with a dramatic sigh. The way I see it, I can indulge her until she finds a date and loses interest in forcing me to come along. In the meantime, a little shopping therapy never hurt anyone.

"Do you think I should ask that hot guy in the cafeteria?" she asks. "You know, the one who only has four fingers on his left hand? Or should I just go stag and see what comes of the night? I wonder if Chris is going . . ."

"He is," I say. "He asked me yesterday, at the library." I have no idea why I've confessed this.

"Well, now you have to go! Why didn't you tell me?"

"Because I knew you would say, 'Well, now you have to go!'"

"Nobody misses their first college homecoming," she says. "That would be crazy."

"That would hardly be crazy," I say, and then because I hear the defensiveness in my voice, I quickly follow with, "What about Murph? Can't you go with him?"

Zoey makes a series of barfing noises that goes on so long, I start to worry about other customers in the dressing room.

"That's not what you said when you had your tongue down his throat at that beach party," I remind her.

"I was desperate," she says. "Get over it."

I put on one of the dresses I've chosen, tight and black with a scooped neck and a high slit up the side. Even though I have no intention of buying it, I still enjoy trying it on, if only for the approval I hope to see in Zoey's eyes when she sees me in it. I step out of the fitting room and do a little spin.

Zoey gives me a quick once-over. "No," she says with an apologetic head shake.

"No?" I'm completely taken aback. "What's wrong with it?"

"You're eighteen, not thirty-five."

I sigh and step back into the dressing room and stare at myself again, confused. I'm certain that my mother would love me in a dress like this.

"This is so dumb," I say. "I'm not even going." Still, I whip off the dress and try on another, now determined to get it right. The next one is a sophisticated black silk gown with a long open V in the front.

When I step out, Zoey again gives me the thumbs-down. "Sorry," she says.

"What now?"

"You look like your mother."

"Okay, whatever. I'm done." I go back into the dressing room and yank off the dress. I feel like crying.

"I just think they send the wrong message," Zoey says through the door.

"What message is that?"

"Like you're trying too hard. You're beautiful. You don't have to try."

"Yeah right." If I were really beautiful, she would've had a different reaction. I feel the ugliness in me leaking out, the chariot ride turning into a pumpkin.

"Hold on a sec," she says, and disappears for a few minutes. When she returns, she cracks open the door and stuffs another dress into my hand. "Now, I know you're gonna say no because it's not black and sexy and mother-approved, but just try this one for me."

I hold the dress up and look at it. It's a silvery-pink shift dress, short but loose. My mother would barf at this.

"No," I say.

"Come on. I really think it will be pretty."

I sigh and hand her back the dresses she has just shot down. Then, because I know Zoey won't let me leave until I try it on and because she's looking at me with those puppy-dog eyes, I close the door to change into the pink thing.

"Do you think this dance will be like prom where they decorate the shit out of everything and hang corny stars from the ceiling?"

I freeze. I don't know what to say, considering I was too busy being locked up in a mental hospital to attend any high school dances. Then, to my relief, Zoey keeps on talking.

"I don't even remember my senior prom. I was so trashed, I fell headfirst out of the limo in front of a teacher and then spent the night puking in the bathroom. That's why I don't drink tequila anymore, or at least, not straight out of the bottle."

I slide the pink dress over my head and then look at myself in the mirror. My reflection startles me. The girl in front of me is young and unguarded, maybe even sweet. All the hard edges of my face have been softened by the blush of the dress, and with my makeup slightly faded from the hot lights and all the taking on and off of clothes, I catch a glimpse of a more vulnerable version of myself, a girl I haven't seen in a long time.

"So what was your prom like?"

"Huh?" I say, stalling. I am still in the mirror, absorbing the face in front of me as I consider how to answer the question. My feet hurt and the lighting is too bright, and all at once I want to sit down on the dressing room stool and tell her everything: that I have never been to a school dance let alone a prom, that I spent my high school years locked up in an institution, that I don't want to go to this dance, but I don't want to miss out either, that I am afraid I'll never be normal, and mostly, that if I tell her all this, she won't like me anymore.

"Oh, my prom? It was stupid," I lie. "All dances are stupid. Also, there is no way in hell I would ever wear this dress."

I open the door and Zoey stands back and gasps. "Oh my God, look at you!" she says, and I'd swear she almost looks teary. "That's the one."

"Seriously?" I say.

She nods vigorously.

I turn back to the mirror and take another look at myself. "Fine. Whatever. Let's just get it and go."

Zoey and I bring our shopping bags back to our room, and then I run up the campus hill because I realize I'm late for my appointment with Liz. When I notice I'm running, I stop. I don't know why I care about getting there on time—or getting there at all, for that matter.

I reach the counseling center and pause to smooth down my hair so it won't look like I was rushing. My heart is still beating too fast when I sit on the yellow waiting room couch, and I don't know if it's because of the running or the unsettled feeling I've had since my shopping spree with Zoey. I think about the dress she talked me into buying, about my face in the mirror when I tried it on, how it felt like looking at a memory.

"Sorry I'm late," I say when Liz comes to get me in the waiting room and ushers me into her office. "I was shopping for a home-coming dress."

"Oh, exciting," she says as she sits and blows on the cup of tea she inevitably won't bother to drink.

"I'm not going."

She raises an eyebrow. "Ah! Thus, the buying of the dress. It's all falling into place."

"It's just to get my roommate off my back. She keeps pressuring me to go. As soon as she finds a date, I'm returning it."

"Seems like an awful lot of effort," she says. "Is there maybe some part of you that wants to go?" She tilts her head and her eyes twinkle like she's trying to weasel the truth from a child.

I hesitate.

"Aha!" she says.

I start to laugh and she smiles at my laughter. Our eyes meet.

"You look happy," she says.

I suppress the laughter, shrug and look away. The room feels too small, Liz's chair too close.

"What happened just now?" she says.

"Nothing."

"You were happy and now you're not happy."

"I wasn't happy."

"You were smiling . . ."

I sink deeper into the couch, fold my arms across my chest. "Whatever."

"No, not whatever. Was it something I said?"

"Was what something you said?"

"Well, you were smiling and laughing and then suddenly you stopped. So I'm just wondering why."

"I don't know. I don't spend my time remembering and analyzing every little thing that happens, every nanosecond of my life."

She doesn't say anything, but I can feel the weight of her stare.

"What do you want me to say? You want me to make something up?"

"Sure," she says. "Make something up. Whatever comes to your mind first."

I look out the window, angry with myself for having brought on this line of questioning. Just beyond the highway, a haze of sun smothers the sea, although every once in a while, the light catches in a particular way and the ocean sparkles gold. "You know what? Never mind. Forget it."

"Cassie."

"What?"

"I don't want to forget it. That's what you do. You want to sweep everything under the rug, pretend like the things that happened in your life don't affect you."

"I'm not pretending. I'm just over it. People do get over things, you know."

"Just like that?"

"Yeah, just like that."

"Okay," she says.

We sit in silence for a long, tense moment. "All right, you really want to know?" I say. "I'm not buying all this therapy bullshit. I don't trust you. I don't trust this. I know what you're trying to do."

"What am I trying to do?"

"Be all nice and mirroring and validating. Trying to make me feel good. Make me think you care."

"You think it's just an act that I could be happy to see you smile. Why would I do that?"

"To suck me in. Make me think it's okay to lower my guard."

"What would happen if you did that?"

I glare at her. "Nothing good."

She nods and leans back. "So if you keep your guard up all the time, nothing bad will happen?"

"Something like that."

"Where do you think that belief came from?"

"I don't know."

"Is that true?"

I look to the window again. The sun is too white, too bright. I turn away from the glare. Something is nagging at me, something elusive and swimming just below the surface ever since I saw myself in that dress. The uneasiness returns and my mind is all fuzzy, like I have the flu. I feel strangely displaced. Time passes. I don't know how long Liz sits quietly watching me, waiting.

"My uncle Billy told my mother he was worried about me," I say finally. "When I was little. He said he thought something was wrong. I don't know why. Or what that has to do with anything. It's just something I remembered after our last session."

She leans forward. "What do you think he meant by that?"

"I don't know. He was a drug addict. My mother didn't seem to take him seriously. I'm sure it's nothing. I don't even know why I mentioned it."

I glance over at the clock. Liz stays fixed on me.

"We still have a few minutes," she says.

"I'm done talking about it," I say and look toward the door.

"Okay. Well, how about this," she says, suddenly sitting forward. She grabs a business card from the table beside her and writes something on it. She hands me the card. "That's my cell number on the back," she says. "If you need to be in touch again before our next session, I want you to feel free to call me, okay?"

I make a scoffing face. "Why would I do that?"

She shrugs. "Maybe you wouldn't."

"But why would you even want me to?" I sit up even further, my body angling toward the door. "You're doing it again. Trying to make me think you give a shit."

"You really think I don't care for you?" she says. "That I wouldn't be there if you needed me?"

"I think you're doing a job."

She tilts her head and stares at me. The room changes, seems strange and unfamiliar, like I'm seeing it for the first time. Liz, too, looks strange, or maybe it's just that I'm really looking at her face today, taking in her features, seeing the whole picture.

A pressure starts in my head like I'm in a crowded, unfamiliar place and I don't know where I'm going and I can't understand the signs. I wonder if it would be weird to just leave. I suddenly sort of want to leave. The silence seems to have its own heartbeat, tense and watchful. It reminds me of childhood games of hide-and-seek, of listening so hard for footsteps. The game seems darker in my memory of it: the sense of being hunted, waiting to get caught, afraid of both being found and never being found.

"I should go," I say.

"Have I upset you?"

"Not at all."

"Are you sure?"

"Yup. I'm fine."

She looks at me with concern, like she knows—as I do—that I'm lying, but she doesn't want to push it.

"Like I said before, I just don't like being messed with."

"You still think I'm messing with you?"

"Kinda, yeah!"

She appears taken aback, or maybe even sad. She looks down at her tea and stirs it as she thinks. "Well, I guess that's the story you know, isn't it?" she says. "Nobody can ever really care for you. People are untrustworthy and manipulative. Bad things happen and no one is there."

"It's not like I'm making it up."

"No, but maybe that's an old story. Maybe now, you can start to write a different one."

I shrug, lean over, look at the clock.

"Do you have somewhere you need to be?"

"Just making sure I don't overstay."

She leans forward abruptly. The sun is reflected in her eyes. "Do it," she says.

"Do what?"

"Overstay."

"Why?"

"Just as an experiment. Kick off your shoes, sit back and overstay."

"I don't get it."

"It's a risk, Cassie. This fear you have is not about what *could* happen but what has *already* happened. And now the ways you protect yourself are the very things that continue to cause you pain. You might not be so afraid of life if you could see that you aren't alone in—"

"I'm not afraid." I stand. "Time's up."

I leave without saying good-bye.

thirty-seven

THE SUN IS just beginning its retreat when I exit the psych building, and there's no warmth to the remaining light. It's the hour of day I like best, when the weather seems slightly removed, without intrusion or demands. Even now, after almost five weeks in college and out of the hospital, there are moments when my freedom is a wonder, when the air on my skin feels like touch to a newborn.

I think about what Liz suggested, that my fear of letting my guard down is not about what will happen but what has already happened. Then my mind wanders to the memory of the day my parents had me locked up, perhaps because of what Liz said, or perhaps because I have avoided looking at it for so long. I have tried to block it completely from my thoughts ever since my mother came back into my life, not wanting to revisit all those awful feelings, not wanting to reignite them. But the memory is insistent tonight, demanding to be looked at. And I sense now that the only way out of the labyrinth is to know where it started, to remember the path that led to where I'm now standing.

Everything seems so vivid and immediate: that seemingly endless drive, the ropes too tight around my wrists and ankles, the sound of my own voice sobbing and pleading for Gavin to help me. And then even worse than the drive, the moment, hours later, when the car finally stopped.

My father and Matthew untied me in the parking lot and led me toward a large brick building with beautiful grounds empty of people. I knew it was useless to fight them, and I didn't have any energy left to try. We entered a reception area paneled with dark, heavy wood. My mother sent Matthew and Gavin back to the car, and a moment later, a middle-aged man appeared and introduced himself to my parents as Dr. Meeks. He barely glanced at me. Meeks led the three of us into an office where two female doctors were already seated. They were obviously expecting me. When I walked in, they greeted me by name.

The three doctors invited us to take seats in the remaining chairs that had been set in a loose half circle around them.

"Cassie," Dr. Meeks said, looking at me finally. "I want to start out by telling you that we're all here to help you."

"That's right," my mother said, her hands folded primly in her lap. She had an expression of deep parental concern on her face that I had never seen before.

"This is ridiculous," I said to Meeks. "I'm not crazy. I have no idea why I'm here."

Meeks gave me a condescending smile. "We just think that maybe you're having some trouble . . . coping."

"Well, I don't know what you've been told to make you think

that, but I would urge you to consider the source." The sound of my voice so calm and mature and reasonable reassured me. "I mean, I may not be getting along too great with my parents right now. Which I can work on. Which I *will* work on—at *home* with them. But—"

"We understand that you tried to kill yourself in the school cafeteria," Meeks said, glancing at my parents and back to me. "Is that true?"

I turned and stared at my mother. "Seriously? That's what you told them to get me here?" To Meeks I said, "Yes, it's true that I briefly considered offing myself last *year*. Obviously I got over it or I'd be dead right now."

I could tell by the expression on Meeks's face that he was not aware of the time lapse. Point one for me.

"I see," he said. "Well, nonetheless, your parents are understandably concerned."

"So concerned that they waited all this time? So concerned that my mother hit me when she found out and called me a stupid asshole and told me she was surprised I didn't go through with my little suicide plan? Did she tell you that I got the idea from her?"

At that, the other two doctors looked up from their notebooks simultaneously and stared at my mother.

I expected her to deny it, but instead she smiled sweetly at the doctors. "At the time I believed I had a brain tumor. So suicide was the only logical choice." She held out her hands as if that explained it.

The doctors exchanged concerned glances and I saw that

the tables were being turned. They were seeing where the true problem lay.

My mother seemed to sense it too because her mouth began to twitch. She looked anxiously at my father, whose gaze remained steadily on the floor, and then back to the doctors. She took a deep breath and sat up straighter. She pushed her blond hair, cut short in a suburban bob, behind her ears. She refolded her hands in her lap.

"Obviously I'm not a perfect mother," she said. "We have our share of problems like all families. I'm sure that Ed and I have made mistakes along the way. But, when she tried to set the house on fire—"

"What?!" I looked to the doctors. Blood roared in my ears.

"—I became concerned for her safety and the safety of my sons—"

"I never set any fires!"

She kept her eyes fixed on Dr. Meeks. "I caught her with a box of matches trying to set the wastebaskets on fire."

My mind spun, searching itself, trying to make sense of things. I had a faint memory of lighting Wade's matches in my room after that big fight with my mother, trying to comfort myself with thoughts of my new and only friend. I remembered that the door had been open and my mother had walked by. But she obviously knew I wasn't trying to set the house on fire. She hadn't even bothered to say anything about it.

"Are you insane?" I said. "How do you even come up with this shit?"

I turned to the doctors. "Can't you see she's just trying to come up with something on the spot?"

"Cassie," my mother said in a soft, nurturing tone. "I know it's hard to hear these things about yourself but trust me, this is for your own good."

I was out of my chair and across the room in two steps. "You bitch!" I screamed in her face. "You crazy, lying bitch!"

She arched back in her chair as if terrified and turned to Dr. Meeks. "Do you see!" she said. "This is what I'm talking about."

"Because you're lying!" I screamed.

"Help me, Dr. Meeks," my mother pleaded.

Meeks picked up the phone.

I turned to him. "Can't you see what she's doing?! She's just saying whatever she has to to get me locked up. She's the real problem! And she can't stand that I won't take her abuse anymore!"

The office doors banged open. Two large male nurses charged toward me and seized me by the arms.

"What are you doing?" I screamed. "Let go of me!" I tried to shake free. Their grips tightened, rendering me helpless, bound.

A sudden crackle of synapses. A spark of memory like a snapshot. Displacing me for a moment in time. A woman's voice in my head. Disappearing as quickly as it came. I shake my head to clear my thoughts.

The nurses pulled me toward the door. My screams turned wild, shrieking, as if my voice could become fists pounding and thrashing to escape. "You have to believe me!" I cried.

I turned to my mother. I looked in her eyes and begged for my life. "Please don't do this to me! I'll do anything. Just tell them the truth."

She shook her head. "This is where you belong."

"Dad!" I shouted. "Help me! You know I wouldn't do that! She's lying!"

He looked to my mother. She stared back at him with challenging eyes.

"Dad, please! You have to believe me!"

His shoulders slumped. He bowed his head. My mother owned him.

She owned all of us.

"No!" I screamed again as the nurses dragged me backward out of the room by my elbows. My mother looked away, leaving me alone once again with the nightmare of what was happening.

By the time I reach my dorm, my adrenaline is surging with the memory and I hate my mother all over again for what she did, for how she lied, for how she just fucking left me there.

But then I think of my mother now, so different from the mother I grew up with, and it's all too confusing, too exhausting. It feels so much easier not to hate, not to be angry, to believe that maybe it really was my fault, maybe she really was just trying to help me, maybe that's why she lied. Maybe everything—my whole life—was just one big misunderstanding. After all, it's true I wasn't perfect. It's true I had been rebellious, even if I felt justified, even if I felt I was saving myself. And it would be so much easier to just believe that it had been my fault. If it was my fault, I could take control now and I could fix it, the bad thing in me, so that nothing like that would ever happen again.

If it was my fault, maybe I could finally have a mother.

thirty-eight

I TELL MYSELF that the only reason I'm going to the dance is to prove something to Liz. I tell Zoey I'm just going to the dance to appease her. But for the last twenty-four hours, I've taken out the dress several times when Zoey isn't around and held it up to myself, trying to judge my own image, to see what Zoey saw when she looked at me in it. In these moments, I find myself imagining the excitement of such a night, the magic of it, and I can almost feel myself stepping into a life that is more, that is really and truly a life.

By Friday, the day of the dance, there is such an anticipatory energy in the air that I almost get swept up in it. I dare to consider that maybe Liz is right—that perhaps the world I'm so defended against is the one of the past, that if I can let my guard down a little now, open myself up to the possibility of new things, life might actually be different. Better.

"Okay, we need to go," Zoey says, standing at the door with curlers in her hair while she shakes her hands to dry her manicure.

We've rented a room at the hotel where the dance will be so we don't drink and drive. Zoey has already packed her overnight bag, but I'm still trying to figure out everything I need to bring.

"I'm sure I'm forgetting something," I say.

Zoey looks at my full-sized open suitcase, already stuffed to the brim with makeup, hair dryer, three pairs of shoes, the dress and pajamas. "I think you're good."

The phone rings.

"Don't answer that," Zoey says. "There are minibar snacks waiting for us."

I move toward the phone anyway, despising the idiotic part of me that hopes it's Chris. I look at the caller ID. "It's my mother."

"Don't."

"Okay," I say. I stare at the phone, letting it ring. Then, at the last second I give in, like always. "I'll just tell her I'll call her tomorrow." I pick up. "Hi, Mom."

There is silence. Then soft crying. "Your father found out about the affair. He's threatening to file for divorce."

I sit down on my bed. My jaw drops, and I notice how weird it is that that actually happens when you're shocked. I'm not even sure if it's the news or the fact that my mother is crying over my father that stuns me more.

"What happened?" I say. To Zoey I mouth, "Holy shit."

"He listened in on a phone call."

"To Pete?"

"No, to *you.*"

The words land with an unexpected thud. I think of my father, and regardless of everything that has happened between us, I feel like a criminal for colluding. Suddenly I understand why Zoey wanted to protect me from being involved.

"What about Gavin?" I say. "Is he okay?" I imagine my poor little brother in the middle of all this.

"He's fine. Cassie," she sobs, "I need you. Please come home."

"You want me to come home?" I'm in shock.

I have waited my whole life to go home, even when I was actually living there. And now, at last, an invitation.

I look up and see Zoey staring at me with widened eyes. I turn away. I don't know how long my mother wants me there, but I'll worry about school another day. If I fail out, so be it. "I'll head out first thing tomorrow."

"Tomorrow?" she says, an edge in her voice.

"It's just . . . we're literally on our way to a dance right now. We already rented a room and I promised Zoey I'd go."

Zoey stares at the floor and her shoulders sag as if she too can hear the silence on the other end of the phone.

"I can't let her go by herself," I say. "And if I came home tonight, I'd get there so late you'd be sleeping anyway. Besides, I want to go. It's the homecoming dance. Nothing will have changed by tomorrow morning, right?"

Silence.

"Mom?"

I see Zoey pull a curler sadly out of her hair.

"I never would have had an affair if you hadn't put it in my head that I didn't love your father," my mother says with quiet menace.

"What? I never said that! *You* said that!" My head feels

like it's underwater, trapped and spinning in the throes of a breaking wave. "You're saying this is my fault?"

Everything is upside down. Her feelings, my feelings, who is right, who is wrong. It's true that I knew the affair was happening, that I was even happy for her happiness. But does that mean I'm to blame? Again to blame? I struggle against the force of an ocean, trying to find the top, the clear sky.

Then I see Zoey staring at me, mouth agape, eyes bright with anger. There is actual horror in her face that stuns me. "It is *not* your fault," she mouths, her eyes boring into me.

"Are you coming or not?" my mother says.

I hold Zoey's gaze. I don't answer my mother right away, don't know the answer still. Then the line goes dead.

"Mom?" I say. "Mom!"

I stare at the phone in my hand. I look at Zoey. Then I call back frantically, but each time I try, my mother picks up without saying a word and hangs up immediately.

Zoey's face softens, seeing my panic. "If you need to go, go," she says. It's all she wants in the world, to attend this dance together, and yet, I can tell that she means it.

I put the phone back in its cradle, stand up and go to my suitcase.

thirty-nine

"WE'RE GOING TO have the best time," Zoey calls to me
for the tenth time as I step out of the shower and grab one of the
hotel's terrycloth bathrobes. She has been walking on eggshells
since the phone call with my mother, eyeing me skeptically when
I tell her that I'm fine, that I'm used to it, that I'm already over it.

"Here. You could use this." She cracks open the bathroom door
and passes me a strange green concoction she has been feverishly
creating from the minibar. "Screw your mother."

"You'd be amazed by how many people have said that to me,"
I say. But underneath, I feel the clatter of dread. I push it away,
determined—for once—not to care, not to let my mother ruin this
night.

I sniff the drink, which smells even more awful than it looks,
and then do a double take to make sure that wasn't smoke I saw
coming off of it. I wait until Zoey is out of sight before I pour it
down the drain.

"I heard that," she says from the bedroom.

I dry off and stare at my foggy reflection in the bathroom
mirror. There is something hopeful and comforting about all the
little shampoos and soaps lined up beside the sink, the soft hotel

lighting, the occasional bursts of lively voices and high laughter moving down the hallway. I glance over at the dress hanging on the door, pink and vulnerable as baby skin. All at once I wish like hell I'd bought something else.

I reach for my eye shadow. My hands haven't stopped shaking since we left the dorm and I hate that. I don't want to care, don't want my mother to affect me. Just as I lean over the sink, Zoey barges back in. "Oooh, can I do your makeup?"

"Um . . . no," I say into the mirror.

"Oh, come on! I promise I'll do a good job. You may not know this about me, but when I was in high school I worked the cosmetics counter at a very high-end department store. I may have been unjustly fired for spraying perfume in the face of a rude customer, but that's beside the point. I promise you'll look amazing."

I look into the mirror and down at my shaking hands. Then I turn back to Zoey, whose eyes are shiny with eagerness. Before I can answer, she runs over and cranks up the hotel's tinny clock radio and orders me to sit on the toilet seat while she pulls up a chair between me and the mirror. Zoey studies my face and then roots around in my makeup bag for what she needs. Soon she is pulling out pots of color, shaking her head yes or no to each item as if they are speaking to her. For the first time in perhaps her entire life, she is completely quiet. She pulls her chair closer and stares at my face. She looks into my eyes, searching them.

"Stop looking at me like I'm made of glass," I say. "I'm telling you I'm fine."

"Okay," she says, "okay." Her brow wrinkles in concentration as she goes to work. Her fingers trace my cheeks and eyes gently, maternally, and I have a sudden nervous urge to laugh. I fight it lest I get stabbed in the eye with blue eyeliner, but the more the laughter sits there pushing against my closed lips, the more hysterical it feels, like it could split off into tears at any moment. I bite my teeth and make myself stop laughing, seek the mask of icy resolve I have come to rely on staring back at me in the mirror. But something has changed in me, and all I see is the water moving underneath.

"Don't forget to use concealer," I say, "and at least two coats of masca—"

"Zip it," she says, angling her chair so I can't see past her. "You're going to look great." Which only makes me panic.

An entirely too-quick fifteen minutes later, she stops and sits back. Her eyes move slowly back and forth across my face. A solemn look comes over her. "My God," she says.

"What?" I say nervously.

"I'm a genius. An honest-to-God genius."

I stand up and look hopefully in the mirror. My face is practically bare. "No way in hell! You're out of your mind." I grab for my makeup bag, but she bats my hand away.

"You are not touching my masterpiece."

"Seriously. Give it. I can't wear just this." I reach for the bag again, but she fakes to the left and dodges out of the bathroom, waving my makeup case like a captured flag in her hand.

I run after her, chasing her around the room. She laughs and screams as I lunge for her, but I am not finding this remotely funny. Finally she stops running and turns, revealing a guilty face and empty hands.

"Where is it? Stop screwing around! I'm serious!"

"I know! *Way* too serious!"

"Zoey!" She doesn't understand that this isn't some little joke to me, that my very survival feels at stake.

She grabs my arm and pulls me back into the bathroom and pushes me in front of the mirror. "Look," she says. "Look how pretty you are."

I resist looking. I think of the hospital, how every time Dr. Meeks would try to make someone talk about their problems in group therapy, James would get very serious and say, "I think the problem with everyone here is that we're all looking into a distorted mirror." Then he and I would crack up laughing because, of course, mirrors in mental hospitals cannot be made with sharps like glass and are therefore warped and fuzzy.

"Please," I say to Zoey.

"Okay, listen," she says. "If you can't trust what you see in the mirror, how about trusting what you see here." She points to herself. "I'm your best friend in the world and I would never mislead you." Our eyes meet for a second and the words *best friend* land in some soft place I didn't even know was there.

"Fine," I say. "Can I at least have my lipstick?"

She sighs and goes and gets me my lipstick. "Be sparing," she says. "Chris doesn't want to kiss a stick of Maybelline."

I put an extra-thick coat on my lips and then dab it onto my cheeks to double as a blush. "Ha!" I say as I watch her face in the mirror. It's still way less than I usually wear, but it's enough to make me feel better.

"Jerk," Zoey says, and rolls her eyes. "Now let's go downstairs. I'm sure your boyfriend is already down there looking for you."

"He's not my—"

"Yeah, yeah. Screw your mother."

The elevator opens onto the hotel lobby, which is teeming with girls in dresses and guys in suits moving at various paces toward the ballroom. Their faces are shiny with excitement as they move stiffly in their formal clothes, reminding me of those toy soldiers at Christmas with their rosy cheeks and wooden bodies. Lights twinkle from the chandeliers, and the crowd is an animated murmur of voices, occasionally interrupted by laughter. The energy is contagious.

Zoey grabs my wrist. "You look amazing," she says in my ear. Then she adds, "As do I," which makes me laugh enough to settle my nerves.

"You really do," I say. "You are stunning and you don't even have to try."

She turns and throws her arms around me and squeezes me tight, and before I can register the shock of being hugged, she lets go and we enter the ballroom. The party is already in full swing, although for a formal dance, hardly anyone seems to be dancing.

"Whatever you do, don't leave me," I say.

I surreptitiously scan the room for Chris while Zoey zeroes in on the food table like a hunter to a moose.

"Oh my GOD!" she says as she drags me by the wrist, beelining for a chocolate fondue fountain rimmed with fruits to dip. "If you can't find me at the end of the night, I'll probably be doing laps in this."

"Helloooo, ladies." Some random guy lurches toward us, a flask tucked inside the waist of his pants. He steps right up to Zoey and peers into her eyes. "You have the most beautiful brown eyes I've ever seen," he slurs. "Wanna dance?"

"Oh Jesus," she says. "My eyes are green. And you're depressing me."

"Is that a no?"

"Is that a bald spot?"

He shrugs and then turns to me. "You have the most beautiful green eyes I've ever seen."

I hear someone clear their throat behind me and Zoey says, "Hi, Chris." I instantly regret dumping that stiff drink down the drain. I turn and there he is, looking somehow taller and older in his button-down and black pants, although there is still that boyishness behind his eyes, like he's embarrassed to be dressed up.

"Wow," he says, standing back to look at me.

"Doesn't she look pretty?" Zoey says.

He nods and blushes, and for one moment I truly feel pretty, actually believe that I am, or at least that I am to somebody.

"You have the most beautiful green eyes I've ever seen," he says with a fake slur. "Wanna dance?"

I laugh, and he grabs my hand and tugs me toward the dance floor.

"Woohoo!" Zoey calls.

"No! Please!" I say, resisting like a stubborn dog on a leash. "I can't!"

He drags me to the middle of the room where a smattering of couples are dancing with each other and a group of random drunk girls are dancing with themselves.

"See! It's way too early. Hardly anyone is dancing yet. And seriously, I'm the worst."

"Shh." He puts his hands around my waist and pulls me close.

I glance around, certain that I will embarrass myself somehow.

"Relax," Chris says. "No one is looking."

Reluctantly I put my hands on his shoulders, and then wonder if that's where I'm even supposed to put them. I look around at other couples to be sure. We start to move, sort of swaying side to side, and I'm like a lumbering elephant the way I can't get in time to the music, don't quite know what to do with my feet.

"Stop trying to lead," Chris whispers with a laugh, and I cringe with humiliation. Just as I'm about to break free and run off the dance floor, he pulls me closer against him. The smell of his cologne surrounds me and his strong shoulder is nice against my cheek. I want to pull away, but even as I do, some long-buried part of me, tender and aching for touch, awakens, makes me want to move closer.

"Now you're getting it," he says.

Encouraged, I start to breathe, to relax a little bit, to forget the other people in the room and my mother and all that has led up to this night. We rock back and forth, and after a while the awkwardness starts to fade, lulled out of me by the music and the swaying. The song changes, and changes again, until I stop hearing the changes at all; the tempo, whether fast or slow, becomes irrelevant to us, the music retreating into background noise. I become aware only of the rough cloth of Chris's jacket against my cheek, of the tender and perplexing act of being pressed gently against another human being, wanted close. Chris rubs his hands up and down my back and the nerve endings on my skin come alive, raw and reaching after a lifetime of not being touched or held. I can feel my breath deepening, my defenses coming down despite myself.

"Let's go outside," he says, and then he is leading me off the dance floor and I am following blindly, hardly aware of my surroundings or myself. We step out onto the terrace and the sudden cool air is like the snap of a hypnotist's fingers, and I remember myself, remember that I don't know how to do this thing I'm doing.

I look back into the ballroom, scan the crowd for Zoey. Chris pulls me toward the railing of the balcony, which overlooks the ocean. He stands beside me and I stare down into the black, breathing sea, giving him my profile so that he won't try to kiss me. I can feel him watching me, until finally it becomes rude for me to keep avoiding his eyes.

"Why do you keep looking at me like that?" I say, even as I know that to speak is to ruin the moment.

He doesn't answer, just turns to face me and puts his hand on the small of my back, guiding me toward him. My breath catches and my heart pumps and booms like the ocean. He slides his hand to the back of my neck.

I want to run.

I don't want to run.

His hand moves to my cheek, fingertips in my hair. I start to speak. He leans down and touches his lips against mine.

The sounds of the party and the ocean bleed together until there is no sound at all. My mind quiets too, moves to a place where there is no fear, no worry that I don't know how to do this, because I am doing it and it's natural and right and so perfect I can't stand it.

My mother was definitely wrong, I think. *He does like me.* I can be liked. The thought abruptly pulls me out of the moment, feels dangerous somehow, full of expectation.

"I have to find Zoey," I say, pulling away, realizing I've been gone too long—both from her and from myself.

Chris follows me inside and there is Zoey, not far from where I left her, only now she is chatting with Murph, whom, if her signature hair-twirling move is any indication, she appears to like again. At least for the night.

I smile and move eagerly toward her the way a kid might race to their mother after a carnival ride—excited to have ventured out, relieved to be returning to their secure base.

"There you are! I was just about to go finish off the shallow end of the chocolate fountain."

I'm shocked to discover how quickly the night is passing, how completely I have lost track of time.

"Holy shit, is the band playing Creed right now?" Zoey says. "I think that may be our cue to leave."

"I could go for room service," I say, thinking I'd like nothing better than to get out of here before anything can ruin this perfect night.

Chris offers to escort me upstairs.

"Well, hold on, you're coming, right, Zo?" I say.

"I'll be up in two seconds," she says, and then looks over at Murph like she's sizing up a piece of chocolate-covered fruit.

"Promise?" I say, nodding my head toward Murph.

"Promise!" she says with an eye roll. "Order me a burger."

Chris and I step into the too-bright elevator, which reminds me of how little makeup I'm wearing. The doors close and suddenly it occurs to me that we are alone in this climbing box with no windows, no escape. I re-press the button to the sixth floor even though it's already glowing. The doors open and I speed-walk ahead of him to my room, sobering up, though I never had a drink.

"Well . . ." I say when we reach my door, "that was fun." I try to make a quick exit into my room but the magnetic key won't work. Chris takes it from me and slides it into the lock. It instantly releases.

Before I can say good night, he kisses me quiet, moving me backward into the room.

I pull away. "Zoey will be up soon."

"Just for a minute?" he says, between kisses. "I don't want to leave you yet."

I start to say no, but then I realize that it would only be because I'm afraid and I don't want to be afraid, want to prove to Liz, to myself, that I'm normal, that I can let my guard down. Besides, it feels so good and natural that I realize I don't actually want to say no. The room is dark, and we almost trip over Zoey's overnight bag before Chris gently lowers me onto the bed, cradling my back and head all the way down. He moves on top of me, and there is that whoosh in my stomach again as he looks into my eyes.

"You okay?" he says.

I nod yes and he brushes my hair away from my face with his hands. He looks at me all tender and sweet, and even though I know it's not, it feels like love the way his eyes flicker with light as they look into mine. I put my hands on his back, surprised by how strong and wide it is, surprised how his weight on top of me is not threatening but securing, anchoring me to this moment, to the earth. He moves over me and all of my thoughts recede as my body takes over. My breathing changes and soon I find it hard to separate his chest from mine.

"I like you so much," he says, smiling.

I want to say, *You too,* am trying to make myself say it, when his hand glides slowly down my waist. For a second I stiffen. I tell my body to relax, to go back to how it felt a moment before, but my nerves start to jangle. I focus on the smell of his cologne and the feel of his back under my hands, the way it feels when he looks into my eyes.

The jangling quiets, and it's okay again. I am in the moment again, and maybe it doesn't feel so bad to have his hand on my waist. He smiles at me and I smile back and wonder if he can see the strain.

"Still good?" he asks, and I say yes, because more than anything else, I *want* to be good, want to be okay. His other hand moves, climbs up my leg. I squeeze my eyes shut, and there is a strange flash in my head like the deadly zap of a bug light. A woman's voice in my head calls my name.

Caasssieeee.

For a split second I lose all sense of where I am. I open my eyes.

Chris is breathing harder now. His hands are everywhere. I want him to stop, but I don't want him to think that I'm weird or a prude. I think of how Zoey wouldn't be scared of any of this, how she would enjoy it.

Sounds become heightened. The tick of the clock and the muffle of voices through the wall next door grow deafening. Footsteps in the hallway, and I pray that it is Zoey, that she will open the door and save me.

Chris's fingers touch the hem of my dress. He pushes the material up slightly. The air hits too far up my exposed legs. I try to move beneath him but his weight has me pinned.

Where is Zoey?

His hands move higher still, and I close my eyes so tightly that I can hear the wind it creates in my head. He's not even Chris anymore—just a weight, a trap, a shadow of something I don't want. His fingers touch my underwear.

"Stop!" I shout, pushing him off of me.

He rolls onto his side. "What's wrong? What happened?"

I sit up. My mind spinning. A flood of thoughts without words. "You need to leave," I say, yanking down my dress.

"What? Why?"

He reaches his hand toward my arm and I jump off the bed like it's burning.

"Don't touch me!" My voice is shaking. "Just get away from me!"

Even in the dark I can see the stunned look on his face.

He stands and places his hands in the air in appeasement. "I don't understand," he says. He moves toward me. "What did I do?"

I back up.

He keeps coming.

"Talk to me," he says.

I'm against the wall now. He's between me and the door.

"Cass."

I glance at the doorknob, willing it to turn, for Zoey to appear. My need to escape is so big, so necessary to my survival that I'd do anything to make it happen.

"Leave!" I scream. "Or I'm calling the cops!"

His mouth drops. "Are you serious?"

"I am totally fucking serious!" I point to the door. "Get out!"

He shakes his head, stops and then shakes it again. "This is crazy," he says. He looks at me in complete disbelief. "*You're* crazy."

Zoey's hairbrush is on the dresser beside me and I pick it up and hurl it past his head. "GET THE FUCK OUT OF MY ROOM!" I scream so loud that I feel like I'm going to shatter.

He dodges the brush and stands back up, wide-eyed. Then he marches out, slamming the door behind him as he goes. For one second I am relieved, can breathe again. Then all at once I start shaking like I'm going to die. I have no idea what the hell is wrong with me. I just shake and shake and wait for Zoey, but she never comes.

My mother was right. About all of it. No one can love me. I am crazy.

forty

IT'S BEEN HOURS since I kicked Chris out of the hotel room and still Zoey does not return.

The shaking does not stop. It worsens. It is an earthquake, rattling my internal beams and supports. I pace the hotel room, back and forth, trying to escape it. My thoughts spin and bang into each other like a crowd running for the exits, finding them blocked. It's a trap. The whole place is a trap. There is no way out of me. My nerves trill like a fire alarm, triggering a flood of sprinklers, all that water spilling everywhere, and nowhere for it to go. I drown in my own panic. Back and forth, back and forth, rubbing my arms up and down, filled with the sickening surety that I am going to die, that my mind will break up into pieces at any moment.

Exhaustion takes over just when it seems it never will. The same nightmare I've had since I was a child returns, the one that woke me up so many nights in the hospital, the one that Dr. Meeks tried to press me to talk about. It sucks me down into its terror. I try to resist, to wake myself up, but just like always, the nightmare wins.

I am playing hide-and-seek with my friends in an old haunted house. I find a good hiding spot in a closet and crouch down low, wait quietly for the hunt to begin. After a while, I realize that no one seems to be looking for me and I start to get worried.

I hear footsteps approaching and someone calling my name. It's someone I know, but I can't picture their face. Whoever it is is counting: twenty-six, twenty-seven. But the voice changes as it counts, becomes inhuman, ghostly and threatening.

I hold my breath, hoping the ghost won't hear me, but then I think that if I'm too quiet, my mother won't know that I need her, and I want desperately for her to come find me.

I start to scream for her. I scream for my mother as loud as I can and I am afraid she won't come, certain she won't come, but then all of a sudden she flings open the door to the closet where I'm hiding and smiles at me. "There you are!" she says.

"Mom!" I say, so relieved and grateful. "Thank God it's you! There's a ghost after me!"

She smiles again, only now her teeth are old and broken. "I know," she says. Then she turns, still smiling, and calls to the ghost, "Yoo-hoo! She's in here!"

I wake with a gasp, waves of panic slamming me, pinning me to the bed. Even with my eyes wide open, the dream feels alive, harassing, demanding my attention. There is something in it this time, something I can't shake. I can feel it just out of reach like a name at the tip of the tongue. The voice. It's familiar. I lie very still, hardly breathing, trying not to feel anything. Every itch or tingle or ache in my body triggers another surge of terror as if my body itself is the threat, as if I have swallowed the ghost and now it is possessing me.

I think of all the foolish hope I had when I left the hospital, how I stood before the ocean trying so hard to believe that I could start over, that I was fine, that I wasn't what they said I was. I stare at the colorless dawn outside the window and think of all my friends who are still locked up. I imagine them looking out on the same bleak morning, trapped in time and yet, unlike me, still able to hold on to the dream that it's possible to really be free from our pasts.

And now, just as in the hospital, in spite of everything my past has taught me, I can't stop myself from longing for my mother.

I wake up around 10:00 A.M., leave the hotel without bothering to check out, call a cab, return to the dorm and immediately start packing. The room seems strange to me. What once looked messy and lived-in now has the quality of sudden, unexpected disaster about it. I pick my clothes up off the floor and stuff them into my suitcase without bothering to fold them. My hands shake so badly, I keep dropping things.

I'm almost finished when Zoey rolls in, still in her homecoming dress, now wrinkled with what looks like chocolate dribble down the front.

"What are you doing?" she says when she notices my entire side of the room has been cleaned out.

"What does it look like I'm doing?" I put my pillow on top of my suitcase.

"It looks like you're leaving."

I walk past her into the bathroom, check the cabinet for anything I might have missed. She follows me.

"I don't understand. Did something happen? Why won't you look at me?"

Her presence makes the hollowness in my stomach ache.

"You're not going to talk to me?" she says.

Some part of me pulls toward her, longs for repair, for the familiar comfort of my friend, but it's like I've gone far into the back of my head and closed the door, and even if I wanted to, I know I'll never be dumb enough to open it for her again.

"Nothing to talk about," I say flatly. "You left me. Now I'm leaving you."

"What? How did I leave you?" she says, and the fact that she doesn't know only makes it worse. "Because I didn't come back to the room last night? Is that what you're all mad about?"

She says this like it's a small thing.

I go to the closet and grab the last few pieces from their hangers. I chuck the rest of the hangers into the trash. Zoey no longer exists in this room. I have made her disappear.

"Don't you think we should talk about this?" she says.

I try to zip my suitcase.

"I mean, I get that you're pissed and I'm sorry I didn't come have a burger with you or whatever, but this is a little ridiculous."

The zipper won't budge so I sit on the suitcase to flatten it down.

"You know, honestly, I'm kinda sick of the way you're always mad at me about something," she says. "I shouldn't have to baby-sit you."

The suitcase finally closes and I stand. I turn to Zoey, steeled with cold hatred. "Well, don't worry," I say. "You'll never have to see me again." I walk out the door and slam it shut. Behind me, I hear the door open again.

"Cassie!" Zoey calls.

I turn the corner, bounce my suitcase down the stairs and leave.

I begin the long trek to the bus stop, but take a detour to the beach one last time, knowing it could be years, if ever, before I see it again. The ocean is choppy and empty of surfers. The water is icy gray; it looks like the kind of cold that cuts. Little white peaks break and shatter. The wind is bigger here, the sun strained. A stormy tide retreats, leaving only wreckage and debris—the bones of the sea.

I think of my surfing lesson with Chris, how far away it seems, like I was a different person then, like we were both different people. Some part of me, small and wiser than my feelings, knows that the difference is only in my mind, that the experience of last night feels bigger, worse, more twisted than it actually was, but I can't stop it from feeling so big, and I don't know why it does, and obviously I must be crazy and Meeks was right—I am not ready to be in the world.

I sit on the beach for a long time, taking in these last hours of freedom, and then I go to the pay phone in the parking lot. I need to call James and let him know that I'm coming back to the hospital. It kills me to have to admit that he was wrong about me, wrong for believing in me, that we were both wrong about that. I tell myself he'll understand, that he will forgive me for my failure. He has to forgive me. He is all I have left.

I look at my watch. It's just after dinnertime there. Most of the patients will be in the TV room. Shelly will be playing Scrabble with herself just outside the group. James will have claimed DJ status over the small stereo by the pool table, pausing between shots to strum the pool cue as if it's an electric guitar. I can see them all in their respective places like a still life. I recall how exciting it was when the pay phone rang on the unit, a novelty in the long, unchanging days. I can practically hear James saying, "If that's the White House calling again, tell the prez I'm busy."

I dial and the phone picks up. It's Shelly.

"Hey," I say, and there is relief in the pure fact that she's okay, that she's still alive. I remember the foreboding I felt on the day I left, staring at her scarred wrists. "It's Cassie."

It takes her a beat too long to remember. But then she calls to the others that it's me, and I want to sit down on the ground and curl up in a ball, both comforted and horrified by the sense of belonging this brings me. Trish jumps on the phone and fires off a half dozen questions about life on the outside, wanting to know how great college is, how happy I am to be free. I avoid my own face in the warped mirror of the pay phone.

"Would you mind putting James on a sec?" I say finally. "I need to talk to him."

There is a pause.

"Oh, shit, you didn't hear?"

"They didn't already discharge his crazy ass, did they?" I say, suddenly remembering that James said he'd be getting out soon.

Another pause.

"Cassie, James killed himself."

"What?"

"They let him out last week and he . . . shot himself."

I clutch the phone between two hands, holding myself up with it. I try to speak but all the wind is knocked out of me, knocked out of the sky.

"Cass, are you still there?"

"I don't understand . . . Are you sure there wasn't some mistake . . . He wouldn't—"

"I'm sure. The funeral was a few days ago. None of us were allowed to go. I'm really sorry."

I can see the ocean from where I'm standing. The sun is not so much setting as fading, the ashy tint of early evening beginning to settle over everything.

Trish keeps talking.

The world looks changed, flattened, like I'm standing outside of it, looking at a picture of it.

She tells me everything she knows, from the group meeting held by the staff to what she read in the newspaper when she was out on a day pass with her parents. I grab on to every detail, as if to know exactly what happened would be to chase it backward, make it unhappen, be with James again so he wouldn't be alone in that unspeakable, definitive darkness of no one there.

It is only when there are no details left for her to tell that I grasp, for just a moment, that he is really gone. I hang up and walk around the parking lot in circles, my arms outstretched in supplication, struggling to hold something they cannot hold.

James.

Circling, circling. My breath comes in gasps. The one person who knew all of me, who knew the worst of me, the ugly, broken, mental hospital me. And loved me anyway. Gone now. And I didn't help him, didn't stop him, didn't even know he was in that much pain. I need to do something, put this news somewhere, deposit it like a bomb and run away from it.

James. Please. No.

I can't. It's too much. There is no one now. Nothing now. Nowhere now. *Please help me,* I think, but the whole world is empty.

I walk toward the ocean, which pushes and breathes like a living thing. The sky has turned dark, and where the water meets it, it looks like the end of the world. I want to walk out into it, to the place where it all stops. I remember how easy it seemed the last time I was out there drowning to just let go, to stop swimming, to surrender to that lethal watery hug.

I take a step. The water is freezing as it seeps into my shoes. But it is only an intellectual cold. My body feels nothing. The ocean tugs me forward with its promise. Just wade out until it swallows me, until I disappear, until it's over. The image of the pink surfboard comes to me, the two fish painted on its nose, swimming in opposite directions. It had felt like a choice then: toward life or away. Now that choice seems gone. I have destroyed everything. James is dead. There is nothing left.

You said we would be fine, James. You said the past was the past, that we could start over. But it just repeats on a loop, pain on top of pain.

I think of my mother. According to Trish, the newspaper said that James had called his mother at work, told her he loved her that afternoon. Had he hoped that she would hear the call of death in his voice, come running, stop him just in time? I recognize the wish, that deep, ancient longing for mother to hear and to come and to soothe. Did I owe my mother that call, that chance? Would she finally hear my need? Would she finally come to my rescue? I turn and look toward the parking lot. Maybe if I tell her I'm sorry. Maybe if I just surrender to her truth, accept all fault. Maybe then.

The night seems huge and desolate around me as I walk small and stunned back to the parking lot. When I get to the pay phone, I realize I'm out of quarters. I call collect. In my distress, it takes a minute to even remember my home number.

The phone rings. I watch the black, churning ocean and think of riptides.

She answers on the third ring, and the operator asks her if she will accept the charges. "Yes," she says.

There is a quick pause.

"Cassie?"

I start to speak but nothing comes.

"Hello? Can you hear me?"

The sound of her voice brings none of the hoped-for comfort.

"Hello?"

Only the sense of going under.

"Cassie!"

Of two dark shadows submerged and fighting each other the whole way down.

I look at the ocean. Toward life or away.

Listen to me, soldier, I hear James say in my head. *Run! Save yourself.*

I can't, James, I think. *I don't know how.*

"Hello? Cassie?"

I remember myself out in the waves, allowing the riptide to take me back and back and back, trusting that eventually I'd be freed.

"Cassie! Are you there?"

I start to answer when I hear that quiet little voice again: the one that saved me once before when I was drowning. Clear and calm and assured. It is the wiser fish. And I realize that in spite of everything that's happened, this time that voice—*my* voice—is a little stronger. *Yes,* it says, *I am still here.*

I watch myself hang up the phone and then stand there staring at it. I'm not sure what I've just done.

On a sudden whim, I dip my finger into the change slot like I did when I was a kid. To my surprise, I pull out a quarter. For all the times I've ever tried that, this is the first it's actually worked.

I look up at the sky.

James, I think, and the loss breaks over me again.

I take a deep breath and pick up the phone one last time.

forty-one

IN THE PITCH blackness I wait, holding my stomach as if my insides will fall out. I rock back and forth, trying to escape my own mind, to push everything away. There are footsteps in the hallway. I squeeze tighter, worried that she'll be angry that I've called her, angry that I need her. A sudden light and she is standing in the doorway.

"Cassie?" Liz says. Her face is creased with concern.

My legs wobble as I stand.

We move into the office and she switches on the lamp in there as well.

I put down my suitcase, sink into the couch.

She watches me worriedly as she takes her seat. "What happened?"

I stare at the floor by her feet, dazed. I want to talk, to get it out, but I'm out to sea, can't find the way in.

"You found this out today?" she says softly of James. The only thing I managed to get out on the phone.

I nod, slowly swimming back. I don't want to swim back to this.

Liz inhales deeply, shakes her head. "It's awful," she says. "I can see how much he meant to you."

Something chokes at the back of my throat. The word *meant*—past tense. Pressure builds in my temples, in my chest a dull scream. I look up at her. "He had just been released from the hospital. He had just gone home."

Liz makes a small, sympathetic sound. Her eyes are round and soft and reaching. The flood pushes against me. I press my arms into my stomach, holding it back.

"I don't understand. He was the one who always talked about getting out. He was the one who said we'd be fine. And then he didn't even try. Why didn't he try?"

"I don't know," she says helplessly. "I wish I knew."

She moves her chair closer. A tightness yields in my chest, allowing her nearness. The sobs come from a place so deep, it's like they're deeper than my body, older than my life.

"It's just . . . we were the same, you know," I say, and my whole body trembles. Something pushes at me, some dark, underwater thing, like the bump of a shark.

"No," she says. "You weren't."

I wipe my tears with the back of my palm, but they keep coming faster. "I'm sorry, I'm sorry! I shouldn't have called you."

"Stop!" she says fiercely.

"I know you have better things to do."

"Listen to me," she says. "There is nowhere else I'd rather be right now. I am honored that you called me."

I roll my eyes, rub my nose on my sleeve.

"I know you can't possibly understand that. Your mother couldn't or wouldn't be with you. And now you think that no one can, that you're too much. But you're wrong. I can. I will."

I glance up at her, try to take it in, but it's only words against a lifetime. I look to the window, helpless, drowning. "But you don't know me. I screw everything up."

"I know that you're here. I know that you're sitting with me and you're talking about this and you're alive. And I'm so glad for that."

"But what's the point? Don't you see? What's the damn point if I push everyone away?"

"You haven't pushed me away."

"Not yet." I lean back, suddenly wanting distance.

"Then who?"

"Chris! Zoey! My mother!"

"What happened with Chris and Zoey?"

I put the palms of my hands to my eyes and shake my head, not wanting to relive it. At the same time, I want it out of me, want the relief of confession. I take a deep breath and tell her everything, the whole story from the hotel room with Chris until this morning with Zoey.

"I told you this would happen. I told you everything would go badly. But you didn't believe me! You said to trust that the world was different!"

The rage is right there, so easy to get to, so much simpler, less painful than the grief. One goes out, the other in.

"I never should have listened to you. I never should have trusted. I knew better and now—"

"And now what?"

"Now everything is ruined! Everything is ruined and I—" I shake my head again, trying to push back the feelings.

"And you what?"

"No! I'm not going to do this!"

"Cassie—"

"*FINE.* I FUCKING HATE YOU FOR IT, OKAY?"

The trembling starts immediately, internally, the old familiar rattle. The room shrinks, the air between us a taut wire. I want to move, to get up and leave, but I am fixed here, frozen, waiting. I cannot back down now, no matter the cost.

The shock of energy dissipates, and I dare to look at her, dare her to challenge my right to this fury. Her eyes are sad, without anger.

"Okay," she says. "You can hate me. I don't like it, but I accept it. I've disappointed you just like everyone else."

I sag into the couch, flattened by the sudden siphoning of rage. The tears return. "I know it's not fair, though . . . to hate everybody, it's not fair. I don't know what's wrong with me. I don't know why I act like this, why I got so crazy with Chris." I look at her pleadingly. "What's wrong with me?"

"You were protecting yourself."

"From what, though? He didn't do anything wrong."

I lean my head against the armrest, too exhausted to even think. All I want is to curl up in a ball and sleep, wake up to find it's all been a bad dream.

"I'm so tired. Can I just lie here for a minute? I just need to close my eyes."

She nods, and I let my lids go heavy. I think of James. His face is right in front of me, that mischievous smile. Always happy, always joking. I think of the funny made-up stories he used to tell about his life. I remember what Meeks said about James being afraid to let anyone know his true self and I wonder if he was right. I hate the thought of that asshole being right about anything, especially James. But what could be so awful that he couldn't let anyone else see it? That he would rather die than reveal it. If he even knew himself.

"He didn't sleep," I say, my eyes still closed.

"What?"

"James. Whenever I had one of my nightmares, the aides would let me come out and watch TV. James was always there. Every time I woke up in the middle of the night, there he was, smoking cigarettes and shooting the shit with the nurses like it was happy hour. I never thought about it."

At the mention of my nightmare, I feel it rise up again, swimming beneath the surface, its dark shadow circling. The familiar footsteps, the sound of someone counting, *"twenty-six, twenty-seven,"* my mother smiling as she invites death in. It nags at me once again.

I open my eyes. "I wonder if it means something," I say. "That he didn't sleep."

Liz is watching me with a soft look on her face, the way a mother might watch a sleeping child. I let my eyes close again and something shudders deep within me, a tiny sigh, like the creaking open of a door, letting in some light, some small sense of safety. I'm tired to my bones, could fall asleep so easily.

Then a flash in my head, again like the zap of a bug light. The woman's voice. *Caasssieeee.*

I sit up suddenly.

"What?" Liz says, looking at my startled face.

"I don't know." I try to shake it away. "This voice. I keep hearing it. The same one from my nightmares." A wave of nausea rolls through me.

"What's it saying?"

Images come at me. Standing in the driveway of my childhood home. My mother's car disappearing around the bend. Matthew and the neighborhood kids playing in the backyard as I walk toward the house. The sense that I could not let my mother down again.

I look up at Liz. "Dora," I say, and the sound of her long-unspoken name still carries a child's electric fear around it.

"Dora?"

"That's the voice. My great-aunt. My mother's best friend. She came to visit us once when I was, like, seven."

"Okay . . ." she says.

"And . . . I don't know. I . . . It's nothing." But my head feels lit up, racing.

"What are you seeing?"

"Just this memory. From when I was a kid."

I'm in my childhood bedroom waiting for Dora. She comes in saying, "Caasssieeee" in her singsong voice. The neighbor's dog is barking. The burn of fall is in the air.

"My mother wanted us to be friends. She made me promise to be good. So I asked Dora to read to me."

I can see Dora beside me, her gray hair like a cloud on top of her head, her powdery makeup settling into the creases of her skin. I'm in my favorite dress, the one with the rooster. She flips open a book of nursery rhymes.

Georgie Porgie puddin' and pie

Kissed the girls and made them cry

When the boys came out to play

Georgie Porgie ran away.

I look up at Liz. Tears start forming in my eyes, but I have no idea why they're there. It's as if my body knows something my mind does not.

And then I remember something else, something new. "I wanted to know why Georgie made the girls cry. I asked her that."

"And what did she say?" Liz asks, leaning forward.

"She said something like, 'Maybe they were bad little girls.' But they didn't look bad. So—"

I lurch back, feeling like I'm standing too close to the edge of a steep, dark canyon. "Forget it," I say to Liz. "This is stupid."

"It's not. Stay with it," she says.

"No." I shake my head.

"Okay then," she says, looking at me intensely. "Just breathe."

But I don't want to breathe. I want to run, to open the door and just run for my life. It feels too dark and threatening, like whatever is there will break my brain apart.

Something comes, a quick picture that appears and then disappears just as fast. I shake my head again, instinctively, involuntarily, like I'm trying to shake it away.

"What is it?"

"I don't know! It's— I'm afraid," I say. But then I think of James. I imagine him, my James, my friend, alone in his house with a gun. And I know that I have to look. That as terrifying as this is, there is more danger in not looking.

I close my eyes. An image flashes in my mind: Dora's face swooping down suddenly. My neck jerks back as her lips mash against my mouth. They are soaked with spit.

"Ucck! Gross! Don't do that!" I say to her.

She laughs innocently. "I'm just being Georgie Porgie," she says.

I wipe my mouth as my whole body shakes with disgust.

Her face changes. "I thought you were going to be nice," she says.

I remember the sense that something was wrong. Everything was spinning, snapshots firing off too fast, the way the world flashes past the window of a speeding car. Dora's big face. The closed door. Red lips, puckered and angry.

Blood surges in my head, both then and now. My heart flutters in my chest like a rabbit's.

"Twenty-six, twenty-seven . . ." It's Matthew counting below my window. Shouting boys scatter like geese, looking for a place to hide.

I try to move away. Dora's hand grabs my wrist. The book of nursery rhymes falls to the floor with a thud.

"Twenty-eight, twenty-nine . . ." I know Matthew is standing in the driveway, his eyes squeezed shut, giving everyone time to hide. I will him to open his eyes. To come inside. To save me.

"Thirty!" he says. "Here I come!"

Dora pushes me back on the bed, pinning me by my shoulders. My thoughts spin wildly, like I'm on a ride going too fast.

She climbs on top of me, pushes up my dress. Her old, wrinkled face is close to mine, watching my terror, enjoying it.

"No!" I say.

Every muscle in my body strains to get away. But she's too strong, too heavy, burying me beneath her. I am trapped, my own body a coffin. I scratch against the seams of myself, clawing to escape.

"Gotcha," Matthew shouts, and whoever he catches groans.

"Be a good girl," Dora whispers with a gruesome smile.

My body kicks and flails and thrashes, but my mind is somewhere else. Way back in a cramped and tiny space in the base of my skull, hiding.

"Cassie," Liz says.

"I'm sorry," I sob. Everything is a jumble. Pieces of recollection fly faster than I can keep up with them. New images and sensations flood me: sharp stabs of pain, her hand over my nose and mouth, a soundless scream, *I can't breathe, I can't breathe.*

"What are you sorry for?" Liz moves her chair closer.

"I don't know!" I say. My breath comes hard like I'm hyperventilating, my body still trying to expel something, throw it up. "Whatever I did!"

I can't look at Liz, won't open my eyes, it's all too awful.

"Cassie, listen to me."

I keep my head down, my hands over my face. The shame is too great.

"Look at me!" she says.

But I can't.

"You did nothing wrong. She was sick! Do you understand me? This is not your fault."

"I know," I say, "I know." But the shame is bigger than my knowing. It is a dark and formless slithering in my body, unchanged by words or logic. It is in the complicity that it was my body that it happened to. "It's just . . . there had to be a reason. If I hadn't been such a nuisance, my mother wouldn't have needed to get away. Or if I just hadn't gone upstairs—"

"No!" she says forcefully. "Sometimes bad things just happen. You want there to be a reason so you can have control, but what happened to you, Cassie, was not your fault."

"But then . . . why me? Why did she pick me?"

"Because you were there! And from everything you told me, it sounds like you had no protection. *That's* the reason!"

Her voice is so fierce and so sure that I dare to look up at her. Liz's presence seems huge, her energy both encompassing and shielding. I feel like an abandoned cub in the face of a lioness. My breath comes in gasps, a child's gulping tears.

"I tried to tell my mother not to leave me with Dora. I hated her. I sensed something. But my mother thought I was just being selfish."

"Listen to me, Cassie. I wish she hadn't left that day. I wish like hell this hadn't happened to you. But I'm here with you now and I'm not going anywhere."

A small sound escapes me, a last mournful yelp. I look into Liz's eyes. They are soft again, holding. Something shifts in me. I can almost hear the click of it in my brain, some internal computer updating, some small bit of suffering released like a balloon. It's hard to process or accept but some part of me recognizes with relief that I am not alone with this anymore.

The light in the room goes in and out of focus—brighter, then blurry like the movement of candlelight. I feel like I'm emerging from a time warp. "Holy shit," I say.

Liz nods, breathing slowly as if she too has just surfaced.

"How could I have forgotten that?"

"Your mind did what it needed to do. It protected you from something too painful to remember."

As she says this, I see again the closed door, feel Dora's adult strength, hear the distant sounds of Matthew laughing and counting, oblivious to my need for rescue. I'd always believed he was the one person who could save me from falling through the Earth, an illusion I clung to long after it had been disproved. Now I realize that I just needed to believe in somebody.

"But why didn't I tell my mother?" I remember her coming into my room, asking me if I'd been a good girl for Dora.

Liz shakes her head as if to say she doesn't know. "Maybe you thought she wouldn't believe you or she would blame you or that she wouldn't do anything to help you."

I think of Dora lying about the candy she said she had brought me, telling my mother I had a "big imagination," setting me up as the liar, letting me know which one of us would be believed. My hatred boils, bigger than me, spilling over my insides. I hate my mother too for believing her, for taking Dora's word over mine. Still, the idea that she wouldn't have protected me seems impossible, that a mother, even *my* mother, wouldn't have saved her own child. "But if I had just told her—"

"Then what? She would have loved you?"

"I don't know. Maybe things would've been different."

"Maybe. Maybe not. We can't know."

"I still should have told her."

"Cassie."

"What?"

"This is not your fault. You were a child! You didn't even have a name for what it was that happened to you."

I let my head fall against the back of the couch. There is so much more I want to say, so many questions I want to ask, but I'm so drained that my voice feels irretrievable, like it has fallen into a deep well. I struggle through my exhaustion to grasp what has happened and what it means.

Not my fault.

I wonder how long that will take to sink in. All these years I'd had the nagging sense of having done something terrible, of *being* terrible. All this time and I wasn't to blame. I stare at the ceiling, my hand on my forehead.

"What?" Liz says.

But I don't know what. There's so much there, all these dark feelings clamoring to be released and yet, surprisingly, there is also relief in the purging, my whole body like a long-held fist finally unclenching after all the years of keeping this memory locked up tight. And there is some hope too, in the knowledge that it wasn't me, that I wasn't the bad one.

I think of James, of how he won't get this chance I'm having, to understand himself better. My heart aches with sorrow. I glance at the clock, realize that I have been here for almost two hours.

I sit forward again, look into Liz's eyes. The memory of my mother pulling out of the driveway returns—the sense of abandonment so pure and true and encapsulating that it is, in some way, the hardest image of all.

"Thank you for being here and, you know . . . helping me," I manage to say, and the tears fall again.

"Anytime, Cassie," she says, and now there are tears in her eyes too.

"So what happens now?" My voice is weak and hoarse. "I mean, what do we do with this?"

"I think we just keep doing what we're doing."

"Okay," I say.

Our eyes meet again and something happens, something so fleeting that it's more like the possibility of something happening. For just one second, I can grasp the idea of a world without terror as its only face, a world where trust is possible. For just one moment, I can imagine.

forty-two

IT IS STRANGE to step outside again, like emerging from a movie theater to the shock that the world has continued in your absence. The trees are alive with movement and all across the campus, windows are lit up like rows and rows of little souls. I notice them—all those lights, all the people whose lives they represent. I have been stuck inside my head too long, afraid to look.

I sit with my suitcase in the campus courtyard for hours, just thinking as the night air moves around me. It's like I've been skinned, the way my whole body is permeated by the slightest wind, the way my edges blur with the night. I am completely raw and vulnerable and deeply sad, and for better or worse, fully present to my life for the first time in a long time.

Eventually, I return to the dorm, exhausted. In the hallway, I stop and stare at Zoey's door. I long to repair things, but I don't have it in me right now to try. I'm so tired, so fragile. I still have the key code to my original room and I am desperate to lie down and make this day be over. I open the door and stop cold in the entrance.

My mother stands in the bare white space, tall and dark as a shadow in her crow-black coat and high boots. The harsh light of the bare overhead bulb makes her face angular and hard.

"There you are!" she says sharply. "Thank God! Where have you been?"

"I . . ." I try to gather myself. To regain my balance. "What are you doing here? How did you get in?"

"The door was unlocked. And what do you mean, what am I doing here? Of course I came right away. I got that strange collect call from you and . . . after the way you treated me the last time we talked, I knew something was wrong. You weren't yourself."

I stiffen, remembering our last conversation, how she blamed me for the affair, hung up on me when I wouldn't come running.

"I got worried you'd fallen into some kind of trouble with that friend of yours."

"I'm not in trouble."

"And then when I got here, your door was cracked open and your room was bare . . . I didn't know if . . . Jesus, you look terrible." She notices my suitcase. "Oh good, you're already packed. We're on the same page then."

I look down at my suitcase. It seems a lifetime ago when I packed it. "What are you talking about?"

"It's my fault for letting you come here when you weren't ready. You're obviously not well." She grabs her purse off the bed. "We can discuss things on the road. I hate driving late at night."

Her energy is overwhelming. I'm so exhausted, need everything to slow down. "I called you because James died," I say.

"James?" She looks at me, confused. "Who's James?"

"My best friend in the hospital," I say. The tears choke at the back of my throat. I wrap my arms around myself, in need of layers. "He killed himself."

"Oh, that's terrible," she says. She sits down on the bare mattress and holds her hand to her mouth. "I'm sorry to hear that."

My throat tightens. Part of me longs to sit down beside her and weep, make it all go away. It would be so easy. To just pretend. But another part of me repels the idea.

"Mom," I say. "There's something else." I know I need to tell her what I remember. The words have been sitting there my whole life, buried, waiting to come out.

She looks up at me. I can feel the longing, the pleading in my eyes. She frowns. "Let me get my keys and we'll go. Whatever it is, you can tell me in the car." She digs hurriedly into her purse. "You know, Matthew thinks I'm crazy, taking you home after all you've put us through—"

"Mom—"

"—but I know you've changed. I know you'll be a good girl. I always thought your father was the cause of your troubles, and if he actually has the balls to go through with this divorce, he'll be gone soon."

"Mom."

"Not that I think he does . . . have the balls. I mean . . . he's bluffing, don't you think? I think he is."

"Mom!"

She looks up. Her eyes are both penetrating and impatient. My voice dries up. I don't know how to say this, these words that will change everything. It's all right there and I know that once it's out, she'll finally see that it was never me, that I was never the problem, that there was this other horrible unspoken thing between us.

"There's something I never told you," I say. "About . . . Dora. Something that Dora did to me." I can feel Liz inside of me, holding me up.

"What do you mean? What . . . something?" Her hands fall into her lap and her body goes very still except for her mouth, which starts twitching. She stares at me, eyes wide and unblinking. Then she looks toward the door, toward the window, her eyes darting desperately, seeking escape.

"She . . . molested me," I say. The words sound so strange said aloud. I don't want to take ownership of them, don't want that word attached to me. I hate that there is still a shame in it for me right now, that even as my mind knows the shame belongs only to Dora, my body still carries it, feels tainted by it.

I watch my mother's face, seeking in her eyes the absolution and reassurance that the child I once was still needs.

She looks at the floor. And then out the window. She does not look at me. When she speaks, her voice is flat and far away. "Your grandmother always hated her, you know. She said Dora messed with Uncle Billy when we were kids. But I don't remember anything like that."

I stare at her, shocked, horrified. I think again of Billy. The game of pool. How I'd fled the basement in terror when he'd reached for the ball that had landed in my lap. How Billy ran after my mother on Thanksgiving, begged her to listen to him, told her he was worried about me.

"So you knew what she was?" The sickening memories of

Dora rush back in. "You knew what she was and you let her into our house?!"

"I only knew what they said," she says innocently.

An ancient scream shrieks in my head, trapped and shattering my brain from the pressure.

She knew. She fucking knew.

I want to smash something, break something. Of course the goddamn room is bare.

All those years. All that damage. And my mother sitting so fucking innocent on the bed, expecting me to understand.

I try to calm myself. Everything is so tight, up in my throat. I hear Liz telling me to slow down, to breathe. I push my pain not away but to the side. Right now, I need something from my mother.

"Well, do you believe me?" I say, because somehow in this moment, this is most important, that she should bear witness, that she should not be allowed to leave me alone with this again. I stand, braced, defiant.

She doesn't say anything, but when I look into her eyes, there is such pure sadness there that I can see that she knows it's true, that she does believe me, even if she can't bring herself to say so.

It's not enough. I want her fury, the outrage of a mother. I want her to know what Dora took from me, what she took from both of us, what my mother allowed her to take.

"She said you wouldn't believe me. She told me you didn't . . . love me." My voice breaks. "She told me I was—bad."

A lifetime of pain sits out in the open, dug up like a casket, the two of us staring into it. And yet, I have learned through Liz that in the uncovering of the past lies the hope of healing it. I look at my mother, pleading with her to come with me, to be with me now at least, even though she could not be with me then. To find the courage.

Her hands tremble. She stands up, then sits again as if realizing there is no way to escape from this. I watch the entirety of it hit her, the understanding of what this means, the guilt at having failed to protect her child, for having deemed her own needs greater. She shakes her head, stops and repeats the gesture. She looks up at me, stunned and helpless. A small gasp or sigh escapes her. Her hands go to her neck, to where the chain that Dora gave her still hangs. She wraps her fingers around its heart and closes her eyes, rocking her body slowly like a little girl. She looks up at me, dazed, lost. Then something in her eyes changes. Her face snaps shut like a purse.

"We really should get going. It's late and I hate driving tired." I stop, stare at her.

"Now where the hell did I put those keys?" She digs back into her bag and then suddenly dumps the entire contents onto the bed. "My God, will you look at all this crap! Can you believe me?" She looks up at me and smiles, sheepish and dazzling. The sun comes out in her face. "Here's the credit card! Maybe we should go charge the hell out of it tomorrow, huh?" She waves it in the air. "Take that, Ed!" She laughs brightly. Then she pulls the keys out from beneath the pile. "Aha!" She holds them up to me, beaming, insisting I play along like usual.

All I can do is watch. All that sunshine, so grossly out of place here.

She tilts her head, making one last plea. Then she puts her smile away, stuffs her belongings into her purse and places it on her lap. She presses her knees tightly together, her eyes on the floor.

"I'm sorry, Cassie," she says. She looks up at me, composed, matter-of-fact. "Dora was like a mother to me. My memories of her are the only good memories I have of my childhood. I can't let you take that away from me."

I stare at her, expecting the scream again, the murderous impulse. Instead there is only a shock of clarity and the feeling of something shutting quietly but firmly, like the small click of elevator doors. I rise above the moment to see the whole. I recognize how unnatural it is for a mother to protect herself instead of her children, to continue to do so even now. There is no pain in this realization and that surprises me too. That facing the truth of who my mother is hurts less than holding on to the illusion that she could ever give me what I needed.

I think of how my whole life I believed it was my fault that my mother didn't love me. How I must have done something terrible to push her away. How I felt deep down, despite all my protests, that there must be something so awful at the very core of me that even my own mother wanted me to disappear. Now I see that it wasn't me. It wasn't even because of Dora. It was something bigger and deeper and, in some way, simpler than I ever realized. For all the time I spent in the mental hospital it was actually my mother who was—still is—ill.

A kind of pity moves into me as I look at her on the bed. I imagine the little girl she was, fighting, like I once did, to survive amidst monsters. Only in her case her brain was unable to survive intact. And now in her desperation to stay afloat, she continues to pull down everyone who would try to love her.

"I'm sorry too, Mom," I say. "I'm sorry for all that happened to you." I step back and hold the door open. She stands up and comes over to me, touches my cheek with her hand.

"You were always a good girl, Cassie," she says. "You always were."

I look into her eyes and I know that underneath the sickness, this is truly what she believes. And I know, too, that she can't hold that, can't stay here, won't believe it tomorrow. Her opinion of me will continue to change, depending on her state of mind, depending on what she needs from me in the moment, depending on how willing I am to sacrifice my truth for her pretend.

I am not willing.

She steps through the doorway.

"Good-bye, Mom," I say.

She turns and looks at me, startled. "What do you mean? You're coming with me."

"I can't," I say. "I just can't." Not now. Not ever. Not because I don't still love her in some way, but because I have to start loving myself.

I close the door, make sure the lock clicks into place, and sit down on the bare mattress, listening to my mother bang angrily on the door until she tires, as if it is only a matter of wood between us. As her footsteps finally move down the hall, it happens so slowly that I'm not sure if I'm imagining it, but I start to feel the current releasing me, like a roller coaster easing gradually into the gate.

I look down at my suitcase and imagine Zoey across the hall.

And then I think again of James.

forty-three

I RUMMAGE AROUND in my suitcase until I find the candle James bought me. It's still wrapped in the hospital toilet paper that I packed it in so it wouldn't get ruined. I unwrap it and put it on my windowsill and light it with his lighter. The little flame shoots up like a life. I turn off the overhead light and sit before the small glow. The flame flickers and moves without wind and I imagine that James is making it happen, that he is here with me, has come back once again because he couldn't leave without saying good-bye.

There is so much I want to say, so much I want him to know. I tell him how sorry I am that he felt so hopeless, and how I wish I had known, had been able to help. I thank him for being my friend and for saving me, both in the hospital and now. I tell him that I love him and that I will miss him. I sit with him for a long, long time, and then I blow out the candle and tell him good-bye.

In the morning, the October sun is sitting at the window, waking me with its warm light. The day seems nearly bursting with it, everything made vivid. I sit up on the bare mattress and put my hands on the glass, and then I push open the window to smell the air and feel the cold. The world is strange, or I feel strange in it—full of hope and sorrow, both at once.

I go across the hall and stand in front of Zoey's door. I think of how we met at the beginning of the school year and, for a moment, I consider knocking, dropping to the floor like I'm sick and green with pneumonia, whispering a hoarse "hospital" when she opens it. In different circumstances, it would probably make her laugh. It seems like something James would do, and the fact that I've thought of it myself comforts me, reminds me of how we keep people with us even when they are gone. It makes me think, too, that maybe the fact that I'm standing here, that I'm working toward being okay, means we can excavate and remove others who don't feel gone enough. It's a leap of faith, to do it differently. To learn a new way.

I knock softly, daring to believe that the world can be different if I am different in it. I hear Zoey moving inside, see the knob turn. I step back and brace. She appears in pajamas and a ponytail. There is surprise in her eyes and then her face becomes unreadable.

"Hi," I say.

"Hi," she says uncertainly.

I am too ashamed to look at her. I stare at a small patch of sand still glued to my leg and will myself to speak. The words are right there to say, but my mouth rejects them like poison, too threatening, too dangerous. I try to push myself out of the way, but my body fights back, clamps down.

Zoey waits. The uncomfortable silence goes on so long that she opens her mouth to say something herself.

"No," I say, "please let me talk first. I'll get there." I press my hands together as if I can squeeze my voice out. I glance quickly at Zoey's face, which softens when she sees me struggle. "I'm sorry," I blurt out finally, and the tears immediately follow, all sorry-ness and sadness and terror at once. My breath rattles as if just to say those words without the sky falling has discharged some long-held fear.

Through my tears I continue. "I don't know how to explain exactly, or if an explanation even matters. But . . . um . . . a lot of things have happened to me that I haven't really dealt with and . . . I obviously have some issues . . . trust issues, clearly . . . but I'm trying to work on them now. I don't know if it's too late or if you can ever . . ."

"I shouldn't have left you," she rushes in. "I promised I wouldn't and then I did. It's my fault."

"No, I'm just messed up, kinda, and . . . and well, you probably know that by now, but there are a lot of other things about me that you don't know . . ."

"I know you're my best friend. What else is there?"

"So, you don't hate me?" I peek out from under myself as if from beneath the covers.

"Seriously? I could never hate you!"

"Do you think I'm nuts?"

"Oh, I think you're totally freaking nuts," she says. "Absolutely bat-shit crazy." She grins that broad, toothy Zoey grin. "How fast can you move back in?"

I go back across the hall to get my suitcase, and by the time I return two minutes later, Zoey is already back in bed asleep. She wakes and sees me and smiles, then drifts off again. On the windowsill beside her bed, the broken cactus is beginning to bloom.

I want so much to stay here and listen to her snoring. But I can't right now. I unpack and take a shower. My bare face in the mirror is an account of the last few days, my nose bright red, my eyes almost swollen shut from crying. I pull out my makeup bag, then decide there's no use trying to fix it. It may not be pretty right now, but it's real and I'm tired of trying to hide myself, of believing that I need to.

I borrow Zoey's biggest pair of sunglasses, take one last look at her sleeping body for courage, and head out onto campus.

I walk quickly, my nerves driving me as I rehearse my speech the whole way there. Only when I reach Chris's building do I wish I had taken more time, put this off a little longer. I need a cigarette or a pep talk from Liz, or better yet, a time machine to go back and undo everything. But as much as I'd love to turn around and go to my room and stick my head under the covers, there is no real thought to doing so.

A bored-looking girl with pink streaks in her hair sits at a desk in the entrance of Chris's dorm, checking student IDs. I flash her mine and tell her I've just come to borrow a book from this guy in my English class whose room number escapes me. "I think he's in 402," I lie, because I have no idea. She checks her list.

"Actually it's 203."

I smile behind my sunglasses even though I sort of wish she wouldn't let me in. My footsteps echo in the stairwell and the sound of myself climbing heightens my anxiety, forces me to be present.

The second-floor hallway smells like gym socks and metal and Irish Spring soap, and loud music blasts from one of the rooms. Chris's door is the second on the right. I knock quickly because I feel out of place and exposed, like I'm in a men's locker room. There is no answer, so I knock again, louder this time, and then lean in closer to listen for footsteps or voices.

A few moments pass, and I imagine that he is eyeing me through the peephole, shushing his friends as he waits for me to leave. I turn and go flying down the stairs, past the pink-haired girl and out the door, relieved to be in the sun again, to be on my way back to the safety of my room.

Halfway to my dorm, I spot Chris in the parking lot. He is with Murph, and the two of them are throwing surfboards into the back of his old, beat-up convertible. The surprise of coming upon him in this way sends my carefully planned speech right out of my head, and just as I'm thinking that maybe I'll do this another time—when I'm better prepared—he looks up.

Shit.

I brace myself, start walking over. Even from a distance I can see his body tense as I approach.

"Hi," I say when I get nearer to him.

He does not respond.

I turn to Murph. "Do you mind if I talk to Chris for a second?"

"Sure," Murph says, and then stands there for another few beats until he realizes that I mean alone. He and Chris exchange glances and then Chris watches Murph walk away as if he wishes he could join him.

My heart sinks, but I know I can't expect anything different.

I wrap my arms around myself. Stare down at the curb. Try to remember the speech. No luck.

"Um, I'm not sure what to say." The sun is glaring, highlighting the awkwardness.

Chris looks toward the street, eyes squinted, making me unimportant with his profile.

This is so much harder than I thought. "I was such a jerk the other night."

He looks at me. No argument there.

"I'm sorry I freaked out on you."

He puts his hands in his pockets, his shoulders still tense, armed against me. "Yeah . . . I don't know what you thought I was trying to do."

I take off my sunglasses, because even though I don't want him to see how awful I look, I want him to see in my face how much I mean what I am saying. "You didn't do anything, Chris. I know you did nothing wrong."

"So what the hell was that then? I mean, you were acting like I was trying to—"

"No, I know. I was a total freak. I completely know that. I'm just really messed up right now." My voice breaks. I will myself not to cry. "I'm sorry."

He nods to himself. "It's fine. I'm over it."

"Okay," I say, hearing the double meaning. "I don't blame you."

Our eyes meet. His face softens a little.

"So . . . I mean . . . are you okay?" he says.

"I am," I say quickly. "Or, I will be."

He gives a small smile as if he's glad. "Well . . . thanks for the apology."

I nod and stand there dumbly. In the distance, I see Murph impatiently shifting his weight.

"I'll go," I say finally, blinking back tears.

I want to say more, to tell Chris that I'm sorry I didn't appreciate him in general, that I was just scared. I want to say that I really did like him and that I shouldn't have acted like I did. More than anything, I want to ask for another chance.

"Thanks for being nice to me," I say. "Because you were and it mattered."

His eyes register several emotions at once, and he pauses as if picking which one to express. "Good," he says finally. "That's good."

The lump in my throat swells. "Well, see you around, I guess."

I start to walk away. Try to remember to breathe, to see that the sun is out, that the picture is bigger than this moment, that life moves, changes constantly, like the ocean.

"Hey," I say, turning. "Can I ask you where you buy one of those?" I point to the surfboards in his car.

"Why? You thinking about becoming a surfer chick?"

"Maybe," I say. "I mean, I'd like to try when the weather gets warm again."

He smiles. "Surf shop down on Bean Street. You need directions?"

"I can find it."

He laughs. "This from the girl who can't find the library when she's standing in front of it."

I laugh too and our eyes meet and that electric energy passes between us once again.

"So . . . maybe I'll see you in the water one of these days," he says.

"Yeah," I say. "I hope so."

I give him a small wave and turn quickly in the direction of my dorm so he won't see me cry.

forty-four

WINTER MOVES IN, white and raw. Snow tumbles into a contagious silence. The retreat is welcome, the need to shutter myself, turn inward. An emptiness has inhabited me, born out of the slightly delayed and disorienting realization that my life is not what I thought it was, that there were chapters missing. Days pass in an out-of-body state as I absorb the shock of all that has happened, as this new, deeper understanding of my history settles in, brings answers to some questions and raises others.

It is a strange thing to discover the mind's capacity to keep secrets from itself. It is stranger still for me to grasp that my identity was formed in the fun-house mirror of a mother who I now realize was mentally ill. Everything I thought I knew about myself needs to be reexamined in light of this new information. Even my perceptions of Matthew shift as I come to realize how much I saw him through the eyes of my mother. It turns out the older brother I both worshipped and felt abandoned by was neither potential savior nor heartless traitor, but rather just a boy as under the influence of his mother as I was. And there is grief in that too, in the realization that we both lost the opportunity to know and see each other as we really were.

The unlovable person I saw myself to be all these years has been replaced with a question mark. Liz says this is a normal part of the process and that I will replace the void with new things, truer things. Which is nice to imagine, and which maybe means I'm on my way to becoming someone who can forgive myself for existing, who can accept that I was not to blame. I've been screaming this my whole life, and yet only now do I feel like I've got any sort of hold on it, that someday it might be something other people can't rip from my grasp.

I spend a lot of time crying in Liz's office about things both remembered and forgotten. All the while, some part of me watches myself with the awareness of how miraculous these tears are, how much lighter I feel for releasing them. A lot of time I cry without having any understanding of why, only that I walk in and the tears start as if they have always been there, waiting for a safe place to land.

I think about Chris often. I tell myself there is still hope, but there are days when I have my doubts, when I wonder if all this work on myself will ever be enough to allow love in, if I'll always be stuck where I am. Liz says that's the thing about life: we only have what's directly in front of us and it's easy to convince ourselves that's all there is. Maybe it's Chris or maybe it's someone else, but I have to allow myself to believe there will be someone someday.

Besides, there is still Zoey, who makes me laugh and points out other cute guys in the cafeteria, tells me all the wonderful things about myself that I can't see. She has her share of heartbreaks too, which don't last more than a night but still, on my better days, make me think that Liz is right: that this is all just a part of things, that maybe we'll look back and remember when we ate too much pizza at two in the morning and played angsty music and worried that we would never, could never, be loved.

In the meantime, there is work to be done, not just in my own head but outside, in the real world. After I barely squeak by first semester, I spend the second hunkered down in my studies, finding that I actually enjoy the work, the sense of efficacy and accomplishment it gives me, the way it grounds me in the present. Each time I turn in an assignment or do well on a test, I am reminded of the fact that I am changing, growing up, recovering enough from my past not only to see a future but to actively move toward one.

Spring brings the end of hibernation, not just for me but for the entire campus. There are Frisbee games and keg parties on the lawn, and the air is charged with youth and hope and infectious happiness.

Zoey and I sign up for an improv group, where she gets to be funny and I get better at letting down my guard, allowing myself to be spontaneous and silly. We drive to Florida for spring break with some of Zoey's other friends who are slowly becoming mine too, and stay at a cheap, disgusting motel and laugh until our stomachs hurt and sometimes have drunken cries upon each other's shoulders about things that are completely ridiculous in the light of morning.

Every once in a while, in the midst of all this bonding and fun, I think of my mother, of that hopeful young girl she was when she went to Dunton, and I feel pity. Sometimes I'm tempted to call her, but inevitably she does something to remind me that she is not safe, whether it's a threatening phone call or an angry, blaming e-mail.

I am learning through my work with Liz that part of being healthy is being able to hold and remember who people actually are instead of who we wish they were. It's a daily struggle against a brain that tends to want to cling to fairy-tale hope, but it's also the only way to guarantee a life surrounded by those who build rather than destroy. In the end, the loss is about letting go of what I never had in the first place.

As soon as the first hints of summer appear, I go to the surf shop to get a wetsuit and board. I end up buying the used pink board Chris once rented for me with its symbol of two fish swimming in opposite directions. The guy behind the counter points to the emblem. "Sign of the water child," he says.

I stay at school for the summer and get a job as—of all things—a lifeguard. On my days off, I paddle out into the waves, usually falling off of them but occasionally managing to catch one and ride it to shore.

To my surprise, the other surfers cheer "nice try!" when I fall, and "good job!" when I don't, and when I paddle back out, they take turns offering me pointers, welcoming me, without reservation, into the tribe.

The world continues to be friendlier than I expect. And each day as the sun sets pink and lovely, I am acutely aware of feeling connected to the surrounding beauty, to the people I've just met, and most of all, to the new piece I have added to the picture of myself: water child.

forty-five

AUGUST COMES HOT and buggy, but with a hint of autumn in the concentrated blue of the sky and the wisps of chill that sometimes slip off the ocean. It's a week before school starts again, my job is over for the summer, and I am with Gavin, who is now almost nine. It's the first time I've seen him since the hospital, and I keep looking at him, can't believe how tall he has gotten, how much we resemble each other.

We have abandoned our beach towels by the lifeguard stand to roam the jagged coastline together, looking for seashells. Gavin is not so much interested in the shells as he is in avoiding the water, which I have been trying to get him into all day, and which he has thus far refused to enter.

He is visiting me here while my parents fight their last and most ugly battle with each other in divorce court back in Pennsylvania. I never thought my father would actually go through with a divorce, but I guess I'm not the only one finding unexpected strength. Who knows, maybe that's the ripple effect of change.

My father and I talked briefly, cordially, when he dropped Gavin off at my dorm, and though I still haven't forgiven him for everything that's happened, it's a start.

Gavin will be living with him now, while Matthew will be moving home after college to live with my mother. Gavin and I do not talk about any of this. Instead we talk about his fear of drowning, which may be hereditary, or may just be a side effect of growing up in a family like ours.

I tell him about the first time I went in the ocean, when Matthew called to me from the water, "Come in! It's no fun by myself!" and I, so afraid, still said yes, answered the call of one love and found, in the Atlantic, another. I tell him how I never imagined all the joy that was just beyond my fear.

Gavin listens intently and smiles. He likes these stories about me and Matthew, about a gentler time in the history of our family, when we were all still connected in some way, when the shadows weren't quite so long. And maybe too he likes to know that there can be meaning in relationships even when they are imperfect or— as is the case with my mother and me—impermanent. That what matters most is what we choose to take away from these relationships. From Matthew, for instance, a love of the sea.

We step over thick manes of seaweed that have been pushed by the tide onto the sand. Gavin tells me that he recently saw Wade Mattell, home from college and playing basketball at the elementary school playground, that Wade says hi.

I smile at the thought. Make a note that I should call him one of these days, spend time remembering not just the bad memories but also the very best of my past.

Something catches my eye between the strands of seaweed. I stop and bend down. Pick up a perfect white conch shell. I hold it to Gavin's ear and tell him to listen.

"Is that really the ocean?" he says doubtfully.

"Some say it's the ocean. Some say it's the sound of your own heartbeat."

"What do you think?" he says.

I smile. "I think it's both."

I brush off the sand with my thumb and put the shell in my beach bag. I will bring it with me, give it to Zoey.

Gavin and I return to our beach towels, where the sun is melting the wax off the two surfboards—mine, and the one I've rented for Gavin.

"Whaddaya say? You want to take this baby for a ride?" I'm no great surfer yet, but I think I'm steady enough to help someone else learn.

He shakes his head, agreeing only to stand at the water's edge and watch. I reapply wax to my board and then his, just in case. Together we head down to the shoreline.

The ocean is yellow green up close and cool and tingly on my hot skin. The waves are small and silky. I wade out up to my waist and then turn to Gavin on the sand. He waves at me and I wave back.

"Come in!" I call.

He shakes his head no.

"Please!" I say. "It's no fun by myself!"

A smile forms on his face as he recognizes the words I've chosen. He looks over his shoulder at the safety of the beach, and then turns back to me and shrugs with helpless resignation. A minute later he has the other board and is wading out to me, moving tentatively forward, like he's walking on glass.

I move toward him, trying not to smile too widely, knowing it will embarrass him and send him back to the shore. He makes funny, disturbed faces as he pushes seaweed out of his way or steps on something strange. I can see the fear evaporating from his eyes as the unknown becomes known. He climbs onto the board and starts to paddle.

He reaches me, breathless, looking around in wonder at where he is in the world. I flip myself over like a seal, and he follows my lead, the two of us slippery and graceful and at home. We emerge laughing and shaking the wet out of our hair, then climb back up on our boards.

The sun is almost white and bounces off the water, off the sand, out of the sky. From the outside breakers someone waves to me and I squint to see who, and then before my brain can even register it, my stomach turns liquid like the sea is sloshing inside of it.

"What are you, a mermaid?" Chris calls to me from across the ocean.

"What are you, a dork?" I call back.

He laughs and then adjusts his board as the biggest wave in the set comes his way. He catches it with ease, showing off as he carves the face, teasingly spraying me with his wake as he rides past. When he is done, he looks back to make sure I've been watching. I give him a thumbs-up, and his wide-open grin is all the reassurance I need.

"Your turn!" he challenges. "Let's see what you've got, O'Malley."

A wave approaches. Smaller than the last, a good learning wave for Gavin.

I turn to him. "Ready?" I say. I signal for him to turn his board toward the beach as I turn mine. "Now paddle," I say. "Paddle!"

But he is instinctual, a born waterman, already paddling. I give his board a little push into the wave before I start paddling for it myself. The ocean catches us both, lifts us together, side by side in motion.

"Jump up!" I say, and he wobbles to his knees before finally climbing to his feet. I throw my arms into the air, look over at Gavin and smile at his smile.

The sun is ours.

The Atlantic breaks.

And we ride it, we ride it, we ride it.

Acknowledgments

Catherine Drayton, my brilliant agent at Inkwell Management, for your wisdom, good humor and faith in me. You are a force and a writer's dream.

Liza Kaplan, my tireless editor, for your passion, vision and insight. I'm so glad my manuscript found you. Also, my amazing publisher, Michael Green, for challenging me to dig deeper, to Talia Benamy for your cheerful assistance, and to everyone at Philomel and Penguin for all the hard work required to make this book happen.

Dylan Kletter, my beloved brother, for your sage counsel and support.

Amanda Fredericks and Marti Daniel Moats, two of my oldest and dearest friends, for countless reads, endless cheerleading and daily comic relief.

John Tashjian for bringing so much fun into my life and for answering the call of every crisis with my three favorite words: "I'm on it."

Melinda Rennert Mizuno for insisting I should write a book, then waiting until I was finished to tell me she was kidding; Ruth Brown for a lifetime of laughter; Jackie Poper, Dan Lane, Dave Hollenbeck, Kathy Conlon Grim, Suzie Paxton, Frank Dino and

Dr. David Neer for various forms of kindness and encouragement; Lori Barnett for refusing to let me drop her English class in eleventh grade no matter how hard I tried; Jen E. Smith for the early advice and help; Cassandra Austin, Erika Ross and Rita Augustine for the wise critiques; and Sophie Smith, who sat on my lap through the early drafts.

Finally, and most important, David Zorn, my first and most-trusted reader, for your patience, humor, gentleness and love. You will always be the best thing that ever happened to me.

Thank you.